The Witch of Woodplumpton

By David Hatton

Proof Reading Services by Julia Gibbs

Also by David Hatton:

The Return

The Medium

The Catfish

The Exhumation

Camp

It's the End of the World as We Know It

All available on Amazon

For Jay,

One for the live list x

This novel is loosely based on the true story of Meg Shelton, also known as the *'Fylde Hag.'* She is supposedly buried beneath a large boulder in the graveyard of St. Anne's Church in the village of Woodplumpton, Lancashire, on the outskirts of Preston. A plaque adjacent to the stone marks the site. The graveyard is open to the public and Meg's tomb is there for all to see.

Little is known about her; however, we know she passed away in 1705 and was the subject of rumours, claiming that she was a witch who liked to cause mischief in the town. She was listed in the records at St. Anne's Church as Margery Hilton, and during this novel her birth name and her alias will be used interchangeably. Her story remains a source of fascination for locals in Lancashire.

The characters in this novel, besides Meg and some of the names referenced in the Pendle Witch Trials, are completely made up. As is the story, although I've used what we know about Meg and the rumours surrounding her fascinating life as a structure for the novel.

I hope you enjoy!

"Everyone loves a witch hunt as long as it's someone else's witch being hunted."

-Walter Kirn

Prologue

Current day

The rickety old coach wheezed to a stop, belching out a cloud of exhaust as it released its weary cargo of twenty dishevelled teenagers. Each one wore a scowl as they grudgingly stepped onto the damp pavement, their grumpiness evident in the early morning mist.

Mrs Finch, their bewildered teacher, surveyed her groggy students with a mix of sympathy and determination. She knew she had a tough sell ahead of her. When she had announced the field trip, she could practically taste the anticipation in the air. They had dreamed of thrilling rides at Alton Towers or the wonders of the Science Museum in Manchester. But reality had dashed their hopes, dragging them instead across the windswept expanse of Lancashire to a remote village graveyard.

As they trudged through the eerie stillness of the mid-morning hour, the village seemed to emanate an atmosphere as cold and lifeless as the graves they were about to visit. Yet Mrs Finch carried herself with an air of quiet determination, her eyes gleaming with an unspoken promise of adventure and discovery.

Mason slouched against the side of the weathered wall, his arms folded tightly across his chest as he surveyed the sleepy village before him. It was a far cry from the bustling streets of London that he longed to roam. Instead, there were just a handful of houses, a quaint pub, and the imposing presence of a stone church. Across the road stood a schoolyard, alive with the laughter of children in matching blue uniforms playing hopscotch.

His stomach churned at the thought of what awaited him inside that church. The solemnity of prayer and the droning hymns that echoed in his mind from countless dull assemblies at school threatened to suffocate him. And to add insult to injury, his mum had packed him yet another uninspired lunch of tuna sandwiches, a sad repetition of the monotony he had endured all week.

His thoughts drifted to the tantalising array of takeaways that would have greeted him in a big city, each promising a culinary adventure far more exciting than the stale sandwiches in his bag. With a pang of longing, he imagined sinking his teeth into a juicy burger from McDonald's or a foot-long from Subway.

Across the road, the sign of The Wheatsheaf pub offered hearty pies and crispy fish and chips. But Mason knew better than to entertain such fantasies. Mrs Finch, with her strict adherence to rules and propriety, would never entertain the idea of her teenage pupils setting foot in a public house.

Mason was the epitome of teenage defiance, his tousled hair falling haphazardly over his furrowed brow. With a permanent scowl etched upon his face, he exuded an air of nonchalance, as if daring the world to challenge his indifference. His eyes, a stormy grey that mirrored the chaotic depths of his soul, were often shadowed by a veil of cynicism. Like most teenagers, nothing was good enough for Mason. In his faded jeans and worn-out sneakers he cut a figure of urban rebellion, a stark contrast to the rural environment he now trod within. His every movement spoke of a restless spirit yearning to break free from the shackles of convention, to carve out his own path in a world that too often sought to dictate his destiny.

Marvin and Kyle, flanking Mason, were his loyal comrades at school. Their synchronised kicks against the weathered stones of the church wall spoke volumes, a silent declaration of their shared disdain for the activities which lay ahead. They'd sooner be back at school kicking a football around the yard.

'Right, boys and girls,' Mrs Finch called in a descending tone. 'Can you all form a line.'

Standing before her students with a posture that seemed to exude authority despite her petite stature, she cast a critical eye over the assembled teenagers, her lips pursed in disapproval. In her fifties, Mrs Finch bore the unmistakable signs of a life lived by the book. Her slender frame was draped in a shapeless beige dress adorned with faded floral patterns, a dress sense that seemed to mirror her own lacklustre existence. Her feet were encased in brand-less trainers, the very epitome of practicality for the rural adventures which lay ahead, while her drab limp hair hung in a bland cascade around her shoulders, devoid of any hint of style or flair.

As the students obediently lined up beside the entrance to the church grounds, a figure emerged from the shadowed depths of the ancient doorway, dressed in a black shirt and the unmistakable white collar of a clergyman. He looked remarkably young for a vicar, with a full head of naturally brown hair that caught the morning sunlight in a cascade of golden hues, as if he was adorned with a halo. He seemed to emit an aura of serenity and calm that drew the eye of even the most restless of onlookers. He couldn't have been long out of college, yet despite his youth there was a gravitas to his presence that commanded respect, a quiet confidence born of unwavering faith and a steadfast dedication to his calling. As he approached the gathered students with a gentle smile playing at the corners of his lips, he extended a welcoming hand.

'Good morning, guys!' He welcomed them with an attempt at a cool demeanour, but Mason and his friends couldn't help but exchange eye rolls, finding him rather unimpressive. 'I am Reverend Thomas, and I am honoured to welcome you to our humble parish. Please, come inside and let us explore the rich history and sacred beauty of this holy place together.'

With a nod of agreement from Mrs Finch, the students followed the Reverend into the hallowed sanctuary of the church. The tour of the church unfolded much as expected, with rows of polished pews stretching out before them like obedient soldiers in formation. An ornate altar, adorned with a striking gold cross, served as the focal point of the refuge, its significance lost on Mason and his pals.

Classic stained-glass windows bathed the interior in array of colours, casting dancing patterns of light across the ancient stone walls. Reverend Thomas, ever the dutiful guide, entertained the pupils with tales of historic figures and vaguely interesting events that had shaped the church's storied past since its humble beginnings in the 17th century. But despite his best efforts the yawns that followed his tales spoke volumes, his stories lost on the tiresome teenagers. For them, the allure of history and tradition faded in comparison to a musical at the theatre or a day of thrills at a theme park, which they'd enjoyed on previous end-of-term excursions at the school.

As Reverend Thomas droned on, his voice echoing hollowly, the students exchanged knowing glances, their eyes alight with a shared sense of impatience. They yearned for something more than mere words and faded relics. Reverend Thomas sensed their frustration and decided to move on to more tantalising subjects.

'Now, let's venture outside, for there's something truly fascinating I wish to share with you in the hallowed grounds of the graveyard,' Reverend Thomas exclaimed, his voice tinged with enthusiasm and a hint of mystique.

Mason couldn't help but roll his eyes in response, a silent protest towards what he perceived as yet another attempt to capture their interest with tales of dead nobodies. Beside him, Marvin couldn't resist the urge to embellish his disinterest with an exaggerated yawn, his theatrics earning a smattering of suppressed chuckles from his classmates.

In the sombre confounds of the graveyard, Reverend Thomas guided the teenagers along a winding stone path, its surface worn smooth by the passage of countless footsteps over the centuries. On either side ancient tombstones cloaked in green moss stood sentinel, their weathered surfaces bearing silent witness to the passage of time. The dedications etched upon the gravestones had long since faded into obscurity, their once-bold inscriptions now mere whispers of the lives they commemorated. Yet, the dates that remained carved into the stone told stories of the parishioners from the church's humble beginnings in the 1600s.

Reverend Thomas came to a halt beside a large boulder that stood at the edge of the path. He turned to face his young crowd, his eyes alight with a quiet intensity.

'Behold,' he whispered, his voice barely louder than a whisper. 'Here lies the key to unlocking the secrets of the past, the gateway to a realm of untold wonders and hidden truths.'

'It's just a big stone!' Marvin heckled, glancing at the boulder which barely reached his knee. Mrs Finch shot him an icy stare, filled with disappointment.

'This is no ordinary stone,' Reverend Thomas continued, his words infused with a sense of wonder and mystery. 'This is the tomb of the Woodplumpton Witch!'

A ripple of astonishment swept through the class, some gasping in disbelief while others exchanged wide-eyed glances of intrigue. But for Mason and his friends, a hint of scepticism lingered.

'There's no such thing as witches!' Mason scoffed. The students turned to him and sighed with apathy at him interrupting the vicar's intriguing story. Marvin and Kyle's sniggering grew more intensely as they felt the lingering stares of their teacher, the vicar and their peers.

'Indeed, young man, while it may be easy to dismiss such tales as mere fantasy, the truth is often stranger than fiction,' Reverend Thomas began, his eyes scanning the faces of his attentive audience. 'Over three hundred years ago, this seemingly unassuming village was gripped by fear and suspicion, as whispers of a supposed witch named Meg Shelton spread like wildfire among the townsfolk.'

He paused for dramatic effect, allowing the weight of his words to settle over the group like a heavy shroud. Around them, the graveyard seemed to come alive with the echoes of the past, the shadows of ancient trees dancing in the mid-morning light.

'Meg Shelton was said to possess powers beyond the comprehension of mortal men,' Reverend Thomas continued, his voice tinged with a hint of awe. 'She was rumoured to have the ability to shapeshift into different animals and to wield magic that could bend the very fabric of reality to her will.'

A murmur of disbelief rippled through the class, mingling with a sense of apprehension that hung heavy in the air.

'And though her existence may be nothing more than a distant memory, the legacy of Meg Shelton lives on in the whispers of the wind and the shadows that dance beneath the moonlight,' Reverend Thomas concluded his story. 'And if you don't believe me, just take a look at this plaque.'

As the group rounded the corner, their eyes fell upon a small plaque protruding from the earth. Etched upon its weathered surface was confirmation of Reverend Thomas's claims.

The Witch's Grave. Beneath this stone lie the remains of Meg Shelton, alleged Witch of Woodplumpton, buried in 1705.

A shiver ran down Mason's spine as he read the inscription, his scepticism momentarily silenced by the weight of history that surrounded them. Around him, the other students stood in humble silence, their eyes fixed upon the plaque as if transfixed by an invisible force.

Reverend Thomas spoke of the rumours that had swirled around Meg's life and untimely death, of the whispered tales of her supposed powers and the fear that had gripped the villagers in the wake of her alleged crimes. He described the events that had led to her final moments alive, painting a vivid picture of a woman condemned by superstition and fear.

But it was the mystery surrounding the manner of Meg's burial that captured the imagination of the students most of all. Reverend Thomas spoke of the strange circumstances that had surrounded her burial, with rumours of dark rituals and covert ceremonies that had shrouded her final resting place in secrecy.

As he spoke, the students leaned in closer, their eyes wide with wonder and disbelief.

'Some say that if you walk around the stone three times and make a wish, Meg will grant it for you. But if you make the same manoeuvre around the stone and say, "I don't believe in witches" the hand of Meg Shelton will appear from the ground and drag you down into the depths of hell.'

As Reverend Thomas bade them farewell with a solemn wave, Mrs Finch took charge once more, leading her pupils on a walk through the picturesque countryside surrounding Woodplumpton. Despite her explicit instructions to wear appropriate footwear, she couldn't help but notice that many of the teenagers had opted for fashion over practicality, their stylish attire ill-suited for the rugged terrain that lay ahead. With a sigh of resignation, Mrs Finch watched as some of the girls struggled to navigate the boggy fields in their impractical heels, their delicate shoes sinking into the soft earth with each hesitant step. Common sense took a back seat to fashion.

'What do you reckon to the old vicar's stories then, boys?' Marvin let out a giggle, and Kyle couldn't hold back a snort of laughter, while Mason stayed suspiciously silent. 'Oh, you don't believe in all that shite, do you, Mason?'

'Nah of course not. It's just a little spooky, that's all. I mean there was a plaque there. It could be real.'

'Anyone can write a plaque, you idiot.' Kyle erupted into giggles and playfully slapped his friend on the back. 'We could put a blue one outside your house saying *First Class Knob Head lived here,* but in your case it would be true.'

'Alright, alright!' Mason shouted, calling time on his friends' jibes. 'Well if you think it's a load of old bullshit, maybe we should come back and test out the theory about circulating her grave. You heard the man, if you circle it three times and say, "I don't believe in witches," Meg will come out and drag you down to hell.'

'Good idea. I could get my brother to drive us over tonight. He's passed his test now,' Marvin said excitedly.

Mason felt a lump form in his throat as he realised he had been bluffing all along, never anticipating that they would actually consider going. The idea of traveling nearly fifteen miles and taking multiple buses to reach this remote village seemed impossible for the three teenagers, and he hadn't expected his friends to come up with a practical solution. *Damn older brothers,* Mason thought.

'I'm not sure I can tonight,' Mason fibbed, scratching his head as he searched furiously for an excuse. 'I've got a... guitar lesson.'

'Whatever, Mason. You're coming. Or are you a coward?' Marvin and Kyle encircled him, casting a shadow over him with their daunting statures, silently imposing peer pressure on their friend with their muscular frames.

'No, I'm not a coward. Fine, I'll come with you,' he reluctantly conceded. Casting one final glance at the church, he felt a wave of nausea wash over him as he contemplated the daunting dare that awaited him that evening.

As the lime green Vauxhall Corsa tore through the winding country lanes, its alloy wheels slicing through the darkness like knives, Mason couldn't help but feel a knot of unease tightening in the pit of his stomach. Marvin in the front passenger seat and Kyle beside him in the back both whooped with excitement, their faces alight with the thrill of the adventures which lay ahead.

In the driver's seat, Marvin's brother Callum gripped the wheel with reckless abandon, his foot pressing down hard on the accelerator as he pushed the car to its limits. With each sharp turn and sudden swerve, Mason's heart leapt into his throat, his knuckles white as he clung to the door handle for dear life like he was riding the Big One at Blackpool Pleasure Beach.

As they neared their destination, the tension in the car grew intense. Mason couldn't shake the feeling that they were treading on dangerous ground, playing with forces beyond their control. And as they finally pulled up outside the graveyard, the echoes of their laughter mingling with the distant howl of the wind, Mason couldn't help but wonder if they had made a grave mistake in coming here.

'Go on then!' Mason pushed Marvin towards the stone which Meg supposedly lay beneath. 'This was your idea.'

'Alright.' Marvin as instructed circled the stone three times and shouted, 'I don't believe in witches!'

They remained silent, waiting for anything to happen. But silence hovered over them.

'Go on, Mason! You do it! Don't be a chicken!'

'Okay,' Mason said, feeling more confident now that he'd witnessed his friends take part with no comeuppance. But an air of caution still followed him. 'I don't believe in witches,' he whispered before walking around the grave three times. After completing his laps, he stopped, closing his eyes, anticipating the worst, his heartbeat thundering in his chest.

A sudden grip around his ankles sent a jolt of shock down his spine.

He turned around to find Callum clenching at his feet.

'You dickhead!' Mason shouted, infuriated and yet simultaneously relieved. 'You scared the living shit out of me!'

The boys cackled, high-fiving each other while Mason grew red with embarrassment.

'Right, let's see what's really beneath this stone.' Marvin went to his brother's car and opened the boot. He fetched out a couple of spades and returned, handing each of his friends a tool.

'You must be kidding me,' Mason protested.

'Hell, no. I want to see if this crazy bitch is actually under here.'

'It's disrespectful to the dead, mate.'

'You heard the vicar, she's a witch!' Kyle slapped his back. Mason fell forward, gripping on to the stone for balance. He knew there was no way of talking his pals out of this. Together they placed their tools beneath the base of the stone and after three attempts they rolled it over. Brushing their hands free of moss and soil, they slowly edged forward to the six-foot cavern beneath it and glimpsed in.

'Holy shit,' said Marvin, his jaw hanging heavy. The boys' eyes widened as they took in the eerie site beneath the notorious stone.

As light flickered to life in the vestry, casting a sudden glow across the graveyard, the boys froze in place, their hearts pounding with fear. They exchanged panicked glances, the realisation sinking in that they were not alone in this desolate place.

'Shit, that vicar must be still here!' Marvin bellowed. 'Come on, let's go!'

With a sense of urgency, they scrambled to replace the stone, their hands shaking with adrenaline as they worked to conceal the evidence of their intrusion. And as the last echoes of the car engine faded into the night, they made a silent vow never to return to the haunted grounds of Woodplumpton again.

Chapter 1

All Hallows' Eve, 1705

Reverend Isaac Armstrong sought refuge in his church as the booming explosions, flashes of lightning and heavy rainfall echoed, as if awakening the souls of those he would later pray for. The unexpected storm arrived shortly after he had completed Evensong, disrupting his brief journey back to the vicarage just a few yards away.

As a clergyman, Isaac presented a biblical appearance with his thick white beard and locks cascading over his ears. His slightly curly wisps on his scalp clung stubbornly as he neared the age of sixty. Having outlived most of the villagers, he acknowledged that his life hadn't included the same strains as theirs. Some might consider the vicar's role somewhat comfortable; he was granted a home, fresh vegetables, and occasional poultry by local farmers. And Isaac spent most of his time indoors and seldom exerted himself.

However, few saw the reality of the role of God's messenger. True, Reverend Isaac spent much of his time indoors at St. Anne's, but the church could be bitterly cold in winter. He remained there from dawn until dusk, and often later. Even when he rested at home, there was little respite. Constant visitors and local parishioners burdened him with their problems, confessions, and the unavoidable local gossip. His neighbours could go home after their day toiling the fields and put work aside until the next day, whilst a vicar was never truly off duty.

Any attempt to find solace in a good book by his fire at night was thwarted by persistent knocks at the door, summoning him to someone's death bed. The experiences he had witnessed over his career haunted him, leaving lasting nightmares. Retirement was an implausible notion. This was a lifelong commitment, which he'd be forced to endure until he was physically incapable of standing to deliver a sermon. His hip and knees were giving him trouble, but he managed to conceal his ailments beneath his long robes, meticulously kept white by his housekeeper, Mrs Norris.

Surveying the sandstone structure which he stood within, he marvelled at the towering oak beams supporting the slate roof. The spire, he hoped, would act as a lightning rod, safeguarding his neighbours' thatched roofs from becoming fiery infernos. Erected in 1639, the church now showed signs of wear and tear over sixty years later. Rain cascaded into the font, serving as a natural source for local christenings.

Kneeling on a wooden stool, he offered prayers before a prominent gold cross that commanded attention on the stone altar. The fixtures surrounding him surpassed his own advanced age. He'd already found a potential successor. One of his altar boys, a young and ambitious blond boy named Alan, had shown interest in pursuing the priesthood. Isaac couldn't help but see a reflection of his own determination in the boy. Like Isaac, Alan had initially supported local parishes with their services before embracing more clerical responsibilities.

While Alan was fortunate to have Isaac as a mentor, Isaac's own journey hadn't been quite as charmed. Recollections of his time as a choirboy at St. Michael's in Clifton stirred unpleasant memories, where a priest would whip the back of his legs for playing the wrong notes on the church organ or for splattering wax on his robes after furiously blowing out the candles. He also held on to unspoken traumas, lingering from the solitary moments with the priest in the vestry. But he'd take those memories to his grave, which was already allotted just a few yards away from where he stood – a bleak perk of the job.

Interrupting his less-than-nostalgic reflections were loud thuds as the ailing mahogany door shuddered from persistent knocking. Isaac rose, offering a respectful nod to the crucifix, and made his way to the door. Why the visitor decided to knock, Isaac could not fathom. God's house was open to all His seekers round the clock. Some nearby churches in the Guild Merchant town of Preston locked their doors at night as the locals sought refuge, hoping for a few shillings from looting the church's relics, raiding the weekly collection or helping themselves to the communion wine.

Yet, this wasn't Preston, nor even a bustling town. Woodplumpton stood as a quaint village in Lancashire, embraced by farmland, a modest row of houses and a nearby watering hole. Isaac was acquainted with every villager by name. The only people he wasn't acquainted with were the men on horseback who passed through the town on a journey to the nearby seaside hamlet, renowned for its black pools and sandy beaches.

Distracted by the persistent knocking, Isaac grumbled, 'Yes, yes, I'm coming!' as he limped over to the entrance. Lifting the steel latch, he swung open the weighty wooden door to reveal a wrinkled face struggling to muster a smile. The figure squinted through the downpour, which had saturated his brown woollen jacket, soiled shirt, and torn trousers. Removing his cap, he wrung it out like a flannel in a tin bath, creating a small waterfall onto the stone path.

'John,' Isaac acknowledged before granting permission to allow the drenched visitor inside. 'You must be freezing. Why didn't you just come in? God's home is your home.'

'I've never been this late, Reverend. I didn't know what the rules were.'

'Well, why in the world have you come at this late hour in these torrential conditions? You must be desperate for my advice.'

Isaac reached for a towel behind the altar, his secret stash of fresh garments and church essentials. Towels were indispensable; one never knew when a child might wet themselves, someone might spill the blood of Christ, or a young mother-to-be might unexpectedly go into labour. In his tenure, Isaac had witnessed it all.

'Thanks, Vicar.' John Cavendish snatched the towel, vigorously rubbing his long black locks before disdainfully tossing the damp garment onto the floor, much to Isaac's dismay. 'I needed to talk to you.'

'Whatever is it?'

'It's about your prayers for All Souls' Day.'

'Oh, yes? Is there someone you want to add? I've already included your dear departed wife, Matilda. And your late mother's name.'

Isaac scratched his head, attempting to recall any other deserving departed soul who might be significant to the Cavendish family, but none came to mind.

'It's more about whom you can take away from the prayers, Vicar.'

'Take away?' Isaac shook his head in disbelief at this extraordinary request. 'This is very unorthodox.'

'I saw the book of names and noticed Meg was in there.'

'Meg Shelton? What about her?' Isaac overlooked the fact that her name was actually Margery Hilton, as few referred to her by anything other than her alias.

'She's a witch,' John stated matter-of-factly.

'I've heard the village gossip, John, and it's rather unkind, don't you think? Margery was a troubled soul but a kind one. She only passed away last month. Her body is barely cold, and we haven't even received her tombstone yet. It feels fitting to include her in our prayers this year.'

'She shouldn't be buried in the church grounds at all. We should've burned her when we had the chance. Just like she burned my crops.'

'I was genuinely sorry to hear about your crops, John, but how could she possibly have been responsible for that? It only happened last week, and I know for a fact that she was buried less than a few feet away from us when it occurred.'

'She's been meddling with my crops for years. She was always an omen when she was alive, and now she's dead, she's somehow gained more power from the beyond.'

'This talk of witchcraft is very ungodly, John. I won't entertain it. She was a dear friend to the village and the parish for decades, even if her friendship went unrequited. I won't let baseless gossip tarnish her legacy, and I won't speak ill of the dead. She had enough of that when she was alive, the poor spinster.'

'Well, you'll regret it, so you will, Vicar. For she will destroy this village and everyone in it given half a chance. If you do plan to pray for her, then I'm telling you now that I won't be here to witness it. Mark my words, she's the devil herself. And you will rue the day that you ever cast eyes on her.'

'It's getting late, John. If there's anything else I can help you with, please do ask me. But Mrs Norris has my dinner on the table, and it'll be getting cold.'

John Cavendish donned his moist cap and returned to the cold, dark night where the rain seemed to be settling. Isaac watched him disappear among the fields and trees across the road from the chapel, thinking what a troubled man he was. No doubt the loss of his crops and indeed his late wife had caused him considerable distress. Loneliness possesses the potential to drive a person to the brink of insanity.

Isaac retrieved his tricorne hat, black overcoat, and a lamp with a lit candle within it before leaving the church. Walking along the paved path beside graves dating back to the church's beginnings, he encountered a diverse range of ages, from elderly ladies to young babies. Too many stillbirths and too many mothers who had departed with them. His job often desensitised him to death, but the loss of the little ones always stung.

Upon reaching the gateway arch, he turned his head to the right and found the grave of Margery Hilton, also known as Meg Shelton. A wooden cross protruded from the ground where her gravestone would soon be placed, currently being etched by the local stonemason. Unlike other graves adorned with flowers, hers remained bare. Isaac picked a daisy from the ground and laid it against the crucifix. Her funeral had been a sombre affair, attended only by the undertakers and a lone teenage boy. She had no family to speak of and certainly no friends. Some onlookers had gathered outside the church, mostly to confirm that the poor woman was indeed deceased.

The toll of the bell tower echoed, serving as a reminder of the time. Isaac limped back to the vicarage, a petite stone cottage merely a hundred feet from the church entrance. Inside, Mrs Norris had already arranged logs on the fire, and the aroma of the stew she had been diligently preparing wafted through the air. Stew proved to be the ideal meal for Isaac, considering the unpredictability of his return home; he would be dismayed if his tardiness resulted in Mrs Norris's culinary efforts going to waste.

'Evening, Reverend.' Despite sharing a home for nearly a decade, they maintained a formality in their address. 'Oh, it's brutal out there. I bet you're glad to be home.'

'That I am, Mrs Norris,' Isaac replied, shaking rain from his hands. He hung his coat and hat on a wooden stand near the door, and discarded his white robe beside the washing paddle, to be attended to by Mrs Norris the next day. Underneath, he wore a simple black shirt and trousers, with a white Roman collar neatly tucked around his neck. On the mantel stood a photograph of Mr Norris, whom she had lost before becoming his housekeeper. Her decision to take on the live-in role was motivated by financial reasons and the additional company of Isaac on potentially lonely nights.

'How was your day?' she asked, placing a bowl of stew on the table as Isaac took a seat. She refrained from joining him, having already eaten earlier in the evening.

'An odd one...' Isaac said. 'John Cavendish visited me and requested that I remove Miss Hilton's name from the All Souls' Day prayers.'

'Miss Hilton?' She scratched her head, pondering the local parishioners.

'Meg Shelton.' Isaac rolled his eyes. Mrs Norris nodded her head in recognition.

'Well, you can't blame him. A few years ago, she'd have been drowned in the pond.'

The pond, more of a flooded ditch, once sat at the east of the village but had since dried up. It featured a ducking tool on the side, where rumoured witches would be lowered into the water. If they survived, they were deemed witches and burned alive. If they perished, they were considered human, but by then, it was too late. Despite generations of dunking, to Isaac's knowledge, no one had survived the ordeal. In later years, it served to punish disobedient women who dishonoured their husbands, stopping short of drowning them.

'Thankfully, we're past the days of the Pendle Witch Trials. As I see it, Miss Hilton was a normal woman who had some bad luck in her life.'

'Did you see the nose on her? And that limp. The Fylde Hag, they called her.'

'I didn't know you were so focused on aesthetics, Mrs Norris,' Isaac replied with an arched eyebrow. Mrs Norris had acquired features resembling Margery Hilton in her later years, but the distinction lay in the fact that *she* had found someone to marry her, whereas Margery remained a spinster throughout her life.

'Well, you can't deny all the strange happenings in this village. Mr Cavendish was a particular victim of her curses.'

'This is very trivial and could be considered blasphemy.' Isaac picked up a spoon, blowing on his stew. 'Surely, if she had any form of demon inside her, that's even more reason to pray for her.'

'I suppose,' Mrs Norris shrugged. 'Anyway, I'm going to bed. Just place your cutlery on the side when you're done, I'll deal with it in the morning.'

'Goodnight, Mrs Norris.' Isaac finished his meal and approached a piano in the corner of the room. Seating himself on a stool, he began playing 'The Goldberg Variations' by Bach, tapping the keys gently to avoid waking Mrs Norris.

Juno, Mrs Norris's white pug, sniffed around his ankles, tickling him with his wet snout. She had brought the dog with her when Mr Norris passed, and despite Isaac's dislike for canines, he couldn't bring himself to tell her to part with her beloved pet so soon after saying goodbye to her husband. Juno was a quiet companion, causing Isaac minimal distress. The vicar patted Juno's head before continuing to play his music – a therapeutic escape after a challenging day at the church. It provided him time to contemplate the significant questions posed by his parishioners.

The journey hadn't been easy. When he first joined the parish, the locals didn't warm to him. Formerly a Roman Catholic community, they were determined to uphold their traditional values, which, despite sharing the same God, felt worlds apart from the Church of England. Eventually, as many churches in the land had undergone multiple transitions through different monarchs' reigns since Henry VIII, the parish became Anglican. The nearest Catholic church was now over an hour's walk away, deemed too far for those without a horse, despite their apparent dedication to their faith. Over time, more people converted and attended his services, although many still sought his counsel for confessions or wanted him to administer Last Rites for the dying, despite it not being a feature of the

Anglican faith; for the latter, he simply offered a prayer, which seemed sufficient for them.

Isaac played until his eyes drooped, and his fingers clumsily hit the wrong notes. He extinguished the log fire with a jug of water and ascended the stairs to bed. The bedroom held two single beds – one for him and another for the occasional guest passing through the town who could not afford a night at the local inn. A candle provided a dim light as he read his leather-bound Bible before placing it on his bedside table. Drifting off to sleep, he thought about Margery Hilton, or Meg Shelton as the locals knew her, chuckling to himself over the absurd notion that she could possibly be a witch.

*

He awoke at dawn, finding that the storms had passed but had left pockets of flooding in the prairies outside his window. In the distance, Pendle Hill asserted its dominance on the skyline. After dressing, he descended the stairs to find a plate of bread and a knob of butter on the table, accompanied by a pot of tea, which he preferred black with a touch of lemon. The house was quiet, but as promised, the dishes from the previous night had been washed and put away. As he broke his fast, he read over his sermon for the day. All Saints' Day was a day to honour, as the title suggests, all the saints, and his sermon resolved around remembrance, gratitude, and a communion of saints.

The tranquillity was abruptly shattered when the door burst open, startling the vicar. Mrs Norris stood behind it, visibly shaken. In her hand was a lead attached to Juno, who nervously sniffed at the ground.

'Mrs Norris, are you all right?'

'Reverend! My goodness!' she cried, panting like her mutt. 'It's the church.'

'What about it?' He cast a fleeting glance out the window, relieved to find it still standing. Its spire remained prominent over the village.

'I was walking Juno. I wasn't able to take him out last night because of the storm, you see. So, I went up towards the church early this morning.'

'Goodness, Mrs Norris, spit it out!' Isaac exclaimed.

'I think I better show you.'

He grabbed his coat and followed her out the door. Her aging pace frustrated him as he was eager to understand the cause of her distress. While not in his prime, he was far more agile than his housekeeper.

'Why don't I run on ahead? What am I looking for?'

'The graveyard, you won't miss it,' she replied, wiping away a tear and covering her jaw in disbelief. Isaac limply jogged ahead, more of a brisk walk at his ripe age. Walking through the gates, he passed the wooden stocks, which had witnessed many locals being punished over the centuries; they stood mostly unused today but served as a reminder for the residents to maintain order. It resembled the leather belt Isaac's own parents had hung on the wall as a threat against childhood disobedience.

He scanned the area for any clues regarding what could have possibly upset Mrs Norris. Then, he noticed it. There, where he had placed a daisy on the bare grave of a former parishioner just hours before, now lay the decomposing corpse of Meg Shelton, exposed for the entire town to witness.

Chapter 2

18 months earlier

'Your turn!' exclaimed Henry, delivering a friendly slap to his buddy's back.

In the quiet stillness of the closed school grounds, James Ashton found himself engrossed in a timeless game of marbles. The path beneath his worn shoes served as the battleground for their competition. As James leaned over the circle of marbles, an array of colours gleaming in the afternoon light meticulously arranged on the ground, his friend's hand slapped his spine, encouraging him to take his turn. With unwavering focus, James set his sights on his opponent's marbles, his fingers expertly caressing the smooth surface of his own.

A flick of the wrist, and James unleashed his marble into the circle with the confidence of a seasoned professional. But the small sphere rolled defiantly out of the chalked arena, eliminating him from the game.

'You've lost your marbles!' Henry's cackle echoed, causing a bashful James to blush.

'You say that every time.'

James ascended from the ground. His once-immaculate black trousers now bore dust and gravel. The pristine cuffs of his white shirt mirrored the battle-hardened landscape of the schoolyard. He dreaded facing his mother when she saw the state of him when he arrived home.

In the midst of adolescence, James found himself trailing behind his peers in stature. At an age where his friends had embraced the lofty heights of their parents, James remained a figure of modest height. Yet, his petite frame had a robustness forged through hours helping his father, who worked as a farmhand on John Cavendish's land.

His mousy brown hair, described as untidy by his teachers, lingered below his ears. Unlike his friends, whose parents had mastered the art of hair-cutting precision, James's mother had not succumbed to such domestic skills. His unruly mane however did provide a sanctuary whenever his acne was particularly angry, where he could conceal his perceived unattractiveness beneath the veil of his locks.

In a time when many families in the county chose the path of home-schooling, in 1661 Alice Nicholson of Bartle, a figure of nobility, had bestowed a generous offering to the village in the form of a free school, which was formed within Woodplumpton Manor. Three years later, a schoolhouse was built in the village centre displaying Miss Nicholson's initials above the entrance like a crest of honour.

The one-storey stone sanctuary offered education for up to sixty children of varying ages, a privilege which was not afforded to many working-class families across England. It proved to be a blessing for James's mother, allowing her to dedicate her time to household chores, as she had never received any formal education herself and was spared the task of educating her son.

'Oi oi!' a voice echoed from behind. Charles Clitheroe, accompanied by the towering figures of William and George, appeared with an athletic sprint. They cast an imposing shadow over James. The trio, with smirks etched on their faces, interrupted the duo's game of Ring Taw.

Not only did Charles, William, and George tower over James in height, but their very presence seemed to embody a contrasting world of privilege. Their unblemished skin spoke of a life untouched by skirmishes with other teenage boys. Tidy haircuts framed their heads at their own mothers' competent hands. Their clothes, tailored in a fashion that showed a refinement James could only dream of, were draped seamlessly on their robust frames, a stark contrast to the loose-hanging garments that clung to James's slender figure.

'Why don't you lads play a proper game?' William said, kicking a ball against the wall. 'Let's play some kickball.'

In this improvised arena, the boys formed teams while Charles assumed the role of goalkeeper, standing before a makeshift chalk-lined goal. Henry and James found themselves on one side, pitted against the opposition, William and George, who engaged in a symphony of passes and tackles, executing manoeuvres with a fluidity that James wished he could mirror. Fearful of the ball and anticipating the impending tackles, James hesitated, standing back beside the goal.

Henry gained possession of the ball and glanced around the amateur pitch. Seizing an opportunity, he passed to an unguarded James, stationed beside what appeared to be an open goal. With a swift and determined kick, James unleashed the ball, sending it soaring beyond the confines of the yard.

'You idiot!' Henry called. 'That would've gone in easily!'

'Sorry,' James bashfully replied.

They played for half an hour, concluding with a fifteen-two score to William and George, much to Henry's humiliation. 'You can go in goal next time,' he grumbled towards James, who bowed his head in shame.

Perched on the weathered wall, the boys delved into mindless chatter of the girls they fancied within the village.

William, with a glint of admiration in his eyes, confessed to a fondness for Charlotte. George, ever the romantic, found himself drawn to the grace of Anne. Meanwhile, the air crackled with a competitive undercurrent as Henry and Charles, entangled in the delicate dance of youthful rivalry, vied for the attentions of Elizabeth, though neither stood a chance. Yet, amidst the chorus of youthful declarations, James Ashton remained a suspiciously silent observer of this romantic display, which the other boys found unsettling.

'You a woofter or summat?' Charles asked, scrubbing his knuckles on James's head.

Before James could respond, Henry stood up and pointed across the road.

'Now there's a *real* game,' he said, chuckling to himself.

The collective gaze of the boys pivoted towards the end of the lane, where the ebb and flow of daily life revealed a figure emerging from the centre of the village. A dishevelled woman draped in a weathered black cloak hobbled down the path with a determined yet faltering gait, clutching on to a wooden staff for support. Her skin, pale and leathery, was etched with the lines of experience that only time could sculpt. Her prominent nose and a singular wart on her chin elicited a mix of both fear and amusement among the boys.

'Here we go, lads!' Charles sniggered.

'Who is that?' James asked, squinting at the old woman.

'It's the Fylde Hag!' William declared. 'Meg Shelton.'

'Who?' James shrugged.

'The local witch. Surely, you've heard of her?'

'No. Never.'

'She's as evil as the devil himself,' Charles explained, placing an arm around James, leaning him into his mysterious tale. 'Some say she brought the plague to Lancashire.'

'What? That's impossible.' James laughed, brushing his friend's arm off his shoulder. He'd learned about the plague in his history class. 'That would make her over three hundred years old.'

'Look at her. She's as old as the sun.'

'She's brought terror to this town. Whole crops have died. Cows' milk soured. And some say she can transform into the shape of animals.'

'It's true,' William said. 'I heard she turned into a duck when the farmer caught her stealing from a local farm.'

'Oh my God! That's terrifying!' James gasped.

Henry sprang into action, fleeing towards a nearby field. The verdant expanse of the Cavendish farm awaited with a treasure trove of ripened tomatoes ripe for the picking. With nimble fingers, Henry gathered a handful of the plump, red jewels. Returning with his harvest, Henry distributed the tomatoes among his friends, passing one to each with a mischievous grin.

'Oh, thanks!' James said, taking a bite. The fresh produce burst with a symphony of sweet and tangy flavours that danced on his taste buds and an earthiness which only ripe picked fruit could offer.

'It's not for eating, you eejit!' Henry barked. 'It's for lobbing.'

Henry took aim. The first tomato sailed through the air, terminating in a splat, leaving a stubborn stain on the black cloak of the unsuspecting elderly woman. The air seemed to freeze for an instant before being shattered by the woman's surprised squeal, a sharp sound that reverberated through the quiet village. As she turned, her glare bore witness to the unruly teenagers, her demeanour transformed from a figure of quiet resilience to an aggrieved victim.

'You little bastards!' she yelled.

William, Charles, and George joined Henry's impulsive mischievous acts, their tomatoes launched in unison toward the bewildered woman. Two of the projectiles found their mark, splattering against the coat of the rumoured witch. Meanwhile, William's aim veered off course, the tomato smashing against the nearby wall.

As the woman recoiled from the unexpected assault, a collage of red and yellow adorned her coat. Undeterred, the woman wiped the yellow seeds from her chest and began to walk towards the boys with an intense glare.

'Go on, James, throw yours!' Henry egged.

A shiver crept down James's spine as he stood frozen, caught in the crossfire between peer pressure and the piercing gaze of the old woman. Her eyes, cold and unforgiving, bored into his very soul, sending a deathly chill through the air. The weight of his decision hung in the balance, suspended between the echoes of mischievous camaraderie and the silent warnings etched in the lines of the woman's face.

'Go on!' Henry's insistence cut through the tense silence, urging James to join the reckless act of his peers. With a reluctant surrender to the collective goading, James, tossed the tomato towards the old woman. The fruit rebounded off her head with an unexpected, comical bounce.

As the woman edged forward, the atmosphere thickened with an eerie tension. Her long, bony index finger pointed directly at the group of disobedient boys.

'I curse the day you were born!'

'Oh shit, she's cursing us! Run!' William yelled. The boys scattered like startled birds.

James collected his marbles hastily, stuffing them into his pocket before pursuing his pals. The gap between him and his friends widened, each step echoing the pounding rhythm of his accelerating heart. As they turned a corner in a desperate attempt to outrun the curse, James stumbled over a dip in the road.

He tumbled face-forward onto the gravelly ground, the jagged edge of a stone meeting his head with a harsh collision.

And all went black.

Upon opening his eyes, the searing sun stung, and his head reverberated with a relentless, pounding ache. He placed his hand over the wound and felt a round bump above his eyebrow. It was moist, and when he inspected his hand, it was red with blood. The pounding of a staff against the rocky ground sent shivers down his spine, and a dark shadow cast out the light.

And then she appeared. Her sagging, wrinkly face loomed over him, her cold dead eyes staring down at his. The protruding nose appeared more prevalent than before, and the wart on her chin could've had its own personality. He screamed, and she placed her cold hands over his mouth.

'Calm yourself, boy,' she said in a gravelly voice. 'I'm not going to hurt you.'

He fell silent, and she removed her hand.

'You've hurt yourself,' she said. Her eyes suddenly softened; she placed her hands over his head, and he winced. 'I can help you. Come on now, get yourself up. I can't lift you. Not at my age.'

He sat up and looked around. The road was empty. Nobody could save him from this potential witch who had the ability to bring a hex upon him. Blood continued to pour down from his head, and he felt a little woozy. The old woman placed a hand on his arm, which felt surprisingly comforting.

'All right,' he resigned himself and stood up, using a nearby wall for balance. He took a seat on the stone wall, and she sat beside him. Placing a hand inside her coat, she took out a small metal flask from a pocket stitched inside. She then lifted out a white linen handkerchief and emptied a clear liquid from the flask onto the cloth.

'Don't worry, it's clean,' she said of the handkerchief. 'When you get to my age, you fall over quite a lot, and you always need to be prepared.'

She dabbed the handkerchief against his head. 'It may sting a bit.'

'Ouch,' he cried. 'What is that?'

'It's gin. The alcohol will sterilise the wound, preventing it from getting infected.'

He scrunched up his eyes and clenched his fists as she gently patted the wound with the moist cloth. 'How do you know all this?'

'I was once a midwife.'

'But you're not anymore?' James asked.

'When you can barely hold your own body upright anymore, parents tend not to want you to hold their new-borns,' she giggled. 'What's your name?'

'James,' he replied.

'Like the old king.'

'That's right.' He nodded. James II had died just three years before, having been removed from the throne sixteen years prior after trying to impose Catholicism on the English and Scottish parliaments. He was succeeded by William, who had reigned with his wife Mary until her death in 1694. James had enjoyed learning about the history of the English monarchy at school.

'Your parents are Catholic then? If they named you after him...' she probed.

'Relaxed ones. They attend St. Anne's these days. The Catholic church is too far away.'

'Who are your parents?'

'You're not going to tell on me, are you?' James gulped.

'Goodness me, no!' she cackled. 'I can see you were being urged on by your friends. I understand peer pressure. I was young myself, you know. Maybe this will be a lesson to you to not always do what your friends tell you to. If they asked you to jump off the roof of your school over there, you certainly wouldn't follow their lead now, would you? Here, hold this to your head for a bit.'

He placed his hand over the handkerchief and looked up, occasionally glancing at his helper.

'My mother is Sarah Ashton. My father is Francis.'

'Oh, the Ashtons. I know them from the church.' While James occasionally attended the church, like most of his friends he spent the hour in Sunday school next door in the vestry with the other children.

'Do you speak to them?' James asked.

'No, but then again nobody really talks to me.' She shrugged nonchalantly.

'My friends say you're a witch.'

'That's what they say.' Meg shrugged her shoulders and laughed.

'Well, are you?'

'Do you think I am?'

James glanced over the shrivelled woman. 'You look like one.'

'Well, thank you very much!' she chuckled. 'You're not so handsome yourself.'

'You seem kind though,' he said, which made her smile.

'I let people believe what they want. If they think I'm a witch, they tend to leave me alone as they're too scared to do anything about it. They fear I'll put a curse upon them.'

'But my friends didn't leave you alone.'

'Well, that's the foolishness of youth, you see. You're not afraid of anything at your age.'

'I'm sometimes afraid,' James admitted.

'Yes, but not of death. That's something which only comes with age.'

'Are you afraid of death?'

'Me? No. Life's too short to worry about dying. It's coming for us all at some point, so why stress about it?'

'That's a good outlook,' James said, before placing a hand over his grumbling belly. 'I'm hungry.'

'Well, we better sort that out.' She stood up and walked away from the wall and down the road back towards the village centre. On their right was a white inn called The Wheatsheaf, which served the locals ale, wine, and gin, as well as providing overnight rooms for passers through. On the left was a row of thatched cottages before the town petered out into fields. The old lady took a right onto a dirt path, passing through gates, and placed a finger on her lips and hushed him as they crept past the farmer's house. Once they were in the open fields, she grabbed a ripe tomato and passed it to the boy, which he devoured.

'My friends said you're called Meg. Meg Shelton.'

'That's what they call me.' She held out a hand, and he shook it.

'I think I've heard that name before.'

'Probably not for good reasons...' Meg replied sceptically. 'There's not many people who have anything nice to say about me.'

'Well, my friends seemed to think you were dangerous.'

'That figures. I'm not very popular around here.'

'People can be very cruel. You seem nice enough to me.'

'You'd be welcome to come to my house sometime if you'd like to give an old hag some company.'

'Where do you live?'

'Cottam Hall,' she replied, pointing up the lane towards a village which was far beyond the reach of his eye. 'In Catforth.'

'But that's massive! Why are you stealing food if you're a member of the aristocracy?'

'I'm far from aristocracy, dear. I have a small house in the grounds. Cuckoo Hall, they call my little hovel, as they think I'm as mad as a bat. I've lived there for decades. I knew the Cottam family, and they let me have a place to stay. I worked for them for a while as a housekeeper outside of my midwifery hours. They've since died, and their son inherited the estate, but the original Lord Cottam gave me the right in his will to stay until the day I die, much to his son's disappointment. He refuses to feed me, though, unlike his father, so I'm left to fend for myself. I have no money, and I'm too old to work.'

'That's tough.' James sighed, suddenly considering his own existence quite privileged.

'It is. So I scavenge around for food from the local land. And try not to get caught by the farmers. Anyway, let's go before we get caught. Do you want to come back to mine for some water?'

'No, I better go home. My dinner will be on the table soon, and Mother will go berserk if I stay out past sunset.'

'Very well. Come and see me sometime, won't you?'

'I will.'

'It was lovely to meet you, James.'

'It was lovely to meet you too, Miss Shelton.'

He turned towards the dirt road and retraced his steps back to the path. When he turned around to wave her off, she had mysteriously disappeared.

Chapter 3

'What are you going to do about this, Reverend?' John Cavendish's bellowing echoed through the vestry as they gathered around the table. Isaac, a reluctant host of the ambush, distributed mugs of whisky to his visitors, setting the stage for a discussion on the latest drama unfolding in the village.

'I don't see what more I can do than rebury her, which I've already done,' Isaac replied.

'But it's the third time she's reappeared this week!' Mary Parr said. She was a young woman, tenderly cradling her baby in her arms. Her long blonde hair cascaded down, framing her face, while a grey linen dress elegantly covered her elbows and ankles. 'I've not let my William come into the village since she first clawed her way out of her grave. He's deeply missing his friends and valuable school.'

'Let's get something straight.' Isaac cleared his throat, his hand calmly resting on the table, while a candle shimmered between the attendees. 'Miss Hilton, or Meg Shelton as you prefer to call her, was exhumed. Someone has waited each night for me to leave the church, and they've dug her up.'

'Ridiculous.' John slammed his hand down, causing both mugs and shoulders to bounce with the impact. 'Who would do such a thing?'

'Well, lots of people don't approve of her being buried in the church grounds, including you, John.'

'What on earth are you insinuating?'

'I'm not insinuating anything. I'm simply saying she had a lot of enemies.'

'And there's a good reason for that,' Joan Clitheroe sniped. She sported white hair and wooden teeth, her tiny frame draped in a blue cloak. 'You know she's cursed the village, don't you? When she was alive, she ruined crops, ruined our milk. My grandson Charles hasn't been the same since she put a hex on him last year. He's not been able to stomach a tomato since.'

'Was that after he pelted the poor elderly woman with said tomato, Mrs Clitheroe?' Isaac raised his eyebrows. 'These are some wild allegations and I've heard more than enough of this hearsay over the years. And as for your dear grandson not being able to eat tomatoes, well, it's hardly a rarity to hear about a young lad refusing to eat his fruit and vegetables now, is it?'

'It's not hearsay, Vicar,' said John. 'She was a witch. I saw it with my own eyes! There's even a constable's report of her turning into a bag of corn.'

'The report which you were the only witness to attest to?'

'Are you calling me a liar, Vicar?'

'I'm saying maybe your eyes were deceiving you.'

'I know what I saw. I'm also sure she put a hex on my wife, which killed her! And you only have to look at the way Meg Shelton died to know something was suspect. Crushed beneath an oak barrel in her own home. Now tell me that's not God's way of getting rid of the old hag?'

'What about you, Mrs Ashton?' Isaac shifted his attention to Sarah, the church warden, diverting the conversation from John's ridiculous claims. Sarah, a rosy, round woman, incessantly scratched at her red hair; lice, a plague in the village, were as common as the rats that scurried beneath their feet. 'What do you make of all this?'

'I've never liked the woman. There are reasons which you all know about, which is why I don't like her, but I won't go over that again today. But she used to creep around my James, inviting him over to her house, teaching him all sorts of bad habits. I used to beg him to keep away from her, but would he listen? Even when we grounded him, he still found a way to get out of his bedroom which I know for a fact we had locked. She must have opened it with her black magic. And she definitely put a spell on his vegetable patch. His potato plants haven't stopped producing.'

'My goodness, how are you coping with all that potato prosperity?' Isaac chuckled. 'Maybe you could give some of your son's home-grown produce to Mr Cavendish, seeing as Miss Hilton apparently has cursed his crops. I can't keep up; is this supposed witch bringing hunger or a flurry of food to the residents of this village?'

'It's both,' Mrs Norris said, sitting in the corner, engrossed in her knitting. 'She's providing for those she liked and cursing those she didn't.'

'This is madness. We shouldn't be blaming the dead. Instead, we should be finding out who keeps digging up her body.'

'Isn't it clear? She's crawling out of her grave to get us!'

'But reaching no more than a foot from her grave. She's not getting very far for someone supposedly so dangerous,' Isaac reasoned.

'Well, something must be done!' Lord Cottam rose, pushing his chair in with a deliberate motion. He wore a tricorne hat, a distinguished pastel green suit, and impeccably crafted leather shoes. A white long wig adorned his head, and a recently groomed moustache added a touch of elegance, finely combed to perfection. 'That woman gave me grief in life, and she's doing it even more in death. These poor women's children can't even get to school without seeing the rotten corpse of a miserable old hag. It's no sight for an infant.'

'And what has any of this got to do with you, Bartholomew?' Isaac replied, using the nobleman's Christian name. 'With all due respect, you live outside of town, you never visit this parish as you have now built your own chapel in that mansion of yours, and your own children are in a private boarding school in Lancaster.'

'My friends here expressed concern, and I care about this village. May I remind you my father thought fondly of this village and donated a lot of money to this church. It's only fair I ensure it maintains its reputation, and I don't think a witch of all people should be buried here. Especially one who continues to resurface.'

'May I remind *you,* Bartholomew, that your father was also fond of Miss Hilton. After all, he gave her a home and ensured she could stay there for the rest of her life.'

'He was too soft for his own good, that man. My mother couldn't stand her.'

'She never expressed those concerns to me,' said Isaac, stroking his beard. 'Miss Hilton was a constant presence in your life and a solid support around your home from what I hear.'

'Well, I'm telling you, Mother didn't like the old hag. She couldn't stand that she lived on our grounds. But Father insisted. Now tell me and these fine people what it is you're going to do about that damn witch? It's the annual village fair tomorrow, and we will have visitors from all over the county. We can't be having bodies rising from the dead. This isn't Easter Sunday.'

Isaac stood up and paced around the room, tapping his fingers together as he mused. His gaze fixed on the painting of The Last Supper hanging on the wall, and he pondered, *what would Jesus do?*

'I'll keep watch tonight. Whoever is doing this will soon be caught. At the very least, I'll save the village from any embarrassment tomorrow during the fair. And if I see one stray finger linger from Miss Hilton's grave tonight without the support of a mere mortal, I'll personally come and tell all of you that you were correct.'

Content for the time being, the villagers departed the church, and Isaac fetched a chair from the vestry. He positioned it a yard away from Margery Hilton's currently unmarked grave. Wrapping a red quilt around his legs, usually reserved for parishioners during the cold winter months, he prepared for his vigil. Isaac blew out his candle, enveloping himself in darkness, keen to catch anyone attempting to disturb Margery Hilton's resting place.

It was a cold, dark night, but it remained dry. 'God must be looking out for me,' he considered, and in gratitude, he whispered a silent prayer. As his eyes drooped, he allowed himself to succumb to sleep. Nightmares plagued his rest, with vivid images of Margery crawling out of her grave and grabbing his leg.

As he opened his eyes, spooked from his nightmare, a boy stood before him gently placing a hand on his shoulder, which made him gasp.

'Are you all right?' asked the boy.

'James. What are you doing here? It must be gone midnight.'

'It's nearly two o'clock. My mother told me you were keeping watch over Meg tonight. I thought I'd come and keep you company.'

'Does your mother know you're here?'

'Does she buggar! No, I sneaked out. It felt like a kind of vigil. I had to be here.'

'You and Miss Hilton were good friends, it seems.'

'She was my best friend. Strange, I know, for a boy.'

'We can't help who we befriend. And she needed your friendship.'

'And I hers.' James bowed his head toward the cross, where she sat beneath its solemn presence.

'You needed each other.'

James reached into his coat pocket, retrieving a silver hip flask. He took a sip and then extended it toward the vicar.

'Would you like a swig, Reverend?'

'What is it?'

'It's whisky. I filled it from my father's cupboard. It'll keep you warm.'

Isaac narrowed his eyes, uncertain about accepting alcohol from the fifteen-year-old. A cold bite in the air caused him to shiver, ultimately persuading him to accept the gracious gift. 'Thank you.'

He took a sip of the whisky. It tasted warm and robust, with hints of oak and a subtle smokiness that lingered on the palate. The liquid provided a comforting burn as it made its way down, instantly warming his cockles.

'It's Meg's hip flask,' James explained. 'She gave it to me when she died.'

'How does a person bestow a gift after their passing?' Isaac stroked his beard, well aware that Margery Hilton had not left a will; after all, she had nothing to her name in life.

'She said if anything happened to her, I could have it.'

'Did she anticipate something would happen to her?' He squinted his eyes, surprised by the boy's startling claim.

'Wouldn't you? If you were the most hated person in town?' James shrugged. 'Besides, she was getting on in life. She had to die sometime, and she knew that time was coming; I just didn't expect it to happen so suddenly. And so suspiciously.'

'Nor did I. Grab yourself a chair from inside.'

James vanished into the church, leaving Isaac to relish the whisky, which now wrapped him in a comforting shield against the frosty night. The windows of cottages across the way began to mist up. Shortly after, James returned with a chair matching Isaac's, settling down beside him.

'Why was Miss Hilton so special to you?' He passed the flask back to the boy who, succumbing to the chill, started to shiver.

'I was with some old pals, they made me pelt a tomato at her. We ran away in fear of what she might do to us. But I fell and hit my head. Instead of punishing me, she came to my aid. She put some gin on the wound to avoid an infection with this very flask.' He lifted the flask and savoured a sip, embracing the burn which accompanied it. 'And I realised she was a lot like me. A bit of an outsider with few friends.'

'But you had your pals,' Isaac said. As he made his way to church each day, he observed James playing with his friends in the schoolyard and considered him quite popular.

'Yes, but they weren't very nice. And I'd always get into trouble with them.'

'I believe Miss Hilton also got you up to mischief too, though.'

'Yes, but that was survivalism on her part. She had to eat.'

'I agree. You have a warm home and food, though.'

'I just went along for fun. And to keep her company.'

'You call her Meg Shelton like the other villagers. Why is that?' Isaac regarded the boy with curiosity. Although claiming to be her friend, he steadfastly refused to call her by her real name.

'She told me that's what her name was. I didn't know her real name was Margery Hilton until she died. At the funeral, in fact, when you read out her name. Why was Meg Shelton an alias?'

'It was something to do with her family, I believe. There's so much rumour about her, though I struggle to decipher what is true and what is local gossip.'

'She liked to keep the rumour factory alive, though.' James chuckled.

'She certainly didn't help herself.' Isaac laughed along with his companion. 'What do you believe?'

'In regards to...?'

'You've heard the rumours that she was a witch. They all seem adamant that there was something mysterious about her.'

James gazed up at the stars and the full moon, offering a natural glow that illuminated the pair as they contemplated Margery's life.

'She was definitely mysterious. She would be hobbling one minute and running the next. And she had a trick of disappearing suddenly. Amazing for somebody who wasn't usually very agile. But a witch? No. What do you think?'

'It's ungodly for me to believe she was anything other than human. I think people thought she was odd, and some had vendettas against her. The witch trials might be over, but it's still common to be considered a witch if you don't follow the norms in society even today.'

'She was also a midwife in her youth. I heard that used to be a source of sorcery for some naysayers.'

'That's true. When I was a boy, any woman who dealt with medicinal substances or could turn her hand to nursing could be seen as a demon. They'd say her medicines were potions. And yet many men are doctors, and nobody says anything.'

'Women need to stay at home to cook and clean. That's what my mother says anyway.'

'Is your mother not worried about where you are tonight?' Isaac asked. He suspected that like most mothers she would be concerned for her son's wellbeing when he was out past dark.

'Nah. She'll be fast asleep by now. I know it's against your faith, but I'd prefer it if you wouldn't say anything.'

'I'll keep a vow of silence in this case.' Isaac winked. 'I have a question though. Your mother seems adamant that Miss Hilton was putting a spell on your door so you could escape to see her. And yet here you are tonight. How have you managed to escape?'

'Oh, Mother doesn't lock the door anymore now that Meg's dead. She doesn't see her as a threat these days.'

'You'd be surprised. She was here only a few hours ago saying she was a curse to the village.' Isaac chuckled. 'Was Miss Hilton letting you out of your room when she was alive?'

'My goodness, no. I just sneaked out the window. There's a tree right outside my bedroom. It doesn't take much for a nimble lad to scale it.'

'And thus another mystery is solved.' Isaac reminisced about his own childhood, recalling the days when he was a young boy scaling trees like a squirrel navigating a forest. How he yearned to be as nimble as he once was.

They conversed for hours until the first light of dawn began to break. A yawn escaped James, and Isaac felt the drip of moisture land on his scalp.

'Come on, it's beginning to rain. I think it's time to go home before your parents catch you. You'll want some sleep before the fair today, no doubt. I think we've done enough here.'

'Yes, whoever is digging her up has missed their opportunity today.'

'Very true.' Isaac stood and neatly folded his blanket. He then lifted the backs of the two chairs and walked toward the church entrance. 'It was lovely talking to you, James. I'm glad you and Miss Hilton had each other.'

'Thank you, Vicar. And thanks for being so kind about her. Few people are.'

'One last thing, James...' Isaac said before James scurried off. '...You said Miss Hilton died not only suddenly but suspiciously. Do you think there was something untoward with her death?'

'I don't just think it, Vicar. I know it.'

'How is that?' Isaac placed the chairs down and scratched his head, staring at James with unwavering curiosity.

'Because I was there.'

Chapter 4

13 Years Earlier

Under the radiant embrace of the sun, the farm stirred to life, the perfect day for the harvest of golden corn. A diligent farmer, John Cavendish rose at dawn, with his loyal farmhand Francis Ashton at his side. Francis had become an integral part of the farm after John secured him a job when the news of his girlfriend Sarah's pregnancy led him away from his previous post serving ale at The Wheatsheaf inn.

Francis confessed to John on an ale-fuelled night beside the worn bar at The Wheatsheaf of his urgent need to marry Sarah before the judgemental eyes of the town labelled their future child a bastard. John compassionately offered the nineteen-year-old a steady position on the farm as well as handing over the keys to a long-deserted cottage that was once inhabited by his mother. The promise of stability was further sealed when John offered the couple a barn reception on his land after their nuptials. It was a generous gesture from John, who often offered the venue for the vibrant annual village fete.

When they first met, Francis had a paunch belly, earned from too many ales down at The Wheatsheaf. Since toiling the fields alongside John, Francis had transformed into a more sculpted figure, gained through the rigors of manual labour. He wore a white shirt bearing the earth's imprint, brown trousers and weathered black shoes. A mop of blond hair, sun-kissed to a golden hue, crowned his clean-shaven face. The biceps sculpted from the laborious hauls of corn sacks transformed him into a handsome man. If only he'd looked this good when he was younger, he considered, he'd have had the pick of the women in the town. But as he considered his two-year-old son, he knew Sarah was the one for him.

The men became rather parched. Matilda Cavendish, John's wife, emerged with refreshments just on time. She had an imposing figure which was softened by her gentle facial features and a cascade of greying red locks. Towering over Francis, she had a complexion in stark contrast to the paleness of the other village wives. The corseted pinafore accentuated her curves, giving her an alluring aura. A fleeting thought crossed Francis's mind – if she had been a few years younger, perhaps he might have sought her affections himself.

The trio savoured Matilda's homemade lemonade before dutifully returning their mugs to her tray. Behind her, Francis caught a glimpse of their expansive home. A large table adorned with bowls and rolling pins took centre stage in the kitchen. A fragrant whiff of fresh bread emitted from a beehive oven beside the kitchen door, constructed from stones once woven into the fabric of their home. The fragrance offered a delightful respite from the customary scent of manure that typically wafted through the village.

'That was lovely, thank you, Mrs Cavendish,' Francis said as he wiped the perspiration from his brow.

'What are you and your wonderful wife doing tonight? Would you like to come over for your dinner?' Matilda suggested.

'We'd love that, thank you.'

'Good. I'll make a pie.' She nodded and retreated to the kitchen, gently closing the door behind her.

'You're a lucky man, John.'

'Don't I know it.' He patted his employee's back. 'Now let's crack on.'

Under the fading glow of the evening sun, they toiled in the expansive fields until the horizon swallowed the last remnants of daylight. The labour was relentless, but John remained persistent in his commitment to farming by hand. Some of his rivals had been persuaded by the allure of modern efficiency such as horse-drawn mechanism, but John recognised the importance of the human touch. Francis was pleased with John's traditional ways as it kept him in a job.

'I think you can go home now, Francis.' John shook his subordinate's hand. 'Good job today. Thank you. Get yourself ready and we'll see you and Sarah over for dinner later. Bring little James with you, of course!'

'Thanks, boss, I will.'

As Francis ambled back to his quaint cottage, the golden hues of twilight weaving around him, John laboured on. The final bags of corn, heavy with the fruits of their day-long toil, were carefully placed in the safety of the barn, shielded from the unpredictable weather which the northwest of England frequently delivered.

John counted the bags of corn. Thirteen sacks stood as a testament to their collective effort. A subtle smile graced John's face, a silent acknowledgement of the money he'd make – enough, he believed, to sustain them through the impending winter months.

With a satisfied glance at the stock, John returned to retrieve the remnants of the day's tools scattered across the field. But as he approached the bounty of fresh vegetables, amidst the vibrant greens and earthy roots, there lurked a familiar yet unwelcome visitor.

A pest.

But not the typical kind found in the form of slugs or fruit flies. No, this was Meg Shelton, the infamous Fylde Hag – a name reverberating through the dark tales from farmers whom she had frustrated along the Fylde coast. Draped in a cloak that barely concealed her distinct features, her unmistakable protruding nose and bony, twig-like form were unmissable even from a distance.

'Oi!' John yelled. 'Meg Shelton!'

Meg swiftly pivoted, her eyes widening in surprise as she concealed her stolen goods within the folds of her cloak. She bolted away, dashing past the farmer who instinctively set off in pursuit. Behind the barn, John eased his pace, the strains of a day's toil and the remnants of a lifetime of ingesting tobacco now taking their toll on his chest. He sauntered past the barn, revealing open fields devoid of hiding places, his gaze scanning the surroundings in search of the elusive intruder.

But Meg was not there.

He retraced his steps to where he had just been, yet there was no hint of her in sight.

As he circled the barn once more, his attention was drawn to the open door where he had been depositing the day's yield. A sly smirk crept across his face as he reached for his shotgun, positioned conveniently by the entrance. With stealthy steps he entered the barn, aiming the firearm towards each corner of the room.

Yet, Meg continued to elude him.

Perplexed, he scrutinized the produce he'd collated throughout the day. Something felt amiss. Had she taken a sack of corn? He meticulously counted the bags.

One, two, three, four, five, six, seven, eight, nine, ten, eleven, twelve, thirteen...

Fourteen...

Was there an extra bag of corn?

Where had it come from?

'I know this is you, Meg. I've heard the tricks you can pull. You can transform yourself into anything. Even a humble bag of corn. Well, I'm done with you.' His finger tightened on the trigger, and a deafening blast shattered the stillness of the barn.

Yellow pops of corn scattered around the barn. The echoes of John's gunshot lingered in the stillness. In the distance, he heard a scream followed by Meg Shelton's eerie cackle. Convinced that she was still in the barn, he walked out, firmly pulled the doors shut, and secured them with a padlock.

'Let's see you try and get out now, you old witch.'

In the distance, a plume of smoke puffed from the chimney of The Wheatsheaf pub, signalling the preparation for the evening crowd. John was aware that Matilda would soon be serving dinner for him and their guests, and he'd need to wash the day's perspiration off himself first. However, an unexpected thirst overcame him. He strolled through the fields toward the inviting glow of the public house, entering and promptly ordering a hearty tankard of ale. His gaze then settled on a vacant stool nestled in the cosy corner beside an oak barrel.

'Constable Kirkham!' John beckoned to the man in the brown uniform adorned with vibrant red collar patches. A white, bushy handlebar moustache decorated his friendly face, and his pot belly found a comfortable perch on the oak barrel serving as his makeshift table. The gentleman, acknowledging the familiar farmer's call, looked up and offered a warm smile.

'John, how are you today?'

'Not good, Constable! Not good!'

'Well it can't be if you're calling me by my official title. I hope this isn't work you're here to see me about.' He slurped his ale, as the white creamy head matted into his tache.

'I'm afraid so.'

'Well this is quite unusual. I don't get much call for trouble in these parts. The odd drunken punch-up perhaps. It's the towns which keep me busy. I'm on night patrol in Preston in a couple of hours.'

'It's that witch Shelton, sir.'

'Oh dear, what's she done now?' Kirkham rolled his eyes. Miss Shelton's antics were a frequent topic of discussion in the village.

'She's been thieving off me again.'

'Oh dear, oh dear, oh dear. Well I'll call round to the Cottam estate tomorrow. Don't you worry. I'll sort it.'

'No need, Archie. I've got her in my barn.'

'What?' Constable Kirkham stood up, intrigued. 'You've caught her?'

'I have indeed.'

'Well I need to see this.'

The two men downed the remains of their drinks and walked back towards the Cavendish farm. John unlocked the padlock and began to slide open the doors.

'I have to say I'm rather excited to finally see her. In all the years I've come to these parts, I've never laid eyes on her. I've heard enough about her though.'

'She's not a pretty sight.'

Inside, the barn was as John had left it. The produce was neatly stacked up, except for one bag which had exploded after firing his gun towards it.

'Where is she?'

John glanced around but his shoulders dropped when he found an empty shack.

'Well she's there.' He pointed towards the burst sack of corn. The detective lifted the bag, hoping to find the infamous woman underneath, but instead, corn rained over the floor.

'I don't understand, John.'

'She ran in here. And then...' He hesitated, suddenly realising how irrational he sounded. 'She transformed herself into that bag of corn. And I shot it. I heard it scream. I thought she might have turned back into her own body by now.'

'Have you been eating some of those mushrooms from the wilderness, Mr Cavendish?' He raised an eyebrow, pondering what substances his old friend might have indulged in. 'Or drinking too much mead?'

'No, I swear. Everyone knows it, speak to the other farmers if you don't believe me. They've seen her transform into all sorts of animals over the years. Granted this is the first time I've heard her convert into a bag of corn.'

'Hmmm.' Kirkham sighed sceptically. 'I'm afraid there's not much I can do. I mean if she has disappeared from here, I haven't much proof she was here in the first place. And if she is here, as you say, as a sack of corn, I think you've already solved the problem.'

He stared at the bag of corn with a hole in the middle where his bullet had torn through.

'I just hope she doesn't turn back into a woman, otherwise I'd have to arrest you for murder,' Kirkham chuckled.

'Well can't you at least write it down? Can't you record it?'

'Aye, yes, I'll do that for you, sure. But next time maybe don't rush me to drink up unless you're sure you have the physical embodiment of Miss Shelton, eh?'

'Yes, of course. I'm sorry, Constable, for wasting your time.'

'Don't worry. Buy me a drink next time you're in The Wheatsheaf.'

'I've got a better option,' John said, breathing in the aroma of his wife's fine cooking. 'Could I interest you in some dinner instead? My wife Matilda has cooked a pie.'

Kirkham sniffed, savouring the enticing aromas emanating from the beehive oven.

'Aye, yes that doesn't sound too bad at all.'

John slapped his friend on the back and guided him toward the kitchen. A bemused Matilda stood in the doorway and let out a sigh.

'You could've warned me we were having extra guests.'

'I'm sorry, love, Archie was doing me a favour. I thought we'd return it in kind.'

'Well, there will be less for everyone else but oh well. I'm sure the Ashtons won't look a gift horse in the mouth. I'm sure they'll be glad of anything truth be told.'

'You always make too much anyway!' It was undeniable. Her meals eclipsed even the transformative feasts of loaves and fishes that Jesus had astonished the wedding guests with.

They settled at the table, soon joined by Sarah and Francis Ashton, who took turns carrying their toddler son James in their arms. Matilda served a butter pie, its thick shortcrust enveloping layers of sliced potatoes, onions, and butter. Accompanying the savoury delight was a mug of mead, brewed with care by Matilda herself.

'This is delicious, Matilda, thank you,' Kirkham said, picking remnants of crust from his moustache.

Once they had all eaten their fill, Matilda gathered their plates and began to wash them with her rag but accidentally dropped it on the floor. As she bent over to retrieve it, a sudden twinge in her stomach made her clutch her waist, emitting a low groan.

'Matilda, are you alright, love?' John rushed to her side, placing a supportive arm around his wife.

'I'm in pain,' she cried. 'I feel like someone has stabbed me.'

The guests all stood up, eager to lend a helping hand. Francis pulled over a seat, urging her to rest. Matilda sobbed, clutching on to her belly.

'It hurts so much.'

Kirkham poured a mug of water and handed it to the ailing host. She sipped it, but moments later she threw up the water, the mead and the pie she'd consumed earlier. Sarah grabbed the rag and began to scrub up the bile, while Francis and John placed Matilda, who had begun to lose consciousness, onto the cold hard floor.

'Archie, what can we do?'

'I'll go fetch the doctor.' Archie dashed out of the cottage, pounding on the door of a nearby dwelling by the vicarage, shouting the doctor's name.

'Is everything alright, Archie?' Reverend Isaac Armstrong poked his head out of the door, drawn by the commotion outside.

'I need Doctor Oldham,' Archie shouted. 'In fact, we may need you too, Vicar.'

'What on earth has happened?'

'It's Mrs Cavendish. She's collapsed. She's unconscious.'

'I'll get my coat.' Isaac grabbed the garment from the hook and joined Archie in calling for Doctor Oldham. The window on the second floor opened and out popped the face of a twenty-something handsome man. He had a thick head of dark hair which flowed down to his shoulders, chocolate brown eyes and an olive complexion. Passers-by could catch glimpses of the wisps of chest hair on the bare man.

'Whatever is the matter?' He rubbed his eyes. 'I was just having a snooze. It's been a hell of a day.'

'It's Mrs Cavendish, she's collapsed in pain.'

'Let me grab my medicine box and I'll be right with you.'

A few minutes later, Doctor Oldham emerged from his front door, clad in a blue overcoat. He continued to button up his white shirt as he closed the door behind him, waving goodbye to his wife, to whom he had no time to explain his sudden departure. As a medic's wife, she was more than used to it.

The three of them ran back to the farm. Doctor Oldham had compounds of mercury and arsenic in his leather satchel, ready to administer to any ailing patient. On arrival they found Matilda on the floor, her skin white and her chest still. Doctor Oldham checked her pulse.

'I'm afraid it's too late for her.' He looked up at her husband with a resigned expression. 'I'm afraid she's died, Mr Cavendish. I'm so very sorry.'

John collapsed into the chair, overcome with grief, and began to sob. Sarah, offering support, placed an arm around him, while Francis attended to the crying James in another room. Doctor Oldham examined the body, and meanwhile Isaac said a prayer. He then dabbed his finger in holy water and made a cross against Matilda's cold forehead.

'If I was to guess, I'd say it was possibly appendicitis. It's hard to say. But it can be quite common and unfortunately deadly. Has she complained of any pain in recent days?' Doctor Oldham asked.

'She did. She just thought it was something she'd eaten. I wish we'd got you over here sooner.'

'There's little we could do to be honest, Mr Cavendish. I'm truly, truly sorry.'

The next morning, they transported Matilda Cavendish's body to St. Anne's Church in a wooden coffin crafted overnight by Francis. After a brief service, officiated by Isaac, she was laid to rest in the church grounds. As they sang a final hymn during the interment, a familiar figure strolled past the church along the road. Catching sight of John Cavendish, she offered a wave.

'It's that bloody witch!'

The mourners turned to see a smiling Meg Shelton, who had curiously developed a limp since John had last seen her running into his barn only the day before.

'She did this to her! I'm telling you! She killed my wife! She put a hex on her!' He turned to Constable Kirkham. 'And look at that limp. I told you that bag of corn I shot was her!'

They all stared at the witch who continued to smile as she hobbled down the road, now clutching at her staff.

Chapter 5

As the first rays of dawn painted the sky in hues of lavender and gold, Isaac stirred from his slumber to the melodic serenade of blackbirds nestled in the secret corners of his lush garden – a symphony that served as his personal natural alarm clock. Eager to see if his night's vigil had been a success, he dressed himself in his black robes, fastening the clerical collar around his neck and rushed downstairs. The night's labour weighed on his mind as he shared a hushed breakfast with his loyal housekeeper, Mrs Norris.

Eager to determine if any further mysteries had unravelled whilst he slept, Isaac departed from the sanctuary of his home with a stealthy purpose. The whole village awaited the outcome of his pursuits.

The churchyard loomed before Isaac. As he entered, his keen eyes were drawn to the conspicuous absence of activity around a particular grave – the final resting place of Margery Hilton, AKA the notorious Meg Shelton. There, beneath the open sky, the earth lay undisturbed, and no ghastly ghoul had clawed its way from the depths.

Relief washed over Isaac, and an unbidden smile etched itself across his face. The night's vigilant watch, shared in secrecy with James, had proven triumphant. The spectre of Meg Shelton, a source of dread among the villagers, remained undisturbed in her eternal slumber at least for another night.

Now unburdened by the village's phantom concerns, Isaac confidently trod the well-worn Roman path towards the Cavendish farm. There John orchestrated the day's festivities. In the face of recent fires that had wreaked havoc on the Cavendish farm, John was determined in his decision to carry on with the annual celebration on his property. Visitors endeavoured to divert their attention from the fire remnants that marred the once-vibrant fields and instead directed their gaze towards the decorated barns.

The quaint village of Woodplumpton, steeped in tradition and history, brimmed with excitement as it readied itself for the annual fete – a jubilant celebration marking the demise of the infamous Guy Fawkes, the man who dared to plot the explosive downfall of Parliament one hundred years before.

As John readied the stage for the impending festivities, Sarah and Francis Ashton embarked on a culinary mission of their own. Their stall, a riot of colours and aromas, bore the fruits of what had survived the fire at the Cavendish farm and their own personal garden, nurtured by the diligent hands of their son James.

Nestled among the lively marketplace, the Clitheroe family's stall had a bounty of freshly baked goods and cheeses, each crafted with the rich, creamy milk sourced straight from their own farm. In contrast, Mary Parr's stall bore a different kind of warmth and sentiment. A display of used baby clothes, each lovingly knitted with a grandmother's touch, spilled across her table.

Amidst the lively celebrations, the distinguished figures of Lord Cottam and his elegant wife Catherine gracefully entered the heart of the festivities. With an air of refined charm, they unveiled a sumptuous array of game from their sprawling estate. The unveiling of pheasants and venison marked a culinary spectacle that transcended the ordinary bounds of Woodplumpton's rustic fare. These gastronomic treasures, usually unattainable luxuries for a town steeped in humble simplicity, for one day a year graced the tables of the impoverished community.

Isaac, now immersed in the vibrant tapestry of Woodplumpton's festivities, moved gracefully between the stalls, extending warm congratulations to each stallholder. Gratitude echoed through the air as they in turn expressed their appreciation for Isaac's noble act of standing watch over Meg Shelton's grave. His guardianship had shielded the village from potential embarrassment, particularly as visitors from afar came in to enjoy the festivities.

As the chimes of the village clock resonated through the air signalling the arrival of noon, a wave of anticipation swept through the crowd. The locals, hungry for the culinary treasures laid out by their fellow villagers, flocked to the Cavendish farm.

In one corner, the savoury aroma of a hog's roast wafted through the air. Simultaneously, a vat of mulled wine bubbled and stirred opposite. David Robinson and his wife Agnes took a keg of ale from the village watering hole, The Wheatsheaf, quenching the thirst of the local revellers.

At the heart of the merriment, a stage adorned with fragrant heather and lavender was graced by a local folk band, The Plumptons. Strings and winds echoed through the community. Couples twirled, laughter echoed, and the vibrancy of Woodplumpton's annual fete reached its crescendo on the impromptu dance floor. From the young to the old, all were swept up in the infectious energy of the music, abandoning themselves to the enchanting pulse of the atmosphere.

As the village of Woodplumpton surrendered to the infectious rhythm of the dance, a collective moment of pure bliss overcame them. In the twirls of their skirts and the stomps of their feet, the recent antics surrounding Meg Shelton's grave faded into the background. Laughter and joy became the focal point, momentarily eclipsing the ghostly whispers of the local churchyard.

The crowd hushed as Abraham, affectionately known as Abe, the charismatic lead singer of The Plumptons, seized the moment. With a mischievous glint in his eye, he announced, 'Our next song is dedicated to a local legend, none other than Meg Shelton!'

In the heart of Woodplumpton, where shadows play their games,

There lies a tale of mystery, Meg Shelton is her name.

A legend whispered in the wind, in every creak and moan,

A spectral dance, a ghostly trance, in the village she's well-known.

Oh, Meg Shelton, in the moonlight's glow,

A ghostly figure, secrets she bestows.

Through the ancient trees, where the whispers grow,

Meg Shelton, in the shadows, her story we'll show.

She slumbers in the churchyard, 'neath the silent stone,

A restless spirit, a mystery to be known.

The villagers, they talk in hushed tones,

Of Meg Shelton's ghost, where the ivy's overgrown.

But in the moonlit night, she comes alive,

A spectral waltz, where the shadows thrive.

Through the misty air, her whispers arrive,

Meg Shelton's legend, forever to survive.

Oh, Meg Shelton, in the moonlight's glow,

A ghostly figure, secrets she bestows.

Through the ancient trees, where the whispers grow,

Meg Shelton, in the shadows, her story we'll show.

In the tavern tales, by the fireplace light,

They spin the yarns of Meg, in the silent night.

A spectral dance, in the pale moon's sight,

Meg Shelton's legend, like a haunting kite.

Through the rolling hills and the ancient lanes,

Meg's spirit lingers, where history remains.

A ghostly guardian, in the night she reigns,

In Woodplumpton's heart, where her story sustains.

But in the moonlit night, she comes alive,

A spectral waltz, where the shadows thrive.

Through the misty air, her whispers arrive,

Meg Shelton's legend, forever to survive.

So let the melodies echo, through the village fair,

In every note, Meg Shelton's tale we share.

A haunting ballad, in the midnight air,

Woodplumpton's legend, for all to declare.

Amidst the cheers and boos that swirled through the crowd, Isaac and James exchanged a glance of shared dismay. Their eyes met across the lively gathering and they rolled their eyes in unison.

'Hello, James,' Isaac greeted the young lad with a warm smile as he approached. James, with a mix of weariness and enthusiasm for the festivities ahead, turned to face Isaac, yawning after a night's vigil. 'How are you feeling today?'

'I'm coping.' James shrugged, brushing off any regrets he had about having stayed up all night.

'I take it your mother didn't discover you weren't in your bed last night?'

'No, thankfully. Her and my father were out like a candle. They'd enjoyed far too many whiskies.'

'I'm surprised there was any left after the amount you poured into that flask.'

'Oh, there's always plenty of whisky in our house. I replaced what I'd used with water. They won't notice.'

'I'll pretend I didn't hear this dishonesty, James.' He raised his eyebrows with a glimmer of disapproval.

'Sorry, Vicar.' James bowed his head in shame but was reassured by a tap on his shoulder. He looked up and found the Reverend towering over him with a beaming smile.

As the day stretched into the late evening, the pulse of Woodplumpton's festivities showed no signs of waning. The melodies of the folk band lingered in the air, intertwining with the raucous laughter and the clinking of glasses.

As the moon ascended, casting its silvery glow on the jubilant crowd, the village entered the grand finale of the evening. John, the orchestrator of the day's festivities, took centre stage once more. In a grand spectacle, he set off a breathtaking array of fireworks, a dazzling tribute that honoured the historical saviour of Parliament nearly one hundred years before.

With the grand finale of fireworks painting the night sky with its dazzling display, the revelry began to fade, and the once-boisterous crowd gradually dispersed. As each hour passed, pockets of villagers made their way home, their laughter and footsteps echoing through the now quieting streets of Woodplumpton. The festive energy waned, leaving behind a tranquil aftermath.

Isaac, wearied from the responsibilities of guarding Meg Shelton's grave and the evening's revelries, yearned for the comfort of his own bed. However the lingering locals, tipsy from a day of sipping spirits, continued to seek his advice. There was no time off for vicars.

'I must go,' Isaac declared, gently waving off the lingering parishioners who sought solace and counsel in the quiet hours of the night. With a sense of duty and a sermon awaiting him the next morning, he trod the familiar path back to the vicarage.

As he passed the church, Isaac's attention was snagged by an unusual sight. In the church grounds, John Cavendish, Sarah Ashton and Lord Cottam had gathered in an impromptu circle. Their expressions were marked by a shared bewilderment, their heads shaking in apparent confusion.

Intrigued, Isaac approached with a curious gaze. The trio, caught up in their own deliberations, looked up at him with a mix of surprise and concern. There was an intense energy surrounding them.

'You promised us this wouldn't happen again,' John grumbled, his tone filled with a mixture of frustration and disbelief. As Isaac neared the perplexed trio, the weight of the situation became clear. His eyes widened with shock as he realised the source of their bewilderment.

Beside their feet lay the lifeless body of Meg Shelton.

Chapter 6

18 Months Earlier

Fourteen-year-old James Ashton wandered around Meg Shelton's humble abode, his young eyes wide with awe and curiosity. The hovel, a stark contrast to the tidy home he was accustomed to, contained intriguing chaos. On every surface, a mixture of potions and peculiar objects lay scattered, each hinting at a life steeped in mystique and the secrets of the supernatural.

The dwelling stood in stark juxtaposition to the immaculate estate that stretched behind it – the grandeur of the Cottam manor and its pristine gardens formed a breathtaking backdrop. Yet the outhouse, which still stood as part of the Cottam estate, seemed to languish in its state of disarray. Despite its unpleasant appearance against the opulence that surrounded it, Lord Cottam seemed unwilling to transform the hovel into a more attractive home.

'You need to get Lord Cottam to fix the roof,' James insisted, his voice carrying a touch of concern. He placed an empty bucket strategically below the leak, diverting the incessant drip that created a puddle on the worn floor.

The modest accommodation offered a glimpse into Meg Shelton's basic existence. Sparse cupboards and meagre furnishings spoke volumes about how she lived, relying on the essentials to get by. The only furniture she owned was a small bed and a table with two chairs, which suggested her existence in the house was merely about eating and sleeping, a mere respite where Meg rested before venturing out to cause chaos for her unsuspecting neighbours. A large oak barrel stood in the corner, propping up old tankards and dirty bowls.

'Ha!' Meg cackled, her laughter echoing across the stone walls. 'Do you think that stuffy bastard cares about me? He wants to drive me out. His father gave me permission to stay here for as long as I live. And his son hopes I'll either die sooner or seek refuge somewhere else if this place continues to fall apart. But I'm not going anywhere.'

Meg's determined gaze softened, and she motioned for James to take a seat on a rickety stool. With a contemplative sigh, she began to unravel the story of her friendship with the Cottam family.

'It was Lord Cottam's father who first noticed me,' Meg explained, her eyes flickering with memories. 'He was different from his son, more open-minded, you see. We struck a deal – I could stay on this land, and in return, I'd support their family around the home. He always took an interest in my herbs and potions. He found value in what others dismissed as witchery.'

James listened with a mix of fascination and empathy, beginning to grasp the intricate web of history and relationships that had woven Meg Shelton into the very fabric of Woodplumpton. The disparity between Meg's humble abode and her connections with the aristocracy underscored the complex dynamics that defined the village and its enigmatic resident.

'As for the current Lord Cottam,' Meg chuckled wryly, 'he's not as fond of our arrangement. He'd rather sweep me away like dirt under a rug. But I stay, for I have as much right to this land as he does.'

'So what are all these potions?'

Meg's eyes twinkled mischievously as James pointed towards the glass jars containing an array of mysterious substances. As James studied the jars, a sense of empathy tugged at him. He could understand how the unconventional life his friend lived might lead villagers to brand Meg as a witch.

'These,' Meg began, her fingers tracing the labels on the jars, 'are my remedies, my lotions, and sometimes, just a bit of magic to mend what the world breaks.' She giggled, fully aware of the mystique her potions carried. 'People call it witchcraft, but I call it survival. The herbs, roots, and secrets passed down through generations hold the power to heal and protect. What I create here is nothing more than what you'd find in a hospital. I learned everything from midwifery, passed down to me by older generations of doctors and carers who had spent years trialling different natural substances on wounds and illnesses. Some worked, while others didn't. But nobody questions whether they may be witches. Sadly they think I am. Maybe because I'm a woman. Men don't like intelligent women. So we get put in our place.'

'I wish the town got to know you better. You seem nice enough to me.' James smiled and placed a comforting hand on the old woman's frail arm.

Meg's eyes softened, touched by the genuine sentiment in James's words. The warmth of his smile and the reassuring hand on her delicate arm spoke volumes, bridging the gap between their generations and social divides.

'You're a kind soul, James,' Meg replied, her voice carrying a hint of gratitude. 'People see what they want to see, but there's more to this world than meets the eye.'

'I'm intrigued by your herbs. We've got a patch of land outside our house on the Cavendish farm. I'd love to grow something myself. But Father spends too much time toiling on John's crops, when we could be growing our own.'

As James shared his aspirations for a green-fingered hobby, Meg's eyes lit up with enthusiasm.

'If you've got the land, young one, don't be afraid to make it bloom,' Meg advised, her weathered hands gesturing towards the unseen potential in the distance. 'Growing something of your own can be a powerful thing. It connects you to the land, to the seasons, and to the very heartbeat of Woodplumpton.'

Meg walked over to the counter beside the window, where the soft glow of sunlight filtered through the worn curtains. Her hands moved with practised grace, lifting out an array of seeds and a small glass jar containing a mysterious brown watery substance.

'Here,' she said, passing the goods to James. 'These will start you off.'

'Why don't you grow your own food rather than stealing from others?' asked James, glancing around the ample meadows which Meg lived amongst.

'Do you not think I've tried?' Meg replied. 'Every time I try to create a small patch for myself, Lord Cottam rips it up and tells me that this is *his* land, not mine. And I have nowhere else to plant them. I have not a penny to my name, so I have no choice but to reap from other people's fields. I only take what I need and nothing more. A girl needs to survive.'

'I better go,' James said, aware that dinnertime was approaching. Graciously accepting the gifts from Meg Shelton, he embraced his newfound friend, the only true confidante in a village where secrets and judgments loomed. Waving her off, James embarked on the forty-five-minute journey back to Woodplumpton.

Entering his house, he was greeted by his parents, and the aroma of dinner filled the air. His mother eyed the goods he had brought from Miss Shelton, a mixture of curiosity and concern etched on her face. She had already faced a scolding from John Cavendish after he reported that James and his friends had stolen tomatoes from his farm and wondered if James's nimble fingers had been at her husband's employer's patch once again. They had a lot to lose if they upset Mr Cavendish.

'What's this?' his mother inquired, eyeing the treasures on the side. 'You've not been looting again, have you?' Her stern tone showed a mother's worry, amplified by the repercussions of his previous misadventures. He had been forced to stay at home for a week and went to bed without dinner on the night of his misadventures.

James, keen to defuse any concerns, replied with an earnest tone, 'It's a gift from my friend Meg. She said I can grow my own vegetables.' He displayed the seeds and the jar of potion, a glimmer of excitement in his eyes.

'Who is this *Meg*?' Sarah's eyes squinted as she attempted to place the name within the roster of local villagers.

'Meg Shelton,' James replied, and his words met with a sudden gasp from his mother. In a swift motion, she grabbed the goods from him and flung them outside, slamming the door behind her.

'God knows what she's given you here, James. That woman is an evil witch! You've possibly brought a curse upon our home. You are not to see that woman again, do you hear me?'

The sudden shift in atmosphere left James standing in the doorway, caught between the conflicting worlds of an ancient village feud and the genuine connection he had forged with Meg. The seeds and potion lay outside, discarded like artefacts of forbidden magic.

'But she's my friend,' James pleaded, his voice filled with sincerity. 'She's a good person. A misunderstood woman...' Before he could continue, Sarah placed a finger against his lips, silencing his words.

'Francis!' she said sternly, turning to her husband. 'Back me up here.'

Francis, momentarily pausing eating his dinner of haggis, looked up at the two most important people in his life. Torn between his wife's concerns for the rumours surrounding Meg Shelton's abilities and the loyalty he felt to his son, he grappled with a way that could please them both.

'I haven't witnessed anything untoward myself,' he began, thoughts lingering on the tales that had woven a web of suspicion around Meg. But his wife's stern stare tipped the balance of his scales. 'But your mother is right,' he conceded, his gaze shifting to James. 'You must not see her again.'

Heartbroken and weary from the turbulent evening, James retreated to his room. Staring out of the window, he let the weight of his emotions cascade into silent tears. He cried himself to sleep.

The next morning, fuelled by a mixture of defiance and grief, James rose before his parents could address the lingering tension which had built up the evening prior. Determined to distance himself from the shackles of their rules, he ran out of the front door.

As he passed the side of the house, a sight caught his attention – a small patch of grass had been dug up, fresh soil scattered around, and wooden canes stood guard in the earth, supporting the promise of a future plantation. James approached the unexpected arrival of a small allotment. Glimpsing closer, he marvelled at the small buds of life emerging from the soil and knew that Meg Shelton had cast her charm upon their previously uninspiring garden.

Chapter 7

'It's time we take action!' John Cavendish declared, his voice resonating with determination. Sarah Ashton and Lord Cottam nodded in agreement. Isaac sighed, the weight of responsibility heavy on his shoulders. He had welcomed them into the vestry after the discovery of Meg Shelton's body lying above the ground, seemingly having escaped her tomb once again. Isaac, resigned to the inevitability of the situation, handed around a mug of whisky to his parishioners. Rubbing his eyes, he braced himself for the storm that the villagers had cooked up just as he'd hoped to retire to bed after a day at the fair.

'Listen...' Isaac interjected, his voice cutting through the passion in the vestry. 'Miss Hilton is not climbing out of that grave. Someone in this village is digging her up. I have to believe this, as anything else would be blasphemous.'

The candlelight cast flickering shadows on the faces of those gathered, uncertainty and scepticism clouding their expressions. The vestry, once a sanctuary, now housed a congregation torn between the tangible reality and the spectral tales that had spun a web of fear. As Isaac sought to redirect the narrative, the vestry became a battleground of beliefs, a clash between the rational and the supernatural.

'But who on earth would dig up a rotting corpse?' Sarah bellowed, her frustration echoing through the vestry. Isaac, stroking his beard, surveyed the three visitors who had disrupted any chance of him getting to bed anytime soon.

'Well...' Isaac mused, fixing his gaze on the trio. 'I have to ask why the three of you were even in the vicinity of the churchyard. Sarah, John, you both live on the farm where we've spent the entire day. While you, Lord Cottam, left the fair over an hour ago. Why are the three of you venturing out to the graveyard at this late hour?'

The question hung in the air, a beacon of suspicion pointing towards those who had fervently called for action against Meg Shelton.

'How dare you! That's slander!' Lord Cottam's voice thundered, his fist slamming down on the table in defiance. 'If you must know, I was passing the church when I left the fair. I nipped into the graveyard to pay my respects to my dear parents. I'll admit, after a drink or two, I become rather reminiscent.' He wiped moisture from his eye, a vulnerable moment in the midst of tension. 'And that's when I saw that old hag had climbed out of her grave again. I immediately ran over to John's house, and he suggested we get Francis and Sarah.'

'Francis is out for the count. He had too many whiskies,' Sarah explained. 'But I had to see this with my own eyes. We can't let this carry on, Vicar.'

Isaac, with a discerning gaze, observed the attire of the three individuals before him. John still wore his Sunday best, a testament to the day of entertaining the locals on the farm. Sarah, in contrast, had donned her nightdress, an unexpected choice for a venture into the churchyard at this late hour. Meanwhile Lord Cottam, displaying a stark contrast in wealth, wore the finest silk — a luxury that few in the village could afford.

As Isaac examined their clothing, a realisation settled in. There wasn't a spot of soil on any of them, nor were they perspiring from the exertion it would take to dig up a corpse. Despite the old woman's body being frail and fragile even in life, it still posed a challenge for anyone attempting such a feat, especially at this late hour.

'Very well. But I stand by my beliefs that somebody in this village is doing this,' Isaac replied. The three sighed with relief, grateful for the absolution from the suspicious scrutiny of their local vicar. However, the pressing issue at hand remained.

'We still need to do something about this, Reverend,' Sarah interjected. 'Whether or not Meg Shelton is crawling out of her grave herself, or whether it's one of the locals playing a prank on us, we can't carry on like this. It's a distraction for the village and is an awful sight for anyone to see. Imagine if my James saw it. He's only a young lad, he'd be scarred for life.'

The shared concern resonated in the vestry, transcending the boundaries of belief and scepticism. The enigma of Meg Shelton's recurring appearances had become a collective challenge that demanded resolution, lest it cast a lasting shadow over the village of Woodplumpton.

'Listen...' Isaac replied, a newfound certainty in his voice. 'Her gravestone is being delivered tomorrow. It isn't much, as she's a pauper after all. But I took a few shillings from the church fund to provide her one. I'm confident the stone will be heavy enough that she couldn't be dug up as swiftly as she is currently. I'm sure whoever is playing this disrespectful prank on the village and on Miss Hilton will be prevented by the weight of her tombstone.'

The vestry, for a moment, fell into a contemplative silence.

'Very well,' Sarah sighed with relief. 'I'm happy with that.'

'Me too,' John Cavendish agreed.

'I concur,' Lord Cottam echoed, his agreement carrying a note of stern resolve. 'However, if these antics continue after the stone is delivered, I'll have no choice but to demand she is removed from the churchyard.'

'Come on, I'm utterly spent. It's time to retire for the night,' Sarah exclaimed, bringing a sense of relief to Isaac. The vicar yearned to return home, seeking the solace of sleep before the demands of the morning sermon. Exiting the vestry, the trio of visitors began to disperse toward their respective homes.

'Wait a moment,' Isaac called, and they turned around, startled by the sense of unresolved matters. 'Is no one willing to assist me in reburying her?' he pointed towards the grave, where Meg Shelton's body still lay exposed.

'Sorry, Vicar, we've got an early start,' John replied, and the others nodded in unison. As they vanished into the enveloping darkness, Isaac sighed, left alone to face the task of reburying the unfortunate spinster. The allure of his bed suddenly felt even more distant.

The next morning, Isaac delivered his sermon to a diminished congregation, scattered across the church pews. Many in the village were recovering from the festivities of the previous day, nursing hangovers in the comfort of their homes. Isaac, in turn, felt a sense of relief with the smaller audience. Exhausted from the late-night task of reburying Meg Shelton's exhumed body, he could now relax without the pressure to muster the usual enthusiasm that captivated his bustling Sunday crowd.

As the sermon concluded, Isaac was pleased to see the arrival of the long-awaited tombstone, punctually delivered by the local stonemason on a horse-drawn carriage. The skilled artisans placed the stone over the once-bare patch that harboured the remains of the alleged witch. Engraved on it were the words, *Margery Hilton, 1640-1705. Rest in Peace.*

Isaac found solace in seeing Margery Hilton's birth name proudly presented on the stone, hoping it would divert the locals' attention from her infamous alias, Meg Shelton. Perhaps now the villagers would allow the woman to finally rest, and the substantial weight of the stone would deter anyone from playing future pranks by exhuming her body.

Eager to share the news with Margery's only friend in the village, Isaac made his way to the home of the Ashtons. It was a quaint two-bedroom stone house with a thatched roof, nestled in the expanse of the Cavendish farm. Smaller than the landowner's grand abode, the modest building provided enough space for the small family, who had once harboured dreams of expansion. Isaac had consoled the bereaved Sarah Ashton through the losses of numerous children over the years. Now, with just one child, they lived comfortably, but the voids in Sarah's heart, spaces meant for additional offspring, cast a lingering sadness within the home that could have accommodated more little feet running around.

'Good news, Mrs Ashton,' Isaac said as she answered the door. She appeared sprightlier than the exhausted figure he had encountered in the churchyard the evening prior. 'The gravestone is firmly covering the ground.'

She sighed with relief and smiled. 'Thanks for letting me know, Reverend. Would you come in for some tea?'

She moved aside to let the vicar enter. Isaac took a seat at their dining table. 'Is James around? I hoped to speak with him.'

She looked at the vicar, confusion etched on her face at his desire to see her son. 'Is he in trouble?'

'Oh heavens no. I just know he and Miss Hilton were friends of sorts and he might want to come and pay his respects now that her gravestone is in place.'

'Oh, I see,' Sarah frowned. 'Well, he's out playing with Henry. He's found some normality now, hanging around with boys his own age since Meg is gone. I think it's healthy. I don't believe it's appropriate for him to visit her grave, with all due respect, Reverend.'

'I understand.' Isaac bowed his head, a tinge of sadness in his expression at her decision. 'Well, send him my regards. I noticed his vegetable patch is flourishing.' He glanced out the window toward the vibrant array of plants, herbs, and vegetables growing outside.

'Yes,' Sarah replied with an air of grievance in her voice. 'He seems to enjoy spending time out there. And I have to admit I do like the produce he brings in. Saves us a few shillings here and there. I just wish his clothes weren't covered in mud all the time.'

Isaac chuckled, 'Well, boys will be boys.'

'Indeed.' Sarah nodded.

Isaac savoured the last sip of tea before gracefully rising from his chair. 'I must bid you farewell. I have matters to attend to,' he declared.

Sarah accepted the empty mug with a smile. 'I'll inform James that you asked after him.'

Exiting their home, Isaac strolled towards James's vegetable patch, marvelling at the impressive variety of produce. He couldn't help but be impressed by how James maintained such an exceptional array. As his own attempts ended in failure, Isaac relied on donations from local farmers and his housekeeper's efforts in their modest garden. The stark contrast only deepened his admiration for the young gardener's skill, and he wondered whether Miss Hilton had offered him something otherworldly to help bring life to his vibrant delights.

Isaac returned to the vicarage, surrendering to the lure of sleep for a few hours. Desperation to recover from the two nights of disrupted rest fuelled his fatigue, and he couldn't help but curse the legendary tales of the humble Margery Hilton. She now lay at peace just yards away, yet Isaac couldn't shake the uneasy feeling that she might still be far from safe, vulnerable to those who harboured ill intentions towards her.

When he awoke, the dim light of dusk filled the room, signalling the approach of Evensong. Isaac dressed and bade farewell to Mrs Norris, who was diligently dusting the house and preparing his evening supper, ready to be served upon his return. As he strolled towards the church, a familiar face caught his eye. Young James Ashton was walking towards the Cavendish farm.

'James!' Isaac called out, offering an enthusiastic wave. James turned and waved back.

'Reverend, how pleasant to see you. I was just on my way home.'

'I hear you are friendly with Henry again. I'm so pleased. I saw your mother earlier.'

'Yes, we were distant for a little while, especially after I started hanging out with Meg, but we're on good terms again now. What did my mother want? Is she still ranting about Meg's body being on display for all of Woodplumpton to see?'

'Actually I was giving her the good news that Miss Hilton's tombstone was now firmly in place. I actually wanted to tell you too. I wondered if you'd like to come and pay your respects, given you two were such good friends. But your mother thought it might not be appropriate.'

'I'd love to! But maybe don't tell my mother.'

'I wouldn't dream of it.'

They walked into the graveyard, and Isaac led the way to the stone, pleased to see it still in its place where it had been earlier that morning. He plucked some petals from the yard and handed them to James, who smiled gratefully. As they approached the front of the stone, something was amiss. The beautifully etched carving from the stonemason was no longer as clear. Thick black paint now covered the tribute that had been visible earlier. Instead of Margery Hilton's name, large black handwritten letters now boldly displayed the name *Meg Shelton*.

'Who would do this?' James asked. 'I know it was how everyone referred to her but to dishonour her grave like this feels particularly cruel.'

Isaac stroked his beard, his mind grappling with the peculiarities of their graveyard. Among its residents were several infamous figures, including murderers and notable enemies of the town. Yet, none had endured as much cruelty towards their final resting place as poor old Margery Hilton.

'There's only one person I can imagine who would want the town to forget her original name. I think I know who might be behind all this...'

Chapter 8

50 years earlier

The Hilton estate graced the outskirts of Barton, a quaint hamlet located north of Preston. Much like Woodplumpton, the town boasted a small collection of houses, originally occupied by the servants of the grand hall and situated on the borough's edge. Vast stretches of farmland enveloped the area. The estate featured a lengthy private drive adorned with trees lining the road. At its culmination, a grand sandstone building stood proudly, commanding the landscape.

Lord and Lady Hilton currently presided over the estate, their home and titles having passed down through generations. Following tradition, their son Christopher stood next in line to inherit the grand abode along with the prestigious title. Much like the neighbouring Cottam family, they represented the pinnacle of aristocracy, having distant connections to the royal family. Among the privileged few in the borough to own property, the Hiltons were known for providing employment and hosting opulent parties for their wealthy acquaintances. Meanwhile, the townspeople served beverages and presented the finest food, only able to watch from the side-lines, never affording a taste of the luxuries enjoyed by the elite.

Margery Hilton, the youngest of the Hiltons' four children, occupied a room on the third floor. Being the last to join the family, she was relegated to the smallest room, and due to a consequence of both her birth order and gender, she was denied any prospects of inheriting such a grand property. As a woman, she had no entitlement to her parents' wealth, and even if she were to marry into affluence, she would remain a resident of her husband's home, devoid of any ownership.

Young Margery, affectionately known as Meg to those closest to her, did not possess conventional beauty. Unlike her older sister Lucy, she hadn't inherited her mother's attractive features. She had a protruding nose and the occasional wisp across her upper lip, and the family's servants were tasked with tending to her physical appearance. Margery, unlike her brother, was unable to attend school, but she was permitted to join excursions with other affluent families. However, as the hairs on her chin began to sprout whilst on holiday, unkind girls noticed her imperfections and cruelly dubbed her 'The Bearded Lady.'

'You should join the circus,' Alice Hutton jibed. 'It's the only chance you have as no man will ever want to marry you.'

The girls' words cut deep, causing pain and embarrassment to Meg. Equally hurtful were the disgusted looks from her mother. Meg's father would occasionally accuse his wife of having an affair, casting doubt on Meg's lineage. 'How could she possibly be mine? Look at her,' he would say, barely able to glance at her.

At almost sixteen years old, Meg was the only daughter still residing at home. Her elder sisters had been married off, a common practice among aristocratic families to arrange unions and continue the blue bloodline. This custom aimed to ensure their daughters were cared for throughout their lives, particularly considering the legal restrictions that prevented them from owning properties or amassing prosperity independently.

In the stark confines of her chamber, she perched delicately on the bed's edge, adorned in a rigid, pastel-green gown with an elegant train. That morning, her mother had meticulously applied layers of white makeup to her face, accentuating the effect with a touch of crimson blush on her cheeks. She felt akin to a chalkboard, susceptible to a mere breath that could disperse the dust-like residue clinging to her face. Her gaze drifted toward the window, where a horse-drawn carriage steadily advanced toward the dwelling. She gulped, apprehensive as she braced for the impending arrival.

'Meg, come hither please!' her mother's voice echoed through the majestic corridor.

Meg drew in a steadying breath and complied with her mother's summons. Descending a sweeping staircase, she entered the grand hall. A stoic suit of armour stood sentinel in one corner, while an impressive fireplace commanded attention as the focal point of the opulent room. Meg's mother meticulously smoothed her attire, scrutinising for any hint of creases or crumbs. Meg sighed in frustration, enduring the ordeal with a sense of humiliation.

The visitor's carriage elicited a distinct squeak as it came to a halt, prompting their diligent servant – a stout woman clad in a black dress adorned with a pristine white apron – to swing open the door gracefully. With a respectful bow, she acknowledged the arrivals.

'Lady Hilton,' Lord Alnwick acknowledged with a courtly bow as he pressed a gentle kiss to her offered hand. 'I am honoured by your warm welcome to this charming abode of yours. The journey was long and the anticipation of our meeting made each moment feel like a timeless venture.'

'It's an honour to receive you in our company, sir. How long did it take you to get here?' she asked.

'In total, a mere three days, with just a brief stopover,' he shared. A man well over thirty years Meg's senior, Lord Alnwick had a portly figure, his belly protruding beneath a face flushed with a tinge of red. He had manoeuvred himself into a distinctive green and black silk collarless coat, worn over a flamboyant yellow waistcoat adorned with large flowers and leaves that sprawled across the fabric. A snap of his fingers set his diligent aides into swift motion, efficiently unloading the carriage of his belongings and ferrying them into the confines of the estate.

'Mother, may I be excused?' Meg asked, a yearning to distance herself evident in her plea. The man before her carried the unmistakable odour of someone who had engaged in a prolonged game of boxing.

'Good heavens, no!' Lady Hilton gasped, aghast at the mere suggestion. 'Lord Alnwick has journeyed all the way from Northumbria to grace us with his presence. We shall convene for tea in the drawing room.'

'And who might this young lady be?' Lord Alnwick inquired with a bow directed towards Meg. Unlike his greeting to her mother, he refrained from kissing her hand, keeping her at a distance.

'This is our daughter Margery,' her mother giggled nervously, gently nudging Meg forward toward the sweaty gentleman. 'The one we spoke to you about.'

Lord Alnwick scrutinized Meg from head to toe, stepping back as if to encompass her entirely. His expression contorted as though catching a whiff of an unpleasant odour. 'Turn around for me, dear,' he requested with an air of scrutiny.

Meg twirled around with a hint of awkwardness, her movements lacking the grace one might expect of an aristocratic lady. In the process, she inadvertently stepped onto her own train, narrowly avoiding a stumble. Her mother responded with an eye roll, followed by a disappointed glare aimed in Meg's direction.

'Are you certain this is the girl you spoke of? The one from the painting didn't quite resemble... this,' Lord Alnwick remarked, a hint of scepticism colouring his words.

Her mother offered a nervous laugh, subtly positioning her daughter behind her as she advanced toward the visitor. 'I assure you, it was indeed my daughter. Perhaps the artist captured her in a particularly favourable light. This hallway can be rather dim at times,' she explained, attempting to dispel any doubts.

'Where is your husband?' Lord Alnwick inquired, casting glances around the corners of the room in search of the absent figure.

'Lord Hilton is presently making arrangements for your visit. He's eager to take you hunting later; our vast estate is teeming with pheasants and deer. It promises to be a splendid afternoon. But first, let's ensure you're comfortably settled with a pot of tea.'

With a snap of her fingers, the servant hurried to the kitchen, while Lady Hilton graciously led her daughter and their distinguished guest to the inviting confines of the drawing room.

The drawing room exuded an air of refined elegance, filled with opulent furnishings and intricate details. The walls were adorned with rich tapestries depicting scenes of pastoral beauty, complemented by ornate golden-framed portraits of ancestors and esteemed figures.

A grand fireplace dominated one side of the room, casting a warm glow that danced across the polished wooden floor. Above, an elaborately detailed chandelier hung from the ceiling, its numerous candles illuminating the space with a soft, flickering light. A mahogany writing desk covered with quills and inkwells stood in one corner whilst decorative swords took pride of place in another.

They settled into their seats as the servant distributed cups of tea, ensuring each guest was attended to with a practised grace. Once tea was served, the servant discreetly retreated to a corner, poised to respond promptly should she be summoned, her presence both unobtrusive and attentive.

'Where's that other daughter of yours? I remember meeting her at the Otterburn estate at their son's wedding? She was a beautiful thing.'

'Oh, you must be referring to Eleanor,' Lady Hilton replied with a warm smile. 'She's married now and living in Yorkshire with the Granger family. Fine people.'

'Oh, what a shame,' Lord Alnwick expressed with a touch of regret. 'I was quite taken with her.' As he continued to praise her absent sister, Meg discreetly kept her head down. Lord Alnwick continued to view Meg with a slightly tilted head, akin to studying an enigmatic painting, as if endeavouring to understand precisely what the artist intended to portray.

'Well Meg's just as suitable,' Lady Hilton affirmed, placing a reassuring hand on her daughter's. 'Meg is unfailingly obedient and quite skilled around the house. Of course, with your extensive staff, her assistance may not be needed, but she's a wonderful addition for entertaining. Once she becomes more relaxed, she becomes the life and soul of the party. Today, she's a touch nervous, as you can probably tell.'

Lord Alnwick responded with a hint of scepticism, 'Mmm. If she's truly the life and soul of the party, why have you kept her away from public view for so long? I don't recall her presence at the Otterburn wedding.'

'Well...' Her mother began searching for an explanation as Meg maintained her lowered gaze, uncomfortable with being discussed as though she was absent. 'She was quite unwell that weekend. Nothing terminal or contagious, of course, but indisposed enough to make the journey up to the north impractical.'

At that precise moment, Lord Hilton made his entrance into the drawing room. The two ladies rose gracefully, executing a synchronised curtsey as he approached. Lord Hilton strode over to Lord Alnwick, and the two men exchanged hearty handshakes, their smiles suggesting a camaraderie that hinted at a long friendship – though in truth, their acquaintance had only been formed through a chance encounter at the Otterburn wedding.

'Samuel, my old friend. How are you? Was the journey down pleasant?' Lord Hilton inquired with a warm smile, exuding an affable familiarity.

'It was a lengthy journey, but at least it remained dry, which is all one can hope for,' Lord Alnwick replied. 'It's a welcome change to see the sun shine in these parts. Whenever I venture to Lancashire, it seems to be perpetually raining.'

'Well, it's delightful to see you, old chap,' Lord Hilton responded warmly. As Meg observed the two men, a sudden realisation struck her – the visitor was both older and wider than her own father. Her father wore a muted brown wool coat that cascaded down to his knees, with buttons that ascended to the hem and featured pleats at the sides. Like the visitor, he wore a white wig. 'I was just saying to your wife how smitten I was with your elder daughter who I met at the wedding.'

'Oh, Eleanor, yes,' Lord Hilton acknowledged with a nod. 'The Otterburn wedding was indeed a memorable occasion. It's always a pleasure to cross paths with old friends and their families.'

'I was saddened to hear she's already taken. She would have been a suitable match.'

'Ah, yes, she got snatched up quite quickly. But our dear Margery here is equally suitable – untouched, unmarred, and very attentive. You won't encounter any trouble from her.' He placed a hand on his daughter's shoulder, prompting her to involuntarily lean forward in an attempt to escape the chill of his touch. The description portrayed her as if she were an object rather than a person, and Meg felt a sense of discomfort at being discussed in such a manner.

'I suppose we better discuss dates for the wedding,' Lady Hilton interjected with an awkward laugh, attempting to navigate the conversation through the delicate terrain of matrimonial arrangements. The mention of wedding dates hung in the air, casting a momentary hush over the room.

'I'm sorry, I don't think that will be happening,' Lord Alnwick replied, casting a disdainful glance at Meg. He rose from his seat, placing his cup on a nearby table. 'Margery seems like a nice girl, but I was expecting someone much prettier. I feel as though you've taken me for a fool, having your artist send the portrait that he did, or maybe he's short-sighted, and you need to find a new one.'

'Samuel, wait!' Lord Hilton intervened, rising from his seat and positioning himself in the path of his visitor before he could make a swift departure. He then turned towards Meg, addressing her with a measured tone. 'Margery, would you mind waiting in your room while I speak to Lord Alnwick?'

Meg swiftly retreated to her room without casting a glance at the visitor or her parents. She left the door slightly ajar, positioning herself to catch the murmurs and discussions unfolding below.

'See, I told you she was obedient,' her father chuckled.

'This really isn't good enough. I know you're keen to marry her off and get her out of your hair, but you can't simply pass her off onto me. I can offer a lot to a potential wife, and I deserve the best,' Lord Alnwick asserted.

'But, Samuel, she would make a wonderful wife, I assure you. Listen, you've had a long journey. Why don't we go and get you rested, have a spot of shooting, and let you mull it over?'

Lord Alnwick pondered the suggestion, acknowledging his fatigue while grappling with the lingering frustration of feeling deceived. The stark contrast between the delivered portrait and the present reality had left him discontented, fuelling a sense of anger that simmered beneath.

'Listen, Samuel, I didn't want to bring this up. I know Margery is not the prettiest, but you're no oil painting yourself. You've been a bachelor for years since you lost Catherine, and with no children to call your own, this could be your last chance. Time is catching up, and if you want to bear an heir, Margery might be your only option. People talk, you know. They wonder what's wrong with you, why you haven't been able to find a wife all these years or produce any children.'

A heavy silence settled in the room, prompting Meg to press her ear closer to the slightly ajar door, eager to catch any murmurs or cues that would reveal the outcome of the tense conversation unfolding below. The weight of the unspoken words lingered, creating an atmosphere which could be cut with a knife.

'Very well,' Lord Alnwick sighed. 'We can set a date for next month. We'll have the ceremony at my estate. I assume that won't be a problem for you and your family to travel up?'

'That will be fine,' her mother interjected, offering a swift affirmation. The agreement was met with a hint of relief, yet an underlying tension persisted.

'That's settled then. Now, grab your weapon, we've got some game to shoot.'

As spring arrived the air resonated with the cheerful melodies of birds, and the landscape transformed with the vibrant blossoming of flowers. The time had come to embark on the journey to Northumbria. The town of Alnwick, once marred by a series of battles during the conflict between England and Scotland, now stood in the era of a settled truce. The monarch had diligently worked towards uniting the two nations, setting the foundation for the emergence of Great Britain.

Meg endured weeks of discomfort as her wedding dress was prepared, subjected to pinches and unwarranted fondling. Throughout this process, her mother's glares intensified every time she reached for her fork, apprehensive that any indulgence might jeopardise the snug fit of the garment. The dress, an heirloom passed down through the family and previously worn by her older sister, bore the weight of expectations and traditions that strained against its seams.

Meg reluctantly donned the wedding dress, fully aware that it would be the most beautiful garment she'd ever wear. However, despite its outward elegance, the dress felt stifling and constricting. The fabric clung to her body, emphasising every contour, and the snug fit made each breath feel like a conscious effort.

It wasn't just the physical tightness that bothered Meg; the dress seemed to carry an emotional weight. The ornate lace and delicate embroidery felt like a metaphorical chain, encircling her neck and tethering her to a future she had little say in. In the reflection of the mirror, she saw not only a bride-to-be but also a symbol of expectations and obligations that stretched far beyond the elegant folds of the gown.

Gazing out of her bedroom window at the gardeners and servants toiling in the estate, Meg couldn't help but feel a pang of envy. While she understood the struggles they faced, grappling with a life devoid of abundant wealth and luxuries, she envied their freedom. Unlike her and Lord Alnwick, they were not burdened by titles, status, or sprawling estates that dictated the course of their lives.

These workers, despite their financial hardships, possessed the liberty to choose their life partners based on love and personal preference. In contrast, Meg was shackled by societal expectations, familial obligations, and the weight of maintaining the family's standing in society. The simple lives of the servants below, devoid of aristocratic constraints, seemed like a tempting alternative to the complex and structured existence she was fated to lead.

Over the years, Meg had cultivated friendships with the servants, a practice her mother disapproved of. Despite the class divide, Meg found solace in conversing with them, listening to tales of their lives that seemed so much freer than her own. Unlike the stiff, formal gatherings of the aristocracy, the servants frequented pubs, indulging in the simple pleasures of getting drunk and letting loose. Their social gatherings were devoid of the stifling judgmental gazes of snobbish attendees, and there was an authenticity to their interactions that she found refreshing.

While the formal parties in the aristocratic circles were laden with plenty of alcohol, Meg noticed that few actually drank it, fearing the repercussions of embarrassing themselves in front of their peers. In these high-society affairs, dancing was meticulously choreographed, and conversations were often veiled boasts and status displays. It made her yearn for the genuine connections and spontaneity she witnessed in the lives of the servants, a stark contrast to the polished but stifling atmosphere of her own social sphere.

With her wedding dress carefully stowed away in her luggage, secured on the back of a horse, Meg's carriage awaited her for the difficult journey to Northumberland. As she glanced around her room, the walls seemed to whisper uncertainties and evoke a poignant nostalgia. She wondered if this departure marked the last time she would set eyes on these familiar surroundings – the room that held the echoes of her laughter, the solace of her solitude, and the countless moments that shaped her youth.

Questions lingered in her mind. Would she see her family again, share laughter with her friends, or revel in the comforting presence of her sisters? The impending journey held the weight of permanent change, and as she glanced over the waiting carriage, the uncertainty of her future loomed large, casting a bittersweet pall over the familiar confines she was leaving behind.

'Come on, dear!' her mother's call echoed through the hallway. With a heavy heart, Meg descended the staircase, a subtle wave of nausea churning in her belly. The weight of the moment, coupled with the uncertainty of the future, bore down on her, making each step feel like a reluctant journey into the unknown.

As the door of the horse-drawn carriage swung open, Meg halted, as if an invisible force had frozen her to the ground. Her parents, gazes filled with expectation, urged her to step into the conveyance, but an unseen weight held her in place.

'I can't do it!' Meg cried, her voice echoing with a mixture of desperation and defiance. 'I can't marry him.' Her parents gasped, their expressions shifting from expectation to shock. The servants exchanged glances, uncertain of how to react.

'Don't be silly, Margery!' her mother barked, employing her daughter's formal Sunday name which she only used in wider company or when she was in trouble.

'No. I won't do it. You can't make me do this!' Meg pleaded, her voice fraught with a resolute defiance that echoed through the air.

'Meg, I will only tell you this once.' Her father leaned over her, his breath heavy with intensity. 'Get in that carriage now, or I will make you.'

Her heart ricocheted across her chest. Adrenaline surged through her bones, flowing with a passion that matched the turmoil within. She struggled to catch her breath, as if her father's hands were squeezing the life out of her, the weight of the impending decision pressing down on her like a suffocating force.

'I said no!' Meg shouted defiantly before retreating into the house. However her father, consumed by anger and determination, followed her, seizing her thin arm and forcefully dragging her back. Her feet scraped along the gravelly ground, her screams shattering the ears of all who bore witness.

Her father pushed her into the carriage, vigorously closing the door before turning to his wife. 'Jane, get in. We're going!'

The servants bowed their heads, unsure of where to direct their gazes in the aftermath of the tumultuous scene. As soon as the doors to the carriage were closed, they scurried away, seeking the refuge of salvation from the lingering tension.

As the reins whipped the horses into motion, Meg watched her home grow smaller and smaller on the horizon. The weight of an impending and unwanted marriage settled on her shoulders, squeezing the air from her lungs. Unable to bear the suffocating prospect, she seized the door and, with a burst of desperation, leaped out before her mother could intervene.

'Margery! Get back here!' her mother screamed, the urgency of her command cutting through the air. The horses came to an abrupt stop. Meg's father, driven by a mix of frustration and concern, ran after her, determined to bring an end to the madness.

'Listen, Margery, if you leave, you will never be allowed back here. Do you hear me? You'll be dead to us!' her father warned.

As Meg looked up at the house that had been her entire life, a flood of memories cascaded through her mind. The familiar façade, once a source of comfort, now stood as a symbol of the shackles she sought to escape. Her gaze shifted to her parents, who had been constants in her life since the day she was born. In that moment of contemplation, she wondered if she could truly leave it all behind, the familiarity of her past wrestling with the uncertain allure of an uncharted future.

'I'm sorry, Father, but I must go. I can't live like this. I can't be like my sisters. I want my own life. Even if it means leaving all this behind,' Meg uttered with a trembling voice, the weight of her decision evident in the tear that escaped her eye. With a heavy heart, she began to walk down the drive alone. Her father stood still, a silent observer, watching his daughter disappear before his very eyes.

'You've brought shame on this family,' Lord Hilton called out, his voice laced with disappointment and anger. 'You are no daughter of mine. You may never use the Hilton name again.'

Chapter 9

'Vicar!' exclaimed Lord Hilton, his voice laced with astonishment as he pushed open the grand oak doors. Isaac had made the two-hour trek to the Hilton estate on foot, quite a feat at his age. Under the uncharacteristically warm Lancashire sun, Isaac's brow glistened with beads of perspiration, each droplet a testament to the uncommon heat that enveloped the quaint village, adding an additional layer of challenge to his journey. 'It is a surprise to see you.'

'May I trouble you for some water?' Isaac's parched voice echoed through the corridor, his body leaning against the wall for support as he sought to regain his strength after the taxing journey. Though the path had been relatively flat and gentle, the unanticipated arrival of an Indian summer in November had turned what should have been a leisurely stroll into a formidable trial.

Over two decades had passed since Isaac last trod upon the hallowed grounds of the Hilton estate. His recollection led him back to a time when the current Lord Hilton was but a young, newlywed man, vigorous and full of life. It was then, amidst the splendour of the estate, that he and his wife had taken residence within one of the stately wings of the grand mansion. Across the manicured grounds, his father, whose noble title and the mansion itself the young Lord Hilton would one day inherit, resided in his own domain, a symbolic reflection of their intertwined destinies.

Time had woven a tapestry of contrasting fortunes upon those who once roamed the halls of the Hilton estate. While Lord Hilton seemed untouched by the ravages of passing years, his sister Margery bore the weight of time more visibly, her countenance marked by the trials and tribulations that life had bestowed upon her.

Lord Hilton's resemblance to his late father at the same age was uncanny, a reflection of the enduring legacy that permeated the aristocratic lineage. Isaac couldn't help but reminisce fondly about the elder Lord Hilton, a man of honour and tradition, whose memory still lingered within the walls of the estate. Despite his affection for the late Lord Hilton, Isaac couldn't shake the pang of regret at Margery's exile from the family fold. He had voiced his concerns to him in the past, deeming her ostracism as harsh and unjust. Yet, he understood all too well the rigid constraints and obligations that governed aristocratic life – the stringent codes of conduct and the relentless pursuit of reputation that superseded matters of the heart. In their world, love often took a backseat to the demands of tradition and societal expectations, a harsh reality that Isaac had learned to navigate with a heavy heart.

'Of course, come in, old friend,' the present bearer of the esteemed title of Lord Hilton replied, his voice carrying a warmth that belied the formalities of his aristocratic standing. With a nod of gratitude, Isaac stepped over the threshold, noting with surprise the absence of a servant to answer his call – a departure from the customary protocol of the past. As he surveyed the familiar surroundings of the grand hall, he noticed the grandeur of the place had waned. Where once stood a pristine sanctuary of opulence, now loomed a hall worn and weathered, mirroring the fatigue of the vicarage he called home.

The absence of the staff, who once moved with silent efficiency through the corridors and lingered in the shadows, did not escape Isaac's notice. He pondered whether the recent change in a now slim-downed monarchy had precipitated a shift in financial priorities, perhaps prompting Lord Hilton to rely more heavily on his personal fortune to sustain the ancestral household.

'How are you?' Lord Hilton inquired, his concern evident as he retrieved a tankard of water from the kitchen and extended it to the vicar. Isaac accepted the offering with gratitude, sipping the cool liquid as though it were from a long-awaited oasis in the midst of a desert. 'I haven't seen you since our Charlotte's christening.'

'Time has flown by indeed,' Isaac concurred with a solemn nod, the refreshing water revitalising his senses. 'I did come to see your father in his final days. It was truly a sombre moment to hear about his passing.'

'We think it was cancer,' Hilton replied, his voice carrying the weight of sorrow as he lowered his head in solemn acknowledgment.

'And how are your wife and the children?' Isaac inquired, his tone delicately avoiding mention of Lord Hilton's late mother, aware of the tragic circumstances surrounding her demise. She had met her untimely end during a hunting expedition, the whispers of speculation surrounding her death casting a shadow over the family for years. Though rumours had swirled for years accusing Lord Hilton himself of responsibility for her death, no conclusive evidence had ever surfaced to substantiate the claims.

'They're all well. In fact, my children have children now. Can you believe it?' Lord Hilton's voice held a blend of astonishment and pride.

'So you're a grandfather now, what a wonderful gift from God.' Isaac's keen eyes noticed a subtle yet significant alteration amidst the artworks adorning the grand hall. Where once the portrait of the former Lord Hilton had commanded precedence, now it was the likeness of the current Lord Hilton that loomed large, asserting its dominance over the room in a striking gold frame.

'And what about you? Are you still at St. Anne's?'

'I am indeed,' Isaac replied. 'I'll be there until my last breath and then I'll be buried there. My plot's already been assigned. We had your sister Margery's funeral there a few weeks ago, I was surprised not to see any of the Hilton family there.' His words were chosen carefully to avoid casting any unwarranted aspersions on Lord Hilton or his family.

'Why would I be?' Hilton shrugged. 'She left our family over fifty years ago and we haven't seen her since. She is no sister of mine.'

'The Lord encourages us to forgive,' Isaac gently reminded the nobleman, drawing upon the tenets of their shared Christian faith. 'Your sister was a troubled woman, very lost and lonely. It was a shame to put her in the ground without anyone who loved her to oversee the proceedings.'

'The only reason I would turn up is to ensure she was actually dead.' Hilton snorted and rolled his eyes, perplexed by his former vicar's attempt to make him feel guilty.

'Well, you were missed,' Isaac stated bluntly, his words carrying a weight of truth that could not be ignored. 'And Margery will be missed,' he added with a solemnity that spoke volumes of the genuine sorrow he felt for the estranged sister who had departed this world without the solace of familial love and acceptance.

'From what I hear, she was a wicked witch who cast spells on the locals. I don't know who exactly is missing her, or whose idea it was to bury her in the church grounds where she was a sorcerer of evil! She brought shame on the Hilton name. Something she is continuing to achieve even now she's dead!'

'Talking of the Hilton family name...' Isaac spotted an opportunity to approach a delicate subject. 'Someone has crossed out the name Hilton on her grave.'

'And?' Lord Hilton shrugged.

'It was if whoever did this was trying to hide the fact that Margery was related to the family.'

'From my understanding, the name she died with was Shelton. That's what my contacts in the village have told me anyway. Why on earth she would need to revert to Hilton after many decades is beyond me.'

'A name is very important to people. She was born with the name Hilton, she never married, so she was buried with the name she was honoured with when she came into this life.'

'Why are you telling me all this?'

Under Lord Hilton's intense gaze, Isaac maintained his composure, meeting the nobleman's scrutiny with unwavering resolve.

'I wondered perhaps...' Isaac stuttered. 'If perhaps it was one of the Hilton family who may have edited the memorial to erase Margery's history with them.'

'That is absurd.' Lord Hilton gasped and snatched the mug from Isaac's hands. 'I think you had better leave. How dare you make such accusations against my family.'

'It was simply a question, Christopher,' Isaac replied, using his Sunday name, which made the nobleman gulp.

'It was a very crude one.'

'Perhaps then you can explain why you have a black stain upon your socks.'

Isaac's gaze subtly drifted downward, noting the peculiar black stain etched into the wool of Lord Hilton's knee-high socks. His eyes then shifted to Lord Hilton's attire above the waist, recognizing the pastel yellow jacket and matching waistcoat as garments that once belonged in his father's closet.

'What about it?'

'Well, it looks remarkably like the stain etched onto your sister's grave.' Isaac's eyebrow arched.

'This is absurd. Take those accusations out of your mouth at once. I was merely lubricating the carriage wheels this morning. There's nothing untoward about it.'

'Very well.' Isaac stroked his chin. 'I shall pray for the soul of whoever is responsible for this crime. We need to get to the bottom of it, as I suspect whoever has defaced the stone has also dug Margery up to scare the town.'

'I heard that she crawled out of her grave herself.'

'That is the ongoing rumour.' Isaac nodded. 'But I believe someone is deliberately trying to harm her reputation rather than letting her rest in peace. Anyway, it's not just you I'm questioning. I'll be asking anyone who knew her. And I'll pray for the soul of anyone who would dare lie directly to a vicar's face.'

'Yes, yes. I admit, I did amend the name on the grave.'

Isaac's eyes widened in surprise at Lord Hilton's unexpected admission. The confession hung heavy in the air, shattering the façade of aristocratic decorum and laying bare the vulnerability beneath.

'But I did *not* dig her body up. That must have been someone else. If not herself.'

'How can I believe you, Christopher?'

'I might stoop low enough to risk a bit of a stain upon my socks. But I would not ruin the finest silk with mud from digging up that hag's grave. Besides I would rather people forget who she was. I know this business of her body resurfacing has brought her even more notoriety amongst the boroughs than when she was alive.'

As Isaac met Lord Hilton's gaze, he saw a flicker of sincerity reflected in the nobleman's eyes. In that moment, amidst the vulnerability and raw honesty, Isaac felt a surge of trust swell within him.

'Very well,' Isaac said. He made his way back to the entrance of the house. 'I'll take this no further. My housekeeper is currently scrubbing away the damage to the grave. Hopefully there won't be long-lasting damage. But please let your sister rest in peace. She deserves that at the very least.'

'Why the hell should I allow her to continue to use our family name when she abandoned us and brought shame upon us?' Hilton grunted.

'Christopher, you're a man and had it so much easier than she. You were able to stay here and inherit this fine home and to choose from an array of girls to marry. Your sister on the other hand was about to be forced to marry a man much older than she who she didn't even like, never mind love, before being shipped off to unfamiliar surroundings for the rest of her life. And when she refused, her family kicked her out of her home and refused to speak to her again. Surely you can have a touch of sympathy for her situation.'

'I suppose.' The droop of Lord Hilton's cheeks and the onset of a mournful gaze painted a sombre tableau across his countenance.

'The last time I saw your father, he spoke of his regret for how he treated Margery. He wished he could reconnect with her. I did try to reach your sister in time but it was too late. Regret is an awful emotion. Don't let your vengeance against a girl who did nothing to you bring you anguish for the rest of your life. Let her have the name.'

With a heavy heart, Isaac turned away from the estate and began his journey back to Woodplumpton. As he glanced back one final time, he caught a fleeting glimpse of Lord Hilton, his mournful visage etched into his memory. Though he hoped his message had made an impact, he couldn't shake the lingering uncertainty that loomed over the estate.

As he walked, thoughts churned within Isaac's mind, the mystery of Margery Hilton's tombstone tarnishing now solved, but a new enigma emerging in its wake. The question of who was digging her up remained an unsettling puzzle, one that gnawed at his conscience like an unresolved chord in a haunting melody.

Chapter 10

1 year earlier

'Come on!' Meg's laughter echoed through the field as she strode with determined intensity, her pace swift and purposeful. The towering wheat stems bowed under her relentless advance, casting shifting shadows across the landscape. Several yards behind, James struggled to keep up, his brow furrowed in both amusement and frustration as he pushed through the dense foliage, his short stature hindering his efforts to keep pace with his mischievous companion.

Despite his exhaustion, James couldn't help but smile at Meg's infectious energy, her laughter a beacon guiding him through the sea of golden wheat. With each step, he pushed himself forward, determined to catch up to his spirited friend and join in her carefree revelry amidst the endless expanse of the countryside.

'Wait for me!' James called. He marvelled at Meg's seemingly boundless energy, her frail form defying expectations as she surged through the field with the vigour of a greyhound. He wondered how she could be hobbling one minute and running the next. Was her transition an act of sorcery or was her limp purely an act? He felt too daunted to ask. 'The farmer is sure to get us.'

'He will if you don't hurry up.'

In their hands, they clutched baskets heavy with corn, their contents acquired through stealth and cunning from Patrick Hutton's farm. As they hurried through the field, the echo of a gunshot reverberated in the air, the deafening sound sending shockwaves through their ears, leaving a lingering ringing sensation in its wake.

The gunshot had erupted in the wake of Farmer Hutton's discovery of the pair, his voice booming across the field as he called out to the thieves who dared to pilfer his prized produce. He reached for his gun, his determination unyielding as he pursued the trespassers through the swaying sea of wheat. His footsteps echoed in the silence, each stride fuelled with rage, his eyes narrowed in steely fury as he closed in on the fleeing figures disappearing into the golden expanse before him.

As Farmer Hutton surged through the field, his figure emerged from the golden waves of wheat. His stature, neither towering nor diminutive, spoke of a lifetime spent toiling under the sun. Bronze skin, weathered and tanned from endless days of labouring in the fields, bore witness to the harsh realities of rural life. A patchy shadow of stubble adorned his lips.

Beneath his flat cap, dark curls peeked out, their moist ringlets clinging to his forehead in the heat of the chase. With a piece of straw clenched between his teeth, he exuded a rugged determination. His attire, a white shirt and black trousers, bore the stains of hard work, the earth's rich soil ingrained into the fabric. And his worn boots trampled the ground with each resolute step.

As the echoes of the gunshot faded into silence, James slowed his pace, his senses on high alert as he crept forward cautiously. He scanned his surroundings, his eyes darting in every direction, searching for any sign of movement amidst the stillness of the wheat field. His heart pounded in his chest, the adrenaline coursing through his veins as he strained to catch a glimpse of either Meg, his mischievous companion, or Farmer Hutton, the irate landowner bent on retribution.

The golden expanse was seemingly endless in its vastness, yet devoid of any discernible presence except for the whispering rustle of the wheat stalks in the breeze. With each passing moment the tension mounted, the uncertainty weighing heavily upon James as he remained poised, uncertain of what lay ahead in the silent aftermath of the chase.

With his heart racing, James wrestled with the conflicting urges within him. On one hand, he yearned to alert Meg to his whereabouts, to ensure they could reunite and face whatever lay ahead together. Yet, on the other hand, the fear of giving away his position to their pursuer loomed large in his mind, cautioning him to remain silent and hidden.

Struggling to find a compromise between these competing impulses, James cast furtive glances around him, searching for any sign of movement or danger, every rustle of the wheat, every whisper of the wind heightening his sense of vulnerability.

James gasped, his heart skipping a beat at the sudden pinch on his arm. Startled, he whipped his head around, only to find himself face to face with the familiar withered hands of Meg. Relief flooded through him.

'Meg!' he exclaimed, his voice a mixture of relief and gratitude. 'You scared me half to death.'

Her weathered face broke into a mischievous grin, her eyes twinkling with amusement at James's reaction. With a playful glint in her eye, she gestured for him to follow her as she melted back into the sea of wheat, her presence a reassuring anchor in the midst of uncertainty.

Following the trail of crushed stems left in Meg's footsteps, James soon found himself standing before a rustic barn nestled amidst the corn. With a sense of anticipation, he followed Meg inside, the wooden door creaking softly as it swung open on weathered hinges.

As he stepped into the dim interior, James's senses were immediately assaulted. Poultry of all shapes and sizes pecked at the scattered seed strewn across the floor, their feathers rustling as they clucked and fluttered in the confined space. The air was thick with the earthy scent of hay and the pungent aroma of animal droppings.

'I know you're out here!'

James's heart skipped a beat as the voice of Farmer Hutton pierced the air, growing louder with each passing moment. Panic surged within him as he realised their precarious situation, the threat of discovery looming ever closer. James watched in awe as Meg's seasoned confidence took charge of the situation. With a reassuring gesture, she placed a finger to her lips, urging silence as she edged closer to the open doors of the barn.

'Don't worry, I've done this before,' she whispered, her voice barely audible over the commotion of the poultry. With precision born of experience, she reached out and scooped up a duck, its tail wagging in protest as she secured her grip around its belly. The bird squirmed and flapped its wings, but Meg's bony fingers held it firm, preventing its escape.

With her back pressed against the barn doors, Meg scanned the shadows on the green ground outside, her eyes keenly searching for any sign of Farmer Hutton's approach.

Meg seized the opportunity as Farmer Hutton's shadow loomed larger and darker against the ground. With a swift and decisive motion, she leaped out from the safety of the barn, hurling the startled duck towards the unsuspecting farmer. As the duck flew through the air, a deafening gunshot shattered the stillness, sending feathers exploding in all directions. They danced and twirled through the air like a heavy snowfall.

The birds surrounding James erupted into a frenzy of fear and commotion, their panicked cries echoing across the barn. Wings flapped frantically, feathers flew in a flurry, and the air was thick with the palpable sense of panic and confusion.

Caught off guard by Meg's unexpected manoeuvre, Farmer Hutton stumbled backward, momentarily disoriented by the sudden onslaught. As James burst out of the barn, his heart sank at the realisation that Meg was nowhere to be seen. Panic surged within him as he scanned the area desperately, searching for any sign of his friend amidst the chaos.

Farmer Hutton clambered to his feet, fury etched across his face as he regained his balance. With a thunderous bellow, he levelled his shotgun in James's direction.

'Stop! Stop or I'll shoot!'

Fear gripped James's heart as he skidded to a stop, the weight of the shotgun's gaze bearing down on him like lead. With a gulp he raised his hands in surrender, his every instinct urging him to comply with Farmer Hutton's command.

Content that the boy was no longer a threat, Farmer Hutton lowered his gun and advanced towards James. Without a word, he seized the tip of James's ear in a vice-like grip, his fingers digging into the flesh as he dragged the petrified boy away from the barn and towards the main road.

James winced in pain as he was forcibly pulled along by Farmer Hutton, his heart pounding in his chest as he braced himself for whatever fate awaited him.

'What's your name, boy?'

As Farmer Hutton dragged him along, James's mind raced with desperation, searching for an alias that would conceal his true identity and offer him a chance at escape.

Amidst the chaos and confusion, he grasped at the fleeting threads of possibility, seeking a name that would grant him anonymity and safety.

After a moment's hesitation, a name emerged from the depths of his subconscious – a name borrowed from a distant memory, a character from a book he had once read long ago. With a silent prayer for luck, James took a deep breath.

'Daniel,' he said.

'Daniel what?'

'Garstang.'

'I haven't heard of that name round here. Where are you from?'

'Coppull,' James lied.

'I'm sure I've seen you before.' Farmer Hutton squinted, glancing over the familiar face. 'Wait, you're Francis and Sarah's son.'

James's heart sank as Farmer Hutton's words pierced the air like a dagger, shattering the fragile illusion of anonymity he had sought to construct.

With a sinking feeling in the pit of his stomach, James braced himself for the inevitable consequences of his actions. There was no denying the truth now, no escaping the repercussions of his reckless behaviour. As he stood before Farmer Hutton, his mind raced with a thousand thoughts and fears, each more daunting than the last.

Caught in the farmer's unrelenting grip, James could only hope for mercy, praying silently that his parents' reputation and good will might yet spare him from the full extent of the farmer's wrath.

As desperation consumed him, James sank to his knees before Farmer Hutton, his hands lifted in a gesture of prayer. His heart pounded with a frantic rhythm, his breaths coming in shallow gasps as he pleaded for compassion.

'Please,' he implored, his voice trembling. 'I beg of you, please don't tell my parents. I didn't mean any harm!'

'Very well.' Farmer Hutton sighed and loosened his grip on the boy's ear. 'But you're going to make up for what your friend stole off me.'

'Absolutely. Whatever you want me to do.'

'Well you can begin by clearing out the coop.'

As James turned to face the poultry barn, a wave of nausea washed over him and the pungent scent of manure simmered in his nostrils. The air was thick with the heavy aroma of accumulated waste.

With a grimace, James stepped inside, his stomach churning at the sight of the disarray that greeted him. Layers of grime coated every surface.

'Please no. Anything else.'

'Do you want me to tell your parents what you've done?'

'No! Please! I'll clean the coop.' James sighed, a glimmer of sadness in his eyes.

'Good. I'll come back at sundown and see how you've got on.'

Over the following hours, James toiled tirelessly in the poultry barn, his muscles straining under the weight of the heavy loads of dung he lifted and carried out. The stench of decay hung thick in the air, threatening to overwhelm him with its noxious odour.

Desperate to shield himself from the putrid substance, James pulled his grey, soiled jumper over his nose, the fabric offering a meagre barrier against the offensive odour. Each breath he took was a battle against the overwhelming stench, his lungs burning with exertion as he continued his laborious task.

Despite the discomfort and the filth that surrounded him, James pressed on, his determination unwavering as he worked to atone for his sins. As James toiled away in the coop, his mind churned with questions and doubts, his thoughts consumed by the absence of his friend Meg. The weight of betrayal hung heavy upon him, a bitter reminder of her abandonment in his hour of need.

Brown sweat poured down his face, mingling with the grime and filth that coated his attire as he worked. With each scoop of dirt, his frustration grew, fuelled by the unanswered questions that tormented his mind. Why had Meg fled, leaving him behind to face the consequences alone? Had she even spared a thought for his safety, or was she content to let him bear the brunt of *her* misdeeds?

The bond of friendship that had once united them now felt frayed and tattered. And as he continued to labour in solitude, the bitterness of resentment seeped into his heart.

As Farmer Hutton returned to the poultry barn, James awaited his inspection with bated breath, his heart pounding with anticipation.

With a critical eye, Farmer Hutton surveyed James's handiwork, his expression unreadable as he took in the remarkable transformation that had taken place in his absence.

Gone were the layers of filth and neglect that had once marred the coop, replaced by a sense of order and cleanliness.

A sense of pride intensified within James as he watched Farmer Hutton's reaction, his chest swelling with satisfaction at the sight of the once-chaotic space now restored to its former glory. And as the birds rushed to Farmer Hutton's feet, with a glimmer of hope that he might have arrived to feed them, James wondered how much longer he would need to stay.

With a nod of approval, Farmer Hutton turned to James with a glimmer of respect shining in his eyes as he offered a gruff acknowledgment of the young man's efforts.

'Not bad, lad,' he said, his voice carrying a hint of grudging admiration. 'Not bad at all. You've done well here. Consider your debt paid.'

Farmer Hutton lifted out his arm. In his hand, a familiar sight caught James's eye – a basket of vegetables. The very basket he'd used to loot from Farmer Hutton's farm which he'd dropped in his pursuit of freedom. He handed the basket back to James. 'Here, have this.'

With a grateful smile, James accepted the basket of vegetables from Farmer Hutton. Though he knew he didn't deserve payment for his efforts in cleaning the coop, the gesture touched him deeply.

'Thank you,' he murmured, his voice filled with genuine appreciation as he looked into the farmer's eyes. In that moment, James realised that his earlier misconceptions about Farmer Hutton had been unfounded – that beneath the surly exterior lay a heart capable of compassion and understanding.

As James arrived home, he carefully tucked the basket of vegetables into the shed beside his own small allotment. He knew that his parents would likely question where he had received such a generous gift.

Amongst the collection of home-grown produce in the shed, the basket of vegetables would blend in seamlessly. His parents would assume that the vegetables were the fruits of James's own labour, and in a way, this was true. Though he hadn't grown them himself, James had certainly worked hard to earn them.

'My goodness, what on earth have you been doing? You haven't been with that Meg Shelton again, have you?'

Sarah gazed at the clothes she had dressed James in just a few hours earlier, a perplexed frown knitting her brow. The clothes had been spotless that morning. But now, as she took in the sight of her son returning home, they looked as though they had weathered a storm. Her eyes traced the smudges of dirt that marred the fabric.

'I was playing kickball with the lads.' James shifted uncomfortably under his mother's scrutinising gaze.

Sarah regarded her son with a mixture of concern and scepticism, her maternal instincts telling her that there was more to the story than he was letting on. But she chose to let it go for now, knowing that pressing him further would only push him away.

'Very well. Why don't you go and take a bath and leave those clothes for me to wash.'

As James nodded in response, a pang of guilt tugged at his conscience, knowing that he had deceived his mother with his half-truths. But for now, he pushed aside his guilt, burying it deep beneath the surface.

As James lay in bed that night, the events of the day played out like a relentless loop in his mind, each moment etched with the weight of guilt and frustration. Despite his exhaustion, he couldn't sleep, his restless mind consumed by a mix of emotions.

The memory of Meg's betrayal gnawed at his conscience like a festering wound, filling him with a simmering anger and resentment. How could she have abandoned him like that? How could she have fled without a second thought, leaving him to face the consequences alone? He had trusted Meg, relied on her friendship, and yet she had let him down in the most crucial of moments. She was the one who led him there. He didn't need to steal food. He was merely accompanying her. And it was he who had to pay the price for her anarchy.

As the silence of the prairie land was abruptly disrupted by the sound of a chip tapping at the window, James sat up. Another tapping followed, and then another, until a small pebble jumped at the glass, causing him to flinch. Curious and somewhat apprehensive, James peered out the window, his heart racing as he searched for the source of the disturbance. And there, below him, he spotted Meg, her face illuminated by a mischievous smile as she waved up at him.

With a sigh of resignation, James opened the window, allowing Meg's voice to drift in.

'Hi there, sleepyhead,' she teased, her eyes sparkling with mischief. 'Sorry for disappearing earlier. I had to make a quick getaway. But I'm back now!'

'You abandoned me! I've had to clear out chicken shit from Farmer Hutton's coop.' James attempted to sound angry in his whispered murmurings.

'I know I'm so sorry. I thought you were behind me.'

'I could've got in a lot of trouble, Meg.'

'I'm sorry about that,' she replied, her voice tinged with amusement. 'I promise I won't disappear on you again. But please come down, I have something for you.'

Angry and yet intrigued by what Meg had to offer him, James felt a reluctant sense of curiosity tug at him, forcing him to relent. With a heavy sigh, he made his way to the window and crawled down the tree outside his bedroom before leaping down to the ground.

The thud that followed was louder than he had anticipated, a sharp jolt of pain shooting through him as he landed on the ground below. For a moment he froze, his breath caught in his throat as he waited for any sign that his parents had been roused from their slumber. But as the seconds ticked by and silence cloaked the night once more, James let out a quiet sigh of relief.

With a wince, James straightened up, pushing aside the pain that throbbed in his limbs as he turned to face Meg. In her hand was a bar of chocolate. As James looked down at the crumbly brown bar of chocolate in her hand, he couldn't help but feel a pang of longing as he licked his lips, the rich aroma of cocoa tantalising his senses. It was a treat afforded usually to the rich or those in the city, a decadent indulgence that he had only ever dreamed of tasting.

'Meg, where did you get this chocolate? It's... well, it's not something you come across every day.'

'Let's just say I have my ways,' she replied cryptically.

As James took the first bite of the chocolate, all thoughts of animosity and resentment towards Meg melted away, replaced by an overwhelming sense of delight and satisfaction. The rich, velvety sweetness of the chocolate enveloped his senses, sending waves of pleasure coursing through him with each indulgent mouthful.

As he handed Meg a piece of the chocolate as a gesture of forgiveness, she accepted it with a grateful smile. Together they giggled like children, their laughter mingling with the night air as they indulged in the delights that wouldn't be usually available to poor rural types.

As they sat side by side, lost in their shared moment of joy, James couldn't help but steal glances at Meg, his curiosity piqued once more by the mystery of how she had managed to secure such luxuries for a woman of her modest means. Yet as he studied her, he couldn't shake the nagging suspicion that perhaps his parents and their neighbours had been right all along – that Meg was more than she appeared to be, a woman of secrets and mysteries hidden beneath her unassuming exterior. Was there something unearthly about this woman after all?

'Ahem.' Startled by the echoing faux cough, James and Meg spun around once more, their hearts pounding with a mixture of fear and apprehension as they searched the darkness behind them.

There, within the light of the moon, stood James's mother Sarah, her features illuminated by a fierce glare that sent shivers down their spines. Gone was the gentle expression of concern he'd received earlier; in its place was a look of unmistakable anger that seemed to pierce through them like a dagger.

'I might have known you'd had something to do with my son coming home covered in mud. You are a bad influence on him. And from what I hear you're a dangerous person who casts spells upon our neighbours.'

'Mother! No, Meg's my friend,' James pleaded.

'Shh, James!' She placed a finger against her lips before turning towards Meg. 'There's something strange about an old woman wanting to mix with young boys. I don't want to see you around my son again, otherwise I will make sure it's the last thing you ever do.'

Chapter 11

'Salve, quod nomen tibi est?'

As James stared back at his teacher, Mr Cuthbert, a sense of confusion washed over him like a wave crashing against the shore. What on earth had he just said? The words that had left his teacher's lips sounded foreign to James, unfamiliar and strange, like a language from a distant land.

James racked his brain, trying to make sense of the Latin question that hung in the air like a heavy fog. He had only ever encountered this strange language once before, during a visit to a Catholic church for a funeral. But in his Anglican upbringing, the language of the church had always been the familiar rhythm of the King's English.

Now, as he sat before his teacher, James found himself at a loss for words, unsure of how to reply to Mr Cuthbert's inquiry. Should he admit his ignorance and risk embarrassment in front of the class? Or should he attempt to cobble together a response based on his limited understanding of Latin?

As the seconds ticked by, James felt the weight of Mr Cuthbert's expectant gaze bearing down upon him, urging him to find an answer. But try as he might, James couldn't seem to summon the words he needed to respond.

With a sinking feeling in the pit of his stomach, James realised that he was well and truly out of his depth. Whatever Mr Cuthbert had said, it was clear that James was ill-prepared to answer in kind. And as he struggled to find a way out of this linguistic impasse, he couldn't help but wish for a return to the comforting familiarity of his native tongue.

'Come on, James, you should be able to grasp the basics. The answer is, "*Salve, nomen meum est Iacobus.*"

James repeated the teacher's prompt as best as he could, stumbling over the unfamiliar words and feeling a sense of frustration building within him. With a heavy heart, he picked up his pencil and began to write down the Latin words on his parchment, his handwriting shaky and uncertain.

As he watched the other pupils in the class eloquently answering Mr Cuthbert's questions with ease, James couldn't help but feel a pang of envy. They seemed to possess a natural fluency in the language, effortlessly weaving together sentences that flowed like poetry. Meanwhile, James struggled to string together even the most basic phrases, his mind grappling with the unfamiliar grammar and vocabulary. It was as if he had been transported back in time to ancient Rome, surrounded by scholars and philosophers whose words he could barely comprehend.

With a sigh of resignation, James couldn't help but question the relevance of learning Latin in the modern world. Where would he ever use this predominantly redundant language? It seemed like a relic of a bygone era, a relic that held little practical value in his everyday life.

As Mr Cuthbert announced that they would move on to mathematics, James felt a sense of relief wash over him. Maths was a subject he felt more comfortable with, a realm where numbers and equations offered a sense of structure and certainty amidst the confusion of language studies.

But as he focused his attention on the sums written in chalk on the blackboard, James couldn't shake the feeling of unease that lingered in the air. Behind him, he could hear the unmistakable sound of sniggering coming from Oliver and

August, their whispers carrying a mocking tone that made his skin crawl.

Desperately trying to ignore them, James buried himself in his work, scribbling down the solutions to the maths problems. But no matter how hard he tried to concentrate, he couldn't shake the feeling of being watched, the weight of their laughter hanging heavy in the air like a dark cloud.

And then, without warning, James felt something ping against the back of his head, followed by a burst of laughter from behind him. Turning around, he saw Oliver and August exchanging smirks.

As James's gaze fell upon the crumpled paper missile lying on the floor beside him, a surge of anger and frustration welled up inside him. How dare they treat him like this, he thought, his jaw clenched tight as he resisted the urge to lash out in retaliation.

'Can I help you boys?' Mr Cuthbert asked, glaring at the unruly lads at the back of the class.

'Sir,' Oliver said, nudging August with his elbow. 'Did you know James was friends with a witch?'

'I wasn't aware, no, Oliver. Maybe you can explain how this is in any way relevant to a maths lesson?'

'Maybe the witch transferred her powers over to him. He might be able to put a hex on us,' August cackled.

'If that were true, August, then surely James would be better at Latin. And I'm sure he'd have supernaturally made you choke on that scrunched-up paper ball you threw at him too.'

As James winced with humiliation, the sting of his inadequacy gnawing at his confidence once again regarding his inability to speak a second language, he couldn't help but feel a sense of injustice burning within him. Why was his teacher continuing to taunt him when he was clearly being subjected to bullying from his peers? It wasn't his fault that he couldn't speak Latin. It just didn't naturally come to him like other subjects.

As the class came to an end, James lingered behind, a sense of unease settling in the pit of his stomach. He knew that leaving the room meant facing the possibility of further confrontation with his enemies, and he wasn't sure if he had the strength to endure it.

As he hesitated in the doorway, William and Henry held back, their concern evident in their expressions.

'Are you all right, my friend?' Henry asked, his voice laced with genuine worry. James met his gaze with a silent nod, a glimmer of sadness flickering in his eyes.

But before James could respond, William interjected with a blunt observation that cut through the air like a knife. 'You don't help yourself, James,' he remarked, his tone matter-of-fact. He reached out to offer James a reassuring pat on the back, but his words hung heavy in the air.

'You've been seen beside Meg Shelton's grave, crying and laying flowers,' William continued, his voice tinged with a hint of disapproval. 'Regardless of whether she's a witch or not, it's a bit weird for a lad like yourself to be sobbing over some old woman who wasn't even a relation.'

James felt a pang of hurt at William's words, his heart sinking at the realisation that even his closest friends harboured doubts and judgments about his friendships. He had thought that his grief for Meg Shelton was a private matter. But now, as he stood before his friends, James couldn't help but feel exposed and vulnerable, his emotions laid bare for all to see. He knew that he couldn't expect everyone to understand or sympathise with his grief, but he had hoped for an ounce of support and understanding from those closest to him.

As James stepped out into the schoolyard, the sight of Oliver and August playing kickball filled him with a sense of dread. He knew that wherever they were, trouble was sure to follow, like a dark cloud looming on the horizon.

Sure enough, as James made his way across the yard he felt a chill run down his spine as he sensed the bullies' eyes boring into him. With a sinking feeling in the pit of his stomach, he quickened his pace, hoping to avoid a confrontation.

But before he could make his escape, Oliver and August had closed in on him, their faces twisted into sneers of contempt. James's heart raced as he realised that he was cornered, trapped like a mouse in a cat's claws.

'Here's the hag's pal,' Oliver sneered, his voice dripping with malice as he shoved James against the wall. James felt a surge of fear coursing through his veins, his breath becoming short, ragged gasps as he struggled to keep his composure.

William and Henry looked on helplessly, their expressions torn between concern and fear. They wanted to step in, to defend their friend against the bullies' cruelty, but they knew that Oliver and August were bigger and stronger than they were. They didn't stand a chance against them.

And so, with a heavy heart, William and Henry watched on in silence, their eyes filled with a mixture of guilt and betrayal. They couldn't bear to meet James's gaze, knowing that their inaction only added to his suffering. But in the face of such overwhelming intimidation, they felt powerless to intervene, forced to stand by and watch as their friend was subjected to the bullies' torment.

Oliver's hand closed around the collar of James's shirt, lifting him effortlessly off the ground and onto the wall. James could feel the weight of Oliver's presence bearing down on him, his breath hot and heavy against his skin as he loomed over him like a vulture circling its prey. He turned his head away, avoiding the odour arising from his breath or them catching sight of his watery eyes.

'Excuse me. Put him down,' a voice boomed out from behind Oliver and August, causing them to freeze in their tracks. With a sinking feeling, they turned around to see the imposing figure of the local vicar, Isaac, standing before them with a stern expression etched upon his face.

Isaac's gaze bored into them like hot coals, his eyes ablaze with righteous fury as he confronted the bullies. Sensing the disapproval radiating from the vicar, Oliver and August quickly released their grip on James, who stumbled to the ground in a heap. Rushing to his friend's side, Henry felt a surge of relief wash over him as James scrambled to his feet.

'What on earth do you think you are doing?'

'Nice dress,' August cheekily replied. 'We're just teaching your little friend here that it's not done to hang around with witches.'

'If you're talking about Miss Hilton, she was a dear friend to some of us in this village and the rumours around her supernatural powers are ridiculous.'

'Well how do you explain her crawling out of the ground?' Oliver sniggered and winked at his friend who held his hand over his mouth.

'And would you know something about that?'

'I don't know what you mean.' Oliver shrugged.

'Get away before I tell your parents and your teacher about how you're treating James.'

As the bullies hastily retreated, their tails between their legs, James and his friends breathed a collective sigh of relief. The tension that had gripped the schoolyard disappeared, replaced by a sense of calm and relief that washed over them like a cool breeze on a hot summer's day.

'Thanks, Vicar,' James said.

'No problem. I actually came to see you. Thankfully it came at an apt time, it seems.'

'We better go,' William said, patting Henry on the arm.

As James and Isaac made their way back to the church across the road, a solemn silence enveloped them like a protective cloak. Entering the church, they found solace in the familiar embrace of the sacred space, its hallowed halls offering refuge from the torment of the school playground. Making their way to the front pew, they took their seats side by side, their eyes drawn to the altar where Jesus hung from a cross.

'Do you think those bullies had something to do with digging up Meg's grave?' Isaac asked, curiously staring at James for a reaction.

'I don't know.'

'They looked strong enough to be able to carry out such a devious act. And their smirks spoke volumes.'

'I don't know if they're clever enough to dream up such a scheme, to be honest.'

'I wanted to ask you about something. When we had that vigil by her grave, before the fair, you mentioned you were at Margery's house the night she died. You seemed to know something about her death. Are you able to elaborate?'

'I don't want to talk about it,' James said, burying his head in his hands.

'If we knew what happened we could tell the constable. The greatest way to honour your friend is to punish those who might be responsible for her death. You spoke as though something untoward had occurred.'

'It did. But I'm too scared to say anything.'

'Has someone got a hold on you? Did they see you? Did they threaten you?'

'No.'

'Was it someone close to you? Was it your mother? I know she disliked you hanging around with Margery. I know your mother was adamant that Margery had brought disruption on the family.'

'It wasn't my mother,' James insisted.

'Then another relative perhaps?'

'It was a relative, but not in the way you think.'

'Lord Hilton?' Isaac suggested.

'No.' James stood up and walked to the church exit. 'I told you I don't want to talk about it.'

'James, don't go.' Isaac stood up and followed the boy, placing a hand on his shoulder. 'I'm sorry, I shouldn't have interrogated you like that. Come, why don't we pray for Margery's soul?'

With a solemn reverence, James and Isaac approached the altar. As they reached the sacred space, they knelt down on the cushion before the Lord, their heads bowed in humble submission.

'Almighty and Everlasting God, in this sacred sanctuary, surrounded by the hallowed presence of Your divine grace, I come before You with a heavy heart and a soul burdened by sorrow. Today, as I kneel before Your holy altar, I offer up a prayer for the soul of Margery Hilton, a beloved member of Your creation who has departed from this earthly realm and entered into Your eternal embrace. Lord, You are the source of all mercy and compassion, the giver of life and the ultimate judge of our souls. I humbly beseech You to look upon Margery with Your boundless love and forgiveness, to grant her peace and rest in Your heavenly kingdom. May Your divine light shine upon her, illuminating the path to everlasting salvation and redemption. Though Margery may have walked a troubled path in this life, fraught with trials and tribulations, I pray that You will grant her the mercy and grace to find solace and redemption in Your infinite love. Forgive her transgressions, O Lord, and wash away her sins with the cleansing waters of Your divine mercy.

'As she journeys into the realm of eternity,' Isaac continued. ...'may Your angels guide her with gentle hands and lead her safely into Your loving embrace. May she find comfort and solace in Your presence, surrounded by the eternal light of Your love. And, Lord, as we meet here today to offer our prayers for Margery's soul, I ask that You grant comfort and consolation to all who mourn her passing. May Your divine peace descend upon her loved ones, filling their hearts with hope and healing in the midst of their grief. In Your mercy, O Lord, hear our prayer and grant eternal rest to the soul of Margery Hilton. May she find everlasting joy and happiness in

Your heavenly kingdom, where she will dwell in Your presence for all eternity. Amen.'

'Amen,' James replied.

With a gentle touch and a reassuring presence, Isaac opened his eyes and placed a comforting hand against James's back.

'You know you can tell me anything anytime,' Isaac said softly, his voice a beacon of compassion in the darkness. 'My door is always open.'

'Thank you, Vicar,' James replied, his voice filled with gratitude and relief. With a grateful smile and a nod of understanding, he felt a sense of peace settle over him, knowing that he had found a friend and confidant in Isaac, a beacon of hope in the midst of life's storms.

Chapter 12

2 years earlier

As the gentle breeze of spring caressed the countryside, painting the landscape with the vibrant hues of new life, Elsie Turner stepped out into her garden, a smile playing upon her lips as she beheld the beauty of nature in full bloom. With the sun casting its golden rays upon the earth, she set about her daily chores, a sense of contentment filling her heart with each passing moment.

Elsie hung out her washing on the line, the colourful array of garments fluttering in the breeze like vibrant flags of joy. Beating her clothes against the weathered stone wall of her cottage, she marvelled at the sight of local lambs frolicking in the nearby fields.

Elsie Turner, a woman of thirty-five years, was a picture of grace and elegance. Her slender figure, draped in the modest yet finely crafted garments, spoke of a quiet dignity and understated refinement. With chestnut locks cascading in soft waves around her face, she possessed a natural beauty that needed no embellishment.

Her hazel eyes, alight with intelligence and warmth, sparkled with an inner vitality that belied her years. A gentle smile graced her lips, softening the lines of worry that occasionally creased her brow, a testament to the responsibilities she bore as a wife and mother in a world of agriculture which was riddled with uncertainty. The weather brought pressure on their ability to grow crops. But thus far, in the previous months, they had been fortunate to enjoy a fruitful abundance of produce.

The rhythmic clops of horses' hooves broke through the tranquil serenity of the countryside, drawing Elsie Turner's attention away from her daily chores. Turning towards the source of the sound, she beheld the sight of her husband Nathanial straddling his horse, his figure silhouetted against the golden rays of the afternoon sun.

As he dismounted from his horse and approached her, Elsie couldn't help but admire the rugged handsomeness of her husband, his weathered features softened by a look of genuine fondness and affection. His eyes, the colour of stormy seas, sparkled with warmth and tenderness as he drew her into his embrace.

'Welcome home, my love,' Elsie greeted him, her voice filled with genuine warmth and affection. 'You're just in time for supper.'

Nathanial returned her embrace with a gentle squeeze. 'I wouldn't miss it for the world,' he replied, his voice tinged with the weariness of a man who had spent the day toiling in the fields.

As Nathanial and Elsie entered their humble cottage, the tranquillity of their home was shattered by the sound of pots crashing to the ground. Instantly alert, Nathanial followed the commotion to the back of the house, his heart pounding with concern.

As he rounded the corner, his eyes fell upon an unexpected sight: an older woman, dressed in a black cloak, scurrying around his greenhouse with frantic urgency. Inside, an array of vegetables that Nathanial had painstakingly grown lined the shelves.

'Who goes there?' Nathanial called out, his voice echoing with authority as he confronted the intruder. Elsie stood by his side, her expression a mixture of alarm and curiosity as she observed the unfolding scene.

The woman froze in her tracks, her eyes wide with fear as she turned to face Nathanial and Elsie. In the dim light of the setting sun, her features were obscured by shadows.

'It's that damn woman again,' Elsie mumbled. 'She's stealing your vegetables.'

As the figure reappeared and hastily scurried out of the greenhouse, Nathanial's instincts kicked into action. With a firm resolve, he instructed his wife to fetch his gun while he swiftly mounted his horse, his heart pounding with determination as he prepared to give chase to the thief.

'It's Meg Shelton,' Nathanial declared with unwavering confidence.

With his trusty steed beneath him, Nathanial set off in pursuit of the fleeing figure, his eyes scanning the horizon for any sign of the elusive thief. The countryside stretched out before him, bathed in the soft glow of the sun, as he rode with purpose, his mind focused on apprehending the culprit and protecting his livelihood.

Elsie strode into the kitchen, her eyes scanning the room with a sense of urgency. Spotting the shotgun propped up against the wall, she wasted no time in reaching for the weapon, her fingers wrapping around its familiar handle with a firm grip.

The shotgun had served her husband well in his duties of protecting their home and providing for their family on hunting trips. As Elsie raced back to the field, her heart pounded with apprehension at the sight of Nathanial lying prone on the ground, his body still and unmoving. Dropping the shotgun, she rushed to his side, her hands trembling as she knelt beside him.

'Don't move, my darling,' she whispered, her voice choked with emotion as she rubbed his chest in a futile attempt to ease his pain. 'I'll get help. Everything will be alright.'

But as she moved to stand, she felt the warmth of Nathanial's hand against her ankle, anchoring her in place. Turning back to him, she met his pleading gaze, her heart breaking at the desperation she saw reflected in his eyes.

'Don't go,' he pleaded, his voice barely a whisper as he struggled for breath. Elsie wavered, torn between the instinct to flee for help and the desperate need to stay by her husband's side.

Kneeling down once more, she took his hand in hers, her lips brushing gently against his forehead as she murmured words of reassurance and comfort. She watched as his breathing slowed, each laboured breath becoming less frequent.

And then, in the stillness of the afternoon glow, Nathanial's chest rose and fell for the final time, his eyes fixed on the endless expanse of the sky above. With a heavy heart, Elsie knew that he was gone, his spirit ascending to the heavens as she remained rooted to the earth below.

Tears streaming down her cheeks, Elsie cradled her husband's lifeless body in her arms, her heart heavy with grief at the loss of the man she loved more than life itself. Breathing heavily, Elsie rose from the ground, her hands shaking with a mixture of rage and disbelief. She glanced up towards the field where Meg had scurried away. She followed her trail to find a black cloak on the floor, the same coat the witch had worn earlier. Within it was a small brown hare, hopping in the evening light. She grabbed the gun and took aim at the animal, aware of the rumours of Meg's ability to shapeshift.

'I know this is you, Meg,' she said, staring down the barrel of the gun with one open eye towards the seemingly innocent creature. 'You killed my husband and now I'll kill you.'

She wasn't a seasoned hunter, leaving those particular chores to her husband but she'd been on enough expeditions with Nathanial to know how it worked. How hard could it be? She pulled on the trigger. The shock of the discharge threw her backwards onto the ground. She sat up and saw the hare gallantly running away with what she was sure was a hint of rebellion in its stride.

'As God as my witness, Meg, I will get you.'

Chapter 13

Isaac sat in the dimly lit vestry of the church, the soft glow of candlelight casting flickering shadows across the walls, and sipped his whisky with a contemplative air. Before him lay an array of black leather-bound books, their pages filled with the stories of generations past.

Opening the first book, the year 1640 scrawled on the front page in faded ink, Isaac traced his fingers over the yellowed pages, his eyes scanning the delicate script that recorded the marriages, christenings, and deaths of every inhabitant of the parish since its inception.

With each turn of the page, Isaac delved deeper into the history of the community he served, uncovering tales of love and loss, joy and sorrow, that spanned centuries. Names and dates blurred together as he lost himself in the passage of time, each entry a testament to the lives that had been lived within the walls of the church.

As Isaac wrestled with James's cryptic words, a sense of unease settled over him like a heavy cloak. The suggestion that Margery Hilton's demise might have been at the hands of a relative lingered in his mind, casting shadows of doubt and suspicion over those closest to her.

James's reluctance to divulge further information only served to deepen Isaac's curiosity, leaving him to wonder what secrets lay hidden beneath the surface of the Hilton family's façade of respectability. Could it be that someone within their own ranks was responsible for Margery's untimely end?

As James reassured Isaac that his mother, Sarah, was not involved in Margery's demise, Isaac's initial relief was tempered by a sense of resignation. He had never viewed Sarah as a likely suspect in the matter, her gentle demeanour and quiet strength making her an unlikely candidate for such a heinous act.

Though determined in her own right, Sarah possessed a gentle spirit and a kind heart, her presence more akin to that of a nurturing caregiver than a ruthless perpetrator of violence. In Isaac's eyes, she lacked the strength and resolve necessary to carry out such a sinister deed, her inner nature more closely resembling that of a mouse than a predator.

But James said it *was* a relative. So who could he have meant? James's father was a possible culprit. Perhaps Sarah couldn't carry out the act, but maybe Francis could? Though he had always appeared indifferent to Margery's antics, perhaps there was more to his stoic façade than met the eye. Could he have carried out his wife's dirty work? Perhaps he was eager to live a quiet life and keep his wife content.

As Isaac contemplated James's cryptic words, a new possibility began to form in his mind. Could it be that James was referring to a relative of Margery Hilton as the possible culprit in her demise? The idea sent a chill down Isaac's spine, as he considered the implications of such a revelation.

James's insistence that it wasn't Lord Hilton himself provided some relief, as Isaac had sensed a sincerity in the nobleman's words during their previous interactions. He had always prided himself on his ability to discern truth from falsehood, and Lord Hilton's demeanour had given him no cause for doubt.

Indeed, Isaac often found that few were willing to lie to a vicar, perhaps out of a fear of divine retribution or a belief that he held a direct line of communication to the heavens above. As a servant of God, Isaac took this responsibility seriously, striving to uphold the trust placed in him by his parishioners and to act as a beacon of truth and righteousness in a world fraught with deception.

As Isaac pondered the circumstances surrounding Margery Hilton's death, he couldn't shake the feeling that her brother, Lord Hilton, was unlikely to have been involved in any foul play. Despite the unsettling notion of her grave being tampered with, Isaac sensed a genuine unease in the nobleman that convinced him of his innocence.

After all, it had been five decades since Lord Hilton had last seen his sister, and there seemed to be little reason for him to suddenly take an interest in her twilight years. Margery's troubled past, concealed beneath the alias of Meg Shelton, had brought anguish to the village, but her true identity remained a closely guarded secret within the Hilton family.

Over the years, the Hiltons had taken great pains to preserve their family's reputation, deflecting inquiries about Margery's whereabouts with tales of scarlet fever or a discreet marriage. Some of their elite friends queried where their invitations to her wedding were, which the Hilton family tiptoed around, blaming her absconding from the first wedding to Lord Alnwick for avoiding a second embarrassment.

No, Margery's association with the Hilton family only came to light after her death, more particularly after her tombstone was erected. Before then, Lord Hilton had little interest in his long-lost sister, therefore Isaac could remove him from his list of suspects for Margery's demise.

As Isaac delved deeper into the investigation, he turned his attention to the other relatives of Margery Hilton, seeking any clues that might shed light on her mysterious death. However, as he contemplated the circumstances surrounding her passing, he found himself at a loss to identify any plausible suspects among her immediate family members.

Margery's parents had long since passed away, leaving behind no direct heirs to carry on the Hilton name other than their only son. Her two older sisters, having married and moved away, now lived lives of luxury under their married names, seemingly detached from the affairs of the Hilton family. With no apparent motive or connection to Margery's fate, they appeared unlikely candidates for involvement in her death.

As Isaac meticulously pored over his books, piecing together the intricate branches of the Hilton family tree, he couldn't help but marvel at the interconnectedness of the residents in the small village. With only six hundred souls to populate the region, it was not uncommon to find numerous relatives among one's neighbours, each link in the chain connecting families in ways both intimate and distant.

Indeed, intermixing and marrying cousins was a common practice in towns of such small populations, where choices for prospective partners were limited. This was evident in some of the web-handed patrons who occasionally visited the church. And the practice was common too among the elite, who sought to maintain the purity of their bloodlines and preserve their social standing through carefully arranged marriages and strategic alliances.

As Isaac's weary eyes scanned the names and connections he had painstakingly transcribed onto the paper, he felt a sense of both determination and exhaustion wash over him. The task of unravelling the intricate tapestry of the Hilton family tree seemed daunting, with hundreds of books yet to explore and countless more potential leads waiting to be uncovered.

As the clock struck three in the morning and the shadows of the church vestry deepened, Isaac couldn't help but wonder how long he could continue down this path and where it would ultimately lead him. The books within his own church were just the tip of the iceberg, offering only a glimpse into the vast network of relationships that spanned the borough and beyond.

With each passing moment, Isaac's mind raced with the possibilities of what lay beyond the pages of the books before him. What hidden truths and buried secrets might be waiting to be unearthed in the chapels of the grand estates and the parishes of the upper-class families? How many more marriages, christenings and deaths had been recorded in the volumes kept hidden from view, waiting to be discovered by an intrepid investigator?

As Isaac's tired eyes scanned the pages of the final book of the evening, they widened in recognition as he came across a familiar name: Lucy Hilton, the older sister of Margery. According to the records, Lucy had indeed married locally, within the very church Isaac now presided over. Her husband was Richard Cavendish, a landowner in nearby Lancaster.

Intrigued, Isaac delved deeper into the connection, discovering that Richard Cavendish was the brother of none other than John Cavendish, a prominent farmer in the area and a vociferous adversary of Margery Hilton. The pieces of the puzzle began to fall into place in Isaac's mind: James had suggested that a relative was responsible for Margery's death, and it seemed that John Cavendish fitted the bill perfectly, albeit a distant in-law of the rumoured witch.

Could James have been aware of the connection between John and Margery? Isaac pondered the implications of this revelation, realising that John had both a familial link to

Margery and a motive for her demise. Blaming her for the theft of his crops and, in his own words, for the death of his wife, John Cavendish certainly had reason to wish Margery harm.

Closing the book with a sense of urgency, Isaac resolved to visit John Cavendish the following day. There were questions that needed answers, and he was determined to uncover the truth behind Margery's death, no matter where the trail might lead him.

Chapter 14

Twenty years earlier

Inside the humble stone cottage, Meg Shelton lay upon the creaking bed, her tired frame a testament to the trials of the day. Her hands, calloused from years of toil, were now still, resting upon her worn apron. The flickering light of a solitary candle cast dancing shadows upon the walls, illuminating the rustic charm of the thatched roof above.

Meg had spent the day as she often did, traveling from homestead to homestead, offering her services as a midwife to those who could afford it. For many families, her presence meant the difference between life and death, a beacon of hope amidst the uncertainty of childbirth. Yet for others the cost of her aid remained out of reach, leaving mothers and infants to face the harrowing ordeal alone.

As Meg drifted into a well-deserved slumber, the creak of the cottage door stirred her from her rest. With a gentle rustle of fabric, Susan, weary from a day spent tending to the grandeur of the Cottam estate, entered the room. A soft smile graced her lips as she approached Meg, her heart swelling with affection for the woman who had become like family to her.

With tender care, Susan leaned down and pressed a gentle kiss upon Meg's forehead, the gesture a silent expression of the bond they shared. Meg's eyes fluttered open, and a warm glow of recognition lit up her tired features as she beheld Susan's familiar face.

'Welcome home, my love,' Meg murmured, her voice a soft lullaby in the quiet of the cottage. Despite the weariness that lingered in her bones, the presence of Susan brought a sense of comfort and solace that eased the burdens of the day.

Susan turned to the kitchen and bustled around the stove, tending to the flickering flames that danced beneath a collection of iron and copper pots. As Meg lay recovering on the bed, Susan prepared their evening meal, the aroma of stew mingling with the comforting crackle of the fire. She chopped root vegetables and diced meat, adding them to a bubbling pot filled with water and a medley of herbs and spices. The stew simmered slowly, filling the cosy space with its rich fragrance. Meanwhile, a pot of oats bubbled beside it, soon to become a simple yet satisfying porridge.

As the savoury aroma of the stew wafted through the air, Meg, now up from her rest, joined Susan by the stove. With a gentle smile, she took hold of the wooden spoon and began to stir the pot.

'It smells delicious,' Meg said, kissing Susan on the cheek.

As they stirred the pot and tended to the meal, Susan's melodic voice filled the kitchen with the timeless lyrics of 'Little Boy Blue.' With Susan's song still lingering in the air, Meg couldn't resist the infectious rhythm, her feet tapping lightly against the stone floor. Catching Susan's eye, she grinned, and in a spontaneous burst of joy she extended her hand. Susan, her cheeks flushed with laughter, eagerly accepted the invitation, and together they twirled and swayed around the stove.

A banging on the door brought their impromptu dance to an abrupt halt, leaving the women exchanging puzzled glances as they made their way to the entrance. Lord Cottam's son's pallid complexion and the urgency in his eyes sent a shiver down Meg's spine. With a trembling hand, Bartholomew Cottam gripped Meg's shoulder.

'It's my father. He's not well,' Bartholomew stuttered.

'Oh my God,' Meg replied. 'What's happened?'

'He's on the floor, clutching his chest.'

With a sense of urgency propelling her forward, Meg wasted no time in grabbing her bag of remedies as she hurried to follow Bartholomew. Through the winding paths of the estate she trailed behind him, her mind racing with thoughts of what awaited her. As they approached the grand manor, Meg's heart pounded in her chest, the weight of responsibility heavy upon her shoulders. She prayed that her knowledge and skills would be enough to ease Lord Cottam's suffering, knowing that every moment counted in the face of such a dire situation.

Inside, Lord Cottam lay on the ground sweating and clutching at his right arm. He'd grown in girth over the years, despite Meg pleading with him to cut down on the steak and the mead. Gout had overtaken his legs and his face was as red as a cherry tomato.

Meg rushed to Lord Cottam's side, her heart sinking at the sight of his distress. She knelt beside him, her hands moving swiftly as she assessed his condition. The symptoms were clear – a heart attack. With practised efficiency, she administered her remedies, applying compresses and administering herbal concoctions to ease his pain and stabilise his condition. Lord Cottam groaned in agony, his face contorted with discomfort as he struggled to catch his breath. Despite the severity of the situation, Meg remained calm and focused, her years of experience guiding her actions as she fought to save the life of the man before her.

As Lord Cottam battled for his life, he reached out for Meg's hand, his eyes imploring her with a silent plea. Amidst panted breaths, he uttered a poignant promise. 'Fear not,' he whispered. 'You shall find refuge within these walls for as long as you draw breath. You have been a true friend to this family.'

Meg's eyes welled with tears as she listened to Lord Cottam's words, his voice strained with effort. She squeezed his hand gently, offering him what comfort she could in his final moments. The weight of his promise settled heavily on her shoulders, a solemn vow of security in the face of uncertainty. She nodded, her voice choked with emotion as she whispered her gratitude. Despite the pain and sorrow of the moment, there was solace in knowing that she would not be homeless again.

With Lord Cottam's passing, the solemnity of the moment enveloped the room like a shroud, leaving a substantial sense of loss in its wake. As Bartholomew Cottam, now the heir to his father's estate, bowed his head in silent grief, a solitary tear traced a path down his cheek. Moved by a surge of sympathy, Meg approached him with tenderness, enfolding him in a comforting embrace. In that fleeting hug, the roles between servant and master seemed to blur. Yet, as the weight of his new responsibilities settled upon his shoulders, Meg retreated with quiet reverence, acknowledging the shift in power and authority. Though she had once cradled him in her arms as an infant, he now stood as her lord and master.

'I thought you were a nurse,' he remarked, his gaze sharp with judgment as it bored into her. 'Why didn't you save him?'

'I'm a midwife,' she clarified evenly. 'I bring life into the world. I'm limited when it comes to saving it.' Their silence hung heavy between them, charged with unspoken tension. 'I'll get you a whisky,' she offered suddenly, her tone softening with sympathy. 'For the shock.' With a respectful nod, she turned and hurried off to the kitchen, leaving him to contemplate her words in the quiet solitude of the room.

When Meg returned, she found the new Lord Cottam standing over his father's lifeless form, his gaze fixed on the stillness of death. At the sound of her footsteps, he looked up, his expression now tinged with a newfound assertiveness. With a confidence she hadn't seen in him before, he reached for the whisky she offered, downed it in one gulp, and handed it back, demanding another. It was a tone unfamiliar to them both, a departure from the gentle demeanour of his father, who had been the epitome of respect and kindness. Meg had gratefully accepted their offer of a home and employment, finding solace in the flexibility they provided in her hour of need. Like Susan, she dutifully tended to the household chores, but her true calling lay in aiding labouring mothers, a service she often had to leave the estate to fulfil. The former Lord Cottam had provided her with a sanctuary and a livelihood, which she cherished deeply.

She gulped, a hint of unease creeping over her as she realised that her new master might not possess the same kindness and understanding as his father. Yet she chose to give him the benefit of the doubt, attributing his abruptness to the shock of his father's passing.

She hesitated for a moment, grappling with the sudden shift in dynamics. While his father had insisted she call him by his first name, she couldn't shake the feeling that her new master might prefer a more formal title. 'Lord Cottam,' she began tentatively, testing the waters with the name, 'I'll summon the undertaker at once.'

The funeral service for the former Lord Cottam at St. Anne's Church in Woodplumpton two days later was a poignant affair, overseen by Isaac. Despite the sombre atmosphere, there was a sense of celebration as they honoured his life. Attendees from all corners of the region gathered, filling the church to capacity and beyond, standing shoulder to shoulder as they paid their respects.

Following the solemn ceremony, the gathering adjourned to The Wheatsheaf pub next door, where Bartholomew graciously hosted an open bar. Amidst the convivial atmosphere, they indulged in a delectable hog roast generously provided by one of the neighbouring farmers.

As speeches were made honouring the departed Lord Cottam, Bartholomew voiced his conviction that his father would have preferred a celebration of his life. The mood lightened further when a young John Cavendish took up his guitar, filling the air with melodious tunes.

'And ye shall walk in silk attire,
And siller hae to spare,
Gin ye'll consent to be his bride,
Nor think o' Donald mair."
O wha wad buy a silken goun
Wi' a poor broken heart!
Or what's to me a siller croun,
Gin frae my love I part!

The mind wha's every wish is pure
Far dearer is to me;
And ere I'm forc'd to break my faith
I'll lay me doun an' dee!
For I hae pledg'd my virgin troth
Brave Donald's fate to share;
And he has gi'en to me his heart,
Wi' a' its virtues rare.

His gentle manners wan my heart,
He gratefu' took the gift;
Could I but think to seek it back--
It wad be waur than theft!
For langest life can ne'er repay
The love he bears to me;
And ere I'm forc'd to break my troth
I'll lay me doun an' dee.'

As John's voice filled the room with the haunting melody, the assembled guests fell into a hushed awe, captivated by the song.

After the wake in the solitude of her humble abode, Meg's tears flowed freely, a testament to the depth of her sorrow at the death of the man who had shown her kindness when she had needed it most. Indeed, in a world where doors had often been shut in her face, he had extended a hand of compassion and generosity, offering her not just shelter, but also dignity and a sense of belonging. As she reflected on his kindness, Meg found herself overwhelmed by gratitude for the man who had seen her worth when others had turned away. Though he was gone, his legacy lived on in the warmth of her memories and the echoes of his kindness that had filled her days with comfort and hope.

In a tender embrace, Susan offered Meg solace and support, her touch a balm to the ache of loss that weighed heavy on Meg's heart. Together, they shared in the grief of saying goodbye to a dear friend, finding strength in each other's presence amidst the sadness that filled the cottage. As the night deepened and the stars twinkled overhead, their bond only grew stronger.

In the eyes of the townsfolk, Meg and Susan's close companionship was perceived as nothing more than the bond between friends, or perhaps sisters, facing life's challenges together as unmarried women in the borough. Despite whispers and speculation that occasionally fluttered through the gossiping tongues of the community, their relationship remained shielded by the understanding that female companionship was more readily accepted than the notion of two men living together. In this way, they found a fragment of acceptance and freedom to live their lives as they saw fit, hidden behind the veils of societal expectations and norms.

Their initial meeting had been marked by a profound moment. As Meg supported Susan's sister through the intense throes of childbirth, their eyes met across the room, and in that fleeting exchange, they recognised something in each other that transcended mere physical attraction.

Meg's skilled hands guided the new-born into the world. With each gentle movement, she navigated the delicate process of childbirth, her focus unwavering as she worked to ensure the safety of both mother and child. As the infant let out its first cries, a chorus of relief echoed through the room, mingling with the sounds of joy and gratitude. The mother, weary but overcome with emotion, reached out to cradle her new-born, her eyes brimming with joyful tears. In that moment, Meg's heart swelled with pride, knowing that she had played a crucial role in bringing new life into the world.

In the cosy ambiance of The Wheatsheaf, bathed in the soft glow of candlelight, Meg and Susan found solace in each other's company as they wet the baby's head. As they shared a mug of mead in a secluded corner, the weight of their secrets seemed to lift. With whispered confessions, they revealed their true identities to one another, knowing that their bond was built on trust and understanding. In the eyes of the world, they were merely two ordinary women, engaged in harmless gossip and idle chatter. But in that intimate moment, they found a connection that transcended societal norms.

In the quiet moments of the night, as the world outside drifted into slumber, Meg and Susan found solace in each other's company. Their covert meetings, cloaked in the cover of darkness, became a sanctuary where they could freely express their deepest thoughts and desires. With each shared secret and stolen glance, their bond grew stronger. Though they were careful to maintain appearances in the light of day, their connection remained devoted.

Over time, Susan settled into Meg's humble abode, and their shared space became a haven where their love could blossom freely. Despite the small confines of their living quarters, they found comfort in each other's presence, revelling in the simple joys of domesticity. Meg's arrangement with Lord Cottam provided them with a roof over their heads, though their secret remained carefully guarded. While Meg maintained the façade of Susan being her friend in front of the late Lord Cottam, she couldn't shake the feeling that he harboured suspicions about the true nature of her relationship with her.

Lord Cottam's silence on the matter brought a sense of relief to Meg and Susan. Despite any suspicions he might have harboured, his acceptance and lack of judgment allowed them to live their lives without fear of repercussion. In his discretion, they found a rare ally who respected their privacy and understood the importance of their bond.

As they sat entwined on the bed, enveloped in a bittersweet embrace, Meg and Susan found solace in the memories of their now departed friend. Tears ran down their cheeks. Suddenly, three sharp knocks shattered their

161

contemplation, heralding the arrival of Bartholomew, the new Lord Cottam.

'Come. Follow me,' he beckoned with a gravity that hung heavy in the air. 'You've been summoned to the reading of my father's will.' With hearts heavy with anticipation, Meg and Susan followed Bartholomew, their fates hanging precariously in the balance. Whilst the late Lord Cottam had assured Meg a home on his death bed, she couldn't be sure that he had put anything in writing.

In the solemn atmosphere of the late Lord Cottam's study, the solicitor presided over the reading of the will, his voice measured as he unravelled the complexities of the document. Before him, an eclectic assembly bore witness to the unfolding testament: relatives, eager heirs to the patriarch's legacy; a local journalist, ever ready to capture a headline-worthy narrative; and amidst them, Meg and Susan, silent observers to their employer and landlord's final wishes. As anticipated, the bulk of the estate was bequeathed to Bartholomew, the newly appointed heir. Yet, amidst the settlements, a singular stipulation emerged.

'Miss Shelton,' the lawyer spoke, his gaze resting upon Meg with a solemnity befitting the gravity of his words, 'shall be granted residence in the cottage on the estate grounds for the duration of her natural life.'

The revelation echoed through the room like a sudden gust of wind, drawing gasps and murmurs from the small assembly. All eyes turned to Meg, who sat in stunned disbelief, her heart a whirlwind of emotions. While she had known of Lord Cottam's intentions, the formal confirmation in his will left her speechless. A sense of gratitude welled within her, mingled with a profound sense of loss for the man who had shown her such kindness. As the weight of the gaze from Lord Cottam's heir lay heavily on her, she found solace in the reassuring grip of Susan's hand.

As Bartholomew Cottam grappled with the weight of his newfound inheritance, a simmering fury ignited within him at the unexpected provision in his father's will. What right did this woman, Meg Shelton, have to claim residence on his land indefinitely? His plans to demolish the rickety old cottage and allocate the space to his own ventures were now thwarted by his father's inexplicable act of generosity towards Meg. Her presence in his property irked him, stirring a tempest of resentment and frustration as he contemplated the implications of his father's decision. Faced with the reality of his father's final decree, with a heavy heart and a sense of resignation, Bartholomew acknowledged that he was indeed stuck with Meg Shelton's presence on his land, at least for the foreseeable future.

At least until her final breath...

Meg and Susan silently celebrated in their home, knowing it would be theirs until Meg's demise. But a banging on the door disrupted their joy. It was Bartholomew Cottam once again. What more could he want?

'Lord Cottam, how may we be of service?' Meg curtsied.

'Well, Meg,' Cottam replied with a sinister smile. 'Congratulations, you will be able to stay here until your dying breath and not a second longer.'

Meg gulped, wondering what Lord Cottam was going to do to her.

'But as for that girlfriend of yours...' Cottam said. The ladies glanced at each other. 'Oh yes, I know about your relationship, you weren't as covert as you may have thought. *She* wasn't in my father's will. She will have to move out immediately. My father might have accepted your lifestyle, but I certainly won't. She has approximately one hour to retrieve her belongings and leave for good. And if you think she'll be back to carry out her duties around my home, you'll be sadly mistaken as from this moment she has been terminated from her employment.'

Meg's heart sank as Bartholomew's words echoed in her ears. She felt a surge of anger and fear coursing through her veins. Susan, who had been standing beside her, froze in shock at the news. This was not the outcome they had expected after the reading of Lord Cottam's will. With trembling hands, Meg managed to utter a response, her voice barely above a whisper.

'But... she's been with me for years. She's not just an employee, she's...' Her words trailed off as Bartholomew's cold gaze bored into her. She realised that arguing with this unreasonable man would be futile. Without another word, she turned to Susan, her eyes pleading for understanding and reassurance. They shared a knowing glance before Susan nodded, silently agreeing to comply with Bartholomew's demands. Meg watched as Susan hurriedly gathered her belongings, her heart heavy with sorrow and uncertainty about their future apart.

Chapter 15

The Cavendish farm lay in ruins, a haunting testament to the devastation that had swept through it. Where lush fields once flourished with vibrant crops, now lay charred remnants of what once was. John Cavendish stood amidst the destruction, his gaze sweeping over the barren landscape, his heart heavy with the weight of loss. Years of tireless effort and unwavering dedication to his land had been reduced to ash in a single blaze. And it was all because of Meg Shelton who had managed to summon a hex upon his crops from beyond the grave.

In moments like these, he longed for the comforting presence of his wife, whose steadfast support had been his anchor through life's trials. But she was gone, a victim of tragedy that John attributed to the curse he believed Meg Shelton had placed upon them. Despite Meg's own demise, John remained persistent in his conviction that her wicked influence endured from her grave, casting a shadow over his crops and his life.

The daunting task of rebuilding his once-thriving empire loomed large before John, providing uncertainty over his future. With his fields laid to waste and his sources of income extinguished, he faced the harsh reality of enduring a long winter devoid of any financial security. Each day would be a struggle, with the spectre of financial ruin haunting his every move. Yet, despite the uncertainty that lay ahead, John remained determined to rise from the ashes and rebuild what had been lost, drawing upon the resilience and determination that had always defined him.

As the sun dipped below the horizon, John bade farewell to his loyal farmhand Francis, his gratitude evident in the hearty pat on the back he offered him. Alone in the kitchen, he settled down to a modest meal of bread and potatoes, a stark reminder of the absence of his late wife's culinary expertise. Often Sarah Ashton, a sympathetic tenant upon his land, would graciously deliver a pot of leftover stew, perhaps intentionally preparing an excess to ensure John had sustenance during leaner times. It was a subtle yet unmistakable gesture of support, a lifeline in the midst of his struggles.

The night cloaked him in a suffocating silence, leaving him with only his thoughts for company. The absence of conversation weighed heavily on him, amplifying the sense of isolation that plagued his evenings. Seeking solace, he sometimes found himself at The Wheatsheaf pub, where the lively chatter and clinking of tankards provided a temporary respite from the solitude that consumed him. It was a fleeting escape, a momentary distraction from the profound loneliness that lingered in the depths of his heart.

A tap on the window disrupted him. He looked up and spotted the vicar waving at him. John smiled, glad of the company, and opened the door to this unexpected visitor.

'Isaac,' John said as he welcomed the vicar inside. He offered him a whisky and they sat together at the table. 'This is a surprise. I don't get many visitors. What brings you to my humble abode?'

'It's a rather delicate subject,' Isaac explained.

'Sounds intriguing,' John replied.

Taking a deep breath, Isaac braced himself for this difficult conversation. Accusing one of his most dedicated parishioners of murder was a weighty task, especially without concrete evidence beyond James's cryptic testimony. Yet, armed with few clues, Isaac knew he had to broach the subject with John. Clearing his throat, he began tentatively, 'John, I hope you'll forgive the gravity of my inquiry, but recent events have left me with troubling questions.'

'Well spit it out, old friend.'

'Were you aware that your brother Richard married Margery Hilton's sister, Lucy?' Isaac asked, watching John closely for any reaction. John's confusion deepened, his brow furrowing as he struggled to make sense of Isaac's line of questioning.

'I was aware of the family connection, Isaac. Meg was at the wedding of course, ugly thing that she was. It was like putting a pig in a dress. She wasn't as odd back then, that began after she scarpered ahead of her wedding. Very quiet girl then, still obeying her parents' demands, just as she should have. But what on earth has this got to do with anything? She hasn't spoken to my sister-in-law or any of the Hilton family for decades.'

'Were the Ashtons aware of your connection?'

'I may have mentioned it once in passing on the farm to Francis. We spend a lot of time together in the fields. There's a lot of time to kill.'

'And what about James, their son? Did he know?'

'Oh I see.' John wiped a bead of sweat from his brow. 'Well I don't see how that would be relevant. I can't see that coming up naturally in conversation. Perhaps Francis may have told his wife and young James overheard them. Why they would discuss it, I have no idea. Why do you ask these questions anyway?'

Isaac nodded, absorbing John's response. 'I understand, John. It's just that James mentioned something peculiar, insinuating that a relative of Margery Hilton might have been involved in her demise,' he explained carefully. 'And considering your family connection, I thought it prudent to explore every avenue. I apologise if my inquiries seem intrusive.'

John appeared both shocked and bemused by Isaac's insinuation. 'So a young boy says a relative of Meg Shelton killed her. And not only did you believe the mumblings of this lad, but you instantly think it's me? Meg must have dozens of relatives. How does James know what happened to her anyway? We all know she was crushed beneath an oak barrel when she was home alone. It was God's will.'

Isaac maintained his composure, understanding the weight of his words. 'I assure you, John, my intention is not to accuse anyone unjustly,' he replied calmly. 'I simply seek to uncover any potential connections or motives that may shed light on this tragic event.'

'What on earth has James been saying?'

'James hasn't said very much at all to be honest. He's so shaken by the whole event, he can't bear to utter what he saw. To be honest, I think he's scared that whatever happened to Margery will happen to him too. But what he did tell me was that it was a relative. He wouldn't offer me any more information. And so, I began to do some digging myself. I've spoken to Lord Hilton too, but he assures me he's had nothing to do with Meg for decades. And after a browse through the church records, I discovered your family connection.'

'But why would that lead you to me?' John angrily replied. He seethed as Isaac sipped on the whisky which John had generously shared with him.

'Well... it's not as though you're without a motive, John,' Isaac said, clearing his throat. 'I mean, you've been very vocal about your distaste for the woman. She was stealing from you, and you believe she was responsible for your wife's death. I wondered if perhaps understandably you may have confronted her and things got out of hand. Or perhaps you accidentally killed her whilst she was stealing from your land and moved her body to her home to cover up what happened. Believe me when I say that if this is the case, I'd have no judgement. That's God's job. But he'd forgive you too if you were honest with me.'

John's face flushed with anger at the implication.

'How dare you accuse me of such a thing!' he spat, his voice rising. 'Yes, I was vocal about my grievances with Meg, but that doesn't mean I would resort to murder! And to suggest that I would hide her body and fabricate such a story is preposterous!'

He stood up abruptly, his fists clenched at his sides.

'You have no evidence, Isaac. This is nothing more than baseless speculation.'

Isaac held up a placating hand. 'John, please, I understand your frustration, but I have a duty to investigate all possibilities. If you truly have nothing to hide, then there's no need to be so defensive.'

John's jaw tensed, but he slowly sank back into his chair, his anger tempered by a sense of resignation. 'Fine,' he muttered through gritted teeth. 'But mark my words, Isaac, you're barking up the wrong tree.'

Isaac nodded solemnly. 'I'll keep that in mind, John. Thank you for your time.'

He rose from his seat, his footsteps heavy as he crossed the room to the door. With a creak, he swung the door open, casting a final glance over his shoulder at John, who remained slouched in his chair, his gaze fixed on some unseen point on the wall.

As Isaac prepared to depart, John's voice halted him in his tracks.

'Isaac,' he called out, prompting the vicar to turn back. 'There's someone else you should consider. She's also related to the Hiltons, albeit distantly. She's the sister of Lord Hilton's wife and, like me, would have cause to seek revenge on Meg Shelton. After all, Meg was also responsible for her spouse's death too.'

Isaac's interest piqued at this revelation. 'And who might that be, John?'

'Elsie Turner,' he replied.

Chapter 16

15 years earlier

The rain poured down on the gathered crowd at St. Anne's Church graveyard, but rather than dampening spirits, it only seemed to heighten the anticipation. Excitement crackled in the air as people squeezed together, eager for a prime view of the main event. Despite the downpour, the atmosphere buzzed with energy, each raindrop adding to the sense of drama and spectacle about to unfold. Indeed, if anything, the rain promised to provide an extra layer of entertainment for the spectacle about to unfold.

Meg Shelton trudged through the rain-soaked fields, her tattered cloak barely shielding her from the downpour, a journey she made most days. In her younger days, she had tended to her own vegetable patch and served as a trusted aide in the grand halls of the Cottam estate. But now, stripped of her privileges by the new Lord Cottam, she relied solely on her earnings as a midwife and the snippets of vegetables she could loot from the nearby farms.

Lord Cottam's refusal to provide her with transportation meant she often arrived too late to assist in births, leaving mothers to suffer alone in their hour of need. With each missed opportunity came the bitter realisation that she would not be compensated for her time or effort. The old lord had always been generous, granting her access to an array of horses stabled on the estate. But since the passing of the late Lord Cottam, his son had assumed control and tightened the reins, denying Meg the means to swiftly reach those in need. She now relied on her own two feet to traverse the muddy paths, a stark reminder of her diminished status in the eyes of the new lord.

He had made her life increasingly difficult since inheriting his father's estate. Although the will mandated that he provide her a home until her death, it was a term that filled him with dismay. So he devised ways to try to coerce her into leaving of her own volition. Stripping her of her job on the estate and the basic luxuries she once enjoyed within the estate grounds were two of the tactics. Furthermore, he neglected the upkeep of her home. Her cottage had become a wretched place, plagued by cold draughts, damp seeping through the walls, pervasive mould, and a leaking roof that flooded her living quarters on rainy days.

But she persevered. She wasn't going anywhere; she had nowhere else to go, and no one else would take her in. So she endured the squalor that her home had become, determined to hold on to the only sanctuary she had left.

She made an attempt to persuade him to construct a new dwelling for her once by suggesting a bet. To entice Lord Cottam into the wager, she made a tempting offer: if she lost, she pledged to vacate the land entirely, relinquishing her claim to the house his father had bequeathed her. This promise gave him free rein to do as he pleased with the property, enticing him further into the bet. However if he lost, he would have to build her a new home on the land.

They agreed on the terms of the bet: if she could outrun one of the hares that darted across his property, he would grant her request. Meg, with her vigour, believed she was capable of the challenge, but she imposed one stipulation: he must not release his black-haired hounds, which appeared to have developed a peculiar fondness for her scent. She couldn't shake the suspicion that Lord Cottam had purposely trained them to deter her from remaining on the estate.

He reluctantly agreed to her terms. A hare was captured, and a distance was set between his opulent mansion and her modest cottage. At the count of three, the hare was set free, and Meg dashed forward. As she suspected, she easily outpaced the creature, bounding ahead with grace. Yet, Lord Cottam broke his promise to protect her from his savage hound. Cruelly, he unleashed the beast, revelling in her distress as it tore into her leg. Amidst her anguished cries, she watched in disbelief as the hare effortlessly hopped past her, reaching the cottage before her.

She endured months of pain, her limp a constant reminder of the vicious dog's attack. When questioned about her injury, Lord Cottam spun a tale of her transforming into a hare herself, implying that the dog had merely acted on instinct. His twisted narrative not only painted him in a more favourable light but also fuelled the rumours of Meg's alleged witchcraft, adding another layer to her already tarnished reputation.

As she lost the bet, Meg didn't receive the promised new home. However, as Lord Cottam had reneged on his side of the agreement, failing to honour the terms they had agreed upon, they reached a compromise to maintain the status quo. Meg would remain on the land, albeit enduring the increasingly inhospitable conditions of her derelict cottage, which grew colder and damper with each passing day.

The cruellest act Lord Cottam committed was casting out Susan. Her expulsion from the estate left Meg shattered, never to fully recover. Forced to return to her family, Susan succumbed to the pressures of societal expectations, marrying a local landowner against her will. On the day of her wedding, Meg passed by St. Anne's Church, where she exchanged a sympathetic glance with Susan amidst the celebratory chaos. Behind Susan's forced smile, Meg detected the weight of her predicament – bereft of choice, desperate, and stripped of her autonomy. Despite their efforts to maintain contact, the persistent rumours surrounding their relationship posed a grave threat to both women, compelling them to part ways and navigate their separate paths alone.

As Meg passed St. Anne's Church once more, her heart sank at the sight that greeted her – a scene of cruelty and injustice. There, in the unforgiving grip of the wooden stocks, was the love of her life, Susan, her head and hands confined as she endured the merciless barrage of vegetables and pebbles hurled by their neighbours towards her. Tears streamed down Susan's face, mingling with the bruises and wounds inflicted upon her. In that moment, Meg felt a surge of helplessness, witnessing the woman she cherished being subjected to such brutality and humiliation.

Beside the stocks, a cruel sneer etched across his face, stood the man Susan called her husband. His eyes glinted with vindictive pleasure as he watched the scene unfold.

'Punish the unruly hag!' he bellowed, his voice filled with contempt. 'This vile woman has dared to disobey her husband!'

Meg's heart sank like a stone in the depths of a dark river. She couldn't bear to witness the brutality being inflicted upon the woman she loved with all her soul. Anguish flooded her being as she watched Susan's agony, her spirit breaking with each lash of the crowd's fury.

'What did she do?' Meg inquired, her voice barely above a whisper.

'Apparently she's been having relations with a woman behind her husband's back,' replied Hilda, her tone tinged with self-righteousness. Known throughout the village as a notorious gossip, Hilda was too engrossed in the spectacle unfolding before her to recognise the woman questioning her as none other than Meg Shelton herself. Hilda's attention, however, remained fixated on Susan, oblivious to the irony of her words given her own taste for spreading rumours about Meg's supposed supernatural abilities.

'Who was the woman she was having an affair with?' Meg inquired, her curiosity piqued. She couldn't help but wonder who held Susan's heart now and why this other woman had not faced the same punishment.

'Some woman named Florence. If you ask me, they were just good friends,' Hilda scoffed, her voice dripping with gossip. 'I reckon he's just using this as an excuse for her not pleasing him in the bedroom, if you know what I mean.' She chuckled, then joined in the cheers as the men continued to pelt Susan with projectiles.

As Meg watched the cruel spectacle, her heart ached for Susan. She knew the rumours circulating about her alleged affair were likely true. Susan was never meant to marry a man, just as Meg herself had not.

Despite the pain of realising Susan had found love with someone else, Meg found solace in the thought that she had experienced some happiness during their time apart, even if it ultimately led to this humiliating ordeal.

As the crowd dispersed and the flogging came to an end, Meg observed Susan being released from the stocks. Her dress was stained red, a mixture of tomato juice and her own blood. Susan appeared shaken, shivering and struggled to stand.

'Now, I hope you've learned your lesson,' Susan's husband grumbled. She silently nodded. 'You will obey me from now on and you will never see that ghastly woman again.'

Tears welled up in Susan's eyes as she silently accepted her fate, meeting Meg's gaze with despair. The poignant memory of their last encounter flooded Meg's mind as she watched Susan endure the cruel punishment. The sympathetic smile she offered now mirrored the one she had given on Susan's wedding day, but the circumstances were vastly different. This time, Susan was shackled not by vows of matrimony, but by literal chains.

Meg couldn't shake the feeling of helplessness as she witnessed her beloved enduring such unjust suffering. She turned away, her heart heavy with anger at the injustice of it all.

Chapter 17

Elsie Turner sat on her porch, the creaking of the rocking chair echoing in the stillness of the countryside. Her gaze was fixed on the expansive fields before her, where tragedy had struck and claimed her husband's life. Yet, Elsie knew deep down that his demise wasn't merely a result of a fall from his horse. No, she harboured a darker truth in her heart – the evil curse cast upon him by the infamous Meg Shelton who, as legend had it, transformed into a hare to evade justice.

Grief had ravaged Elsie, leaving behind a mien weathered by sorrow and loss. Each line etched into her skin told a tale of heartache, while the weight of her sorrow burdened her form, rendering her frail and gaunt. The once vibrant spirit had waned, leaving behind a hollow shell haunted by memories of her beloved.

Since he left her, the farm had fallen into disrepair. The once thriving fields now lay barren, the crops withered, and the animals neglected. Overgrown grass swayed in the breeze. While some attributed the farm's decline to the absence of manpower, Elsie remained convinced that it was the sinister work of the local witch, casting her wicked spells to ensure her misery knew no end.

Lost in her reverie, Elsie failed to notice Reverend Isaac ascending the three steps onto her porch. It wasn't until his hand gently rested on her shoulder that she snapped out of her trance, realising she was no longer alone.

'Elsie,' Isaac began with a tone of genuine remorse, 'I'm deeply sorry to find you in such distress. I've been remiss in my duties as a vicar; I haven't stopped by since the funeral to inquire about your well-being. Time seems to have slipped away from me.'

Elsie offered him a reassuring smile before returning her gaze to the emptiness before her. 'I can hardly claim to be a model Christian myself,' she admitted softly. 'I haven't set foot in St. Anne's since...'

'I'm sure God will forgive you for that,' Isaac interjected, taking a seat beside her on the bench. 'You've had more than your fair share of burdens to bear.'

'I couldn't bear to see *her* either,' Elsie confessed.

'*Her* being Meg Shelton?' Isaac inquired, receiving a nod in response. 'I understand your sentiments. Many in the village share similar feelings towards her, despite her death.'

Elsie remained quiet.

'There's been some unrest regarding her grave,' Isaac revealed. 'I'm endeavouring to uncover the culprits.'

'She'll be behind it, mark my words. She's a witch,' Elsie asserted firmly.

'Well, we can agree to disagree on that,' Isaac replied diplomatically.

'What brings you here, Vicar?' Elsie asked, her tone indicating her lack of energy for entertaining visitors. She had grown accustomed to solitude in recent years, finding solace in the quiet of her own company.

'I didn't realise you and Meg were related,' Isaac said, prompting a surprised reaction from Elsie who remained silent.

'I believe your sister is married to Lord Hilton, Meg's brother?' Isaac continued.

Elsie's expression darkened at the mention of Meg's family ties. 'She brought shame on that family,' she muttered bitterly. 'She left long ago, and nobody wanted anything to do with her after. How did you come by this information anyway?'

'John Cavendish told me,' Isaac replied. 'I recently discovered his familial connection, and upon further inquiry, he revealed your link to Meg as well. Though, as in-laws, rather than by blood.'

'Given she strayed from the family nearly fifty years ago, I hardly consider her a relative,' Elsie retorted. 'She doesn't deserve to bear the Hilton name. That's why she's a Shelton. Well, until you ordered that tombstone.'

Isaac's response was unwavering. 'She'll always be a Hilton, whether you like it or not,' he asserted. 'You can't change where you come from, only where you're headed.'

'Why do you have this sudden interest in Meg's relations?' Elsie asked through clenched teeth, her frustration palpable.

Isaac hesitated, carefully choosing his words. 'You wouldn't have any reason to wish harm upon Meg, would you?' he ventured cautiously.

Elsie's response was swift and sharp. 'What, besides the fact that she murdered my husband?'

Isaac chose to overlook her accusation, considering it absurd. He understood that grief could stir up a multitude of emotions, but he found it implausible to believe that Margery Hilton could have committed such a deed. Evidence suggested that his death was the result of an accident.

'I know you're relieved that she's gone,' Isaac remarked, carefully treading around the sensitive subject. 'But I'm simply asking if you have any idea who might be responsible for her death.'

Elsie's response was laced with defensiveness. 'If you're insinuating something, Vicar, I'd rather you be straightforward about it.'

'I'm not making any accusations,' Isaac clarified, maintaining his composure. 'I'm merely seeking answers. We believe that a relative played a role in her demise, and I'm determined to uncover the truth.'

'And what if the finger pointed to me?' Elsie challenged, her tone sharp with suspicion. 'Would you report me to the authorities? Have me thrown in jail? Or worse, see me hanged?'

'Elsie, anything shared with me remains in confidence. However, I would pray for your soul,' Isaac said solemnly. 'I'd wish for whoever did this to repent for their sins, to feel remorse for their actions, and seek forgiveness from God.'

'I'm not sorry for anything,' Elsie grumbled defiantly.

'So, did you?' Isaac inquired, his tone gentle yet probing.

'Did I do what?' Elsie retorted.

'Kill Meg Shelton?' Isaac shrugged, maintaining his composure.

'I wish I could claim responsibility for that,' Elsie admitted bitterly. 'How I'd relish the opportunity to wrap my hands around her throat and witness the life fade from her eyes. But no, Vicar, it wasn't me. Truth be told, there's hardly anyone who didn't have a motive to end Meg Shelton's reign of terror. She was an evil witch who instilled fear in this town.'

'But there aren't many individuals in the area who can claim a familial connection,' Isaac pointed out.

'Someone like me? I wouldn't even consider myself family,' Elsie scoffed. 'And I certainly wouldn't broadcast such a link. In the past, they'd have tarred and feathered me just for being associated with her. Times may have changed, Isaac, but the stigma remains.'

'I suppose you have a point. It's uncertain how many people could be linked,' Isaac conceded. 'I've searched through the church's records and found no other connections, distant or close.'

'There was, however, a child. A son,' Elsie revealed, her voice tinged with a hint of apprehension. 'If she were my mother, I'd certainly harbour ill feelings towards her.'

'A son?' Isaac gasped, taken aback by the revelation. 'But how is that possible if she was never married?'

'You don't need a marriage certificate to conceive a child, Vicar,' Elsie remarked dryly.

'I understand the concept, Elsie. But when did this happen?' Isaac pressed further.

'I've already said too much,' Elsie replied cryptically, rising from her seat. 'It's not my place to spread rumours. I can't confirm if it's true, and I certainly won't expose some innocent soul as Meg Shelton's offspring. Nobody deserves that fate.'

'And what if he was the one who ended Meg's life?' Isaac questioned, his curiosity piqued.

'Well then,' Elsie smiled enigmatically. 'I'd extend my hand in gratitude. And then take their secret to the grave.'

With that, Elsie retreated into her home, leaving Isaac pondering in the wake of her revelation. The fields where Meg once roamed now held a newfound significance. If he could uncover the identity of her long-lost child, perhaps he would finally unlock the mystery behind Meg Shelton's demise.

Chapter 18

34 years earlier

A winding road stretched away from The Wheatsheaf pub, its rubbly path disappearing into the darkness of the night. Those making their way home after a few tankards of ale relied on flickering candlelight to guide their stumbling steps along the uneven terrain.

Constable Ivan Lovelace embarked on his journey back to his own residence, a modest cottage located just outside the village. Normally, the walk took him about twenty minutes, but tonight he debated whether to take a shortcut across a field. Recent rains had left the grass soggy and muddy, a sure way to stain his trousers, and he couldn't afford the time to clean them before his morning shift.

He had spent the evening in the company of his peers, men of a similar age who had all capped off their arduous day's work with a drink. They had laboured in the local fields while he had patrolled the streets of Preston, apprehending thieves and safeguarding homes left vulnerable by their absent owners, who were toiling away elsewhere.

The alcohol had taken its toll on him, blurring his vision and slowing his once-nimble legs. He knew he needed to sober up before he could undertake his duties the next day, so he had set aside some bread at home for that purpose.

Ivan had been serving as a constable for ten years, a decision that brought reassurance to his family. His father had passed away at a young age due to the toll that heavy farm work had taken on his body. Unlike farm labour, which was often seasonal, policing offered a reliable source of income throughout the year. There were always wrongdoers to apprehend.

His wife Olivia would likely be waiting patiently at home, perhaps already in bed. Although she occasionally grumbled about his late nights, she understood the demands of his position and allowed him the occasional evening out with his friends. Ivan suspected she passed the time with her own circle of friends, exchanging the latest local gossip. There was always plenty to discuss – rumours of illicit affairs, scandalous secrets, and mysterious disappearances. The village was a hotbed of whispered stories, from covert romances to hidden pregnancies and hasty adoptions, each laden with its own share of family shame.

The spectre of witchcraft still lingered in the village, despite the Pendle trials having long concluded. Suspicion often fell upon unmarried women, particularly those engaged in certain professions, casting a shadow of doubt upon their reputations. Ivan had heard countless rumours of local women supposedly transforming into animals and placing curses upon crops. However, without any tangible evidence or proof of wrongdoing, there was little he could do. The whispers persisted, but without concrete accusations, they remained nothing more than unsettling tales whispered in the dark.

One name that frequently surfaced in the gossip of the village was that of Meg Shelton. A peculiar character, so they said. Ivan had spotted her on more than one occasion, nursing a gin or two in the corner of The Wheatsheaf. She always seemed to keep to herself, with few willing to engage her in conversation. Despite local pleas to the landlord to bar her from the premises, their requests were sternly rebuffed. The pub relied on custom, after all.

Meg was a ghastly sight, they said, with a nose like a cavern and haggard features that seemed to repel any semblance of charm. Rumour had it that her family had made numerous attempts to marry her off, all of which had failed miserably. They had long abandoned her to her solitary existence. Few knew the details of her background, but Ivan couldn't quite grasp the extent of the negativity directed at her. She was simply an unsightly loner, nothing more. If only he had a penny for every man who fitted that description in the village he would be richer than the Hiltons and the Cottams combined.

As he stumbled down the road, his foot caught on a hidden pothole, sending him crashing to the ground. The candle he held flickered out, plunging him into total darkness. Only the faint glow of the moon and stars offered any guidance toward his home. He cursed under his breath, feeling the dampness of a puddle seeping into his trousers.

'God damn it,' he muttered, realising he'd be in trouble with his superiors come morning. It was expected that he arrive at work in a spotless uniform.

'It's a miserable night, isn't it?' came a gravelly voice from the shadows. Ivan squinted, trying to discern the figure responsible for the voice and its whereabouts. Slowly, the figure emerged into the minimal light, revealing a woman draped in a cloak.

She stood beside him and helped him to his feet, brushing down the mud from his trousers. Upon closer inspection, Ivan recognised the distinct features he had often glimpsed at The Wheatsheaf.

'Meg Shelton?' he asked, surprised.

'That's me,' she whispered.

'Thank you for your help. What on earth are you doing down here at this time of night?' he inquired, puzzled.

'You never know when a lone pedestrian might need some help,' she sniggered, placing a hand over her mouth.

'Well, thank you for your help. May I wish you a good night. Get home safely,' he said, tipping his hat and preparing to continue his walk home.

'Shilling for my time?' she asked, holding out her hand. He stopped and turned around. He knew the woman was poor. Anyone who had seen her clothes could see she had it tough. And in The Wheatsheaf, she nursed the same drink all evening when she was in there.

He fiddled around in his pocket and pulled out a shilling, tossing it towards her. She caught it in her hand and rubbed it on her cloak, then bit it to test its legitimacy before holding it up to the light.

'Thank you, kind sir. I'll give you a lot more for two shillings,' she suggested.

'What do you mean, offer me more?' he asked curiously.

'Well, you know. It's a dark night and you're on your own. I'm on my own. For an extra shilling, I could make sure we weren't alone on this cold evening,' she implied.

'I'm a constable, you know?' Ivan said sternly.

'Are you telling me constables don't have needs?' she shrugged.

'I could arrest you for even suggesting this. I could have you flogged outside St. Anne's,' he threatened.

'Never mind,' Meg said, holding up her hands. 'I'll take my shilling and go home.'

'Wait,' Ivan called as she began to walk off. 'I could still arrest you just for even suggesting it.'

'Well, why don't you?'' she said, holding her nerve. He looked at her as if he had never seen her before. Yes, she was still the same woman whom he'd encountered around the village, but under the cover of darkness and to his blurred, ale-filled eyes, she wasn't as hideous as he remembered.

'I'll offer you a proposal. You give me whatever you were offering for free, and I'll say no more about it,' he proposed.

'Very well,' Meg said.

She clasped his hand firmly and guided him into the shadowed embrace of the nearby forest.

Chapter 19

In the heart of the rolling countryside, nestled amidst verdant meadows and ancient oaks, stood the venerable walls of a 16th-century nunnery. Its façade, weathered by centuries of wind and rain, exuded an aura of timeless tranquillity. As Isaac approached the building, the scent of wildflowers mingled with the faint echoes of Gregorian chants, hinting at the devout seclusion within.

Tall, wrought-iron gates guarded the entrance. Beyond them, a cobblestone path wound its way through meticulously tended gardens, where colourful blooms nodded in silent devotion to the heavens above. The main building rose majestically, its sandstone walls softened by ivy that climbed gracefully towards the sky. Stained-glass windows depicted scenes of biblical significance, casting colourful patterns of light onto the polished floors within.

Isaac approached the imposing double oak doors of the convent, their aged wood polished to a warm shine by countless hands over the centuries. With a firm yet respectful knock, he awaited entry into the sacred sanctuary beyond.

Moments later, the doors creaked open, revealing a figure cloaked in the traditional black and white habit of the order. Her face, weathered by the passage of time and marked by the lines of devout devotion, bore the unmistakable aura of one who had dedicated her life of service to God.

'Welcome, Reverend,' she greeted him with a gentle smile, her voice soft yet infused with a quiet strength that spoke of a lifetime of faith. 'Please, come in. Sister Agnes will show you to the parlour.'

With a nod of gratitude, Isaac stepped over the threshold. Within the secluded confines of the convent, silence reigned, broken only by the soft rustle of habits and the hushed whispers of prayer. Candlelit corridors led to tranquil chapels, where flickering flames illuminated altars adorned with golden icons and fragrant incense perfumed the air.

In the refectory, long wooden tables awaited the sisters, where simple meals were shared in communal silence. Above, the dormitory housed rows of narrow beds, each adorned with a simple crucifix, offering solace to those who sought rest after long hours of prayer.

'It's not often we have a Protestant vicar here,' Sister Agnes whispered, her voice carrying the weight of centuries of tradition. They took a seat at the table.

'Well, I'm on a particular mission today,' Isaac replied, his tone earnest yet respectful as he followed her down the quiet corridors of the convent.

'Well, I suppose we all worship the same God, don't we?' Sister Agnes remarked with a gentle smile, her words echoing the universal truth that transcended religious divides.

The elderly nun who had greeted him at the entrance returned with a tray of tea, the delicate fragrance wafting through the air as she set it down before them. Isaac offered his gratitude, and with a nod, the nun quietly withdrew, leaving Sister Agnes and Isaac alone in the peaceful confines of the convent.

'So what can I do for you?' Agnes slurped her tea and fixed her gaze on her guest with curiosity.

'Well...' Isaac took a deep breath. 'I'm trying to unravel a peculiar case. A parishioner of mine has recently died, and there's a suspicion that she may have had a son. Now, in all my time at the church, I've never heard her mention a child. However, I'm aware that she was never married and faced some especially trying circumstances. And considering this is a convent...'

'You're wondering if she might have given birth here, and we would have arranged for the child to be placed with an appropriate family?' Agnes suggested. Isaac silently nodded in agreement. 'Well, there is a possibility that she may have, but I have to say we run a confidential service here. We have to protect the mothers who seek solace within our care as I'm sure you respect the confidentiality of the parishioners in your care.' Her tone was gentle but firm.

'And as you should,' Isaac replied, acknowledging the sanctity of the convent's discretion. 'Believe me, I know more than anyone how important it is to keep the trust of those who seek our guidance and support. However, the person in question has since died, and I wondered if we could provide some answers to her son who may still be with us.'

'But it's not just the mother we have a duty to, Reverend,' Sister Agnes raised her eyebrows, her expression grave with the weight of responsibility. 'We also have to consider the feelings of the parents who came to us to adopt. Who knows what they've told their son or daughter about the adoption. It's not for us to meddle. And we have to consider the feelings of the child themselves. If they weren't aware, the news could be disruptive. If they did, they might not want to be found.'

Isaac nodded solemnly, his expression reflecting the gravity of the situation. He gently patted his index finger against his lip as he carefully weighed Sister Agnes's responsibilities. 'I understand, Sister Agnes,' he began, his voice measured. 'The thing is, I have a strong reason to believe that people's lives are in danger, and I'm keen to ensure the safeguarding of my parishioners. If there's even a chance of understanding if my departed patron had birthed a son, it could be lifesaving. I assure you, God would will you to help me.'

'If it's within God's interests, He will find a way to sort it out. My hands are tied, I'm afraid, Vicar,' Sister Agnes replied with a gentle yet resolute tone, her hands clasped together in a gesture of finality. 'Now, if there's anything else I can help you with, please do not hesitate to ask.' With a graceful motion, she rose from her seat and led him towards the entrance, her demeanour calm and composed despite the weight of their conversation.

'I am so grateful for your time, Sister Agnes, and I completely respect your vow of silence on the matters of the people you have aided,' Isaac expressed with genuine appreciation, tipping his hat respectfully. The nun who had greeted him upon his arrival already had the door open for his departure.

'Wait,' Sister Agnes interjected before Isaac could make his exit through the entrance gates. 'I'm curious, who was the woman you mentioned, the one who might have sought our support?'

'It was Margery Hilton, Sister,' Isaac responded. 'Though locally, you may know her as Meg Shelton.'

The two nuns exchanged a silent glance, their eyes revealing a shared surprise. Without uttering a word, they understood each other's thoughts perfectly.

'Does that name mean anything to you?' Isaac inquired with a hint of uncertainty. Sister Agnes drew in a deep breath.

'I believe it's best if you come back inside.'

Sister Agnes took him to a courtyard, which echoed with the laughter of novices engaged in their studies, while older sisters tended to the herb gardens or sought quiet contemplation in secluded alcoves. In this haven of piety and devotion, the sisters lived out their days in humble service to their faith, their hearts lifted by the promise of eternal grace and their souls nourished by the unyielding embrace of divine love.

They settled on a wooden bench tucked away in the corner of the courtyard, far from the prying ears of the sisters who went about their daily routines. Though devoted to their faith and committed to the church, they found solace in the occasional indulgence of gossip, even if it was only among themselves.

'Meg Shelton was part of your congregation?' Sister Agnes whispered, her voice barely audible.

Isaac nodded solemnly. 'For quite a long time, yes. She was a woman of little means, abandoned by her family, and unfortunately, often misunderstood by the community. She endured hardships, and I fear the locals weren't as compassionate as she deserved.'

'You are aware of her reputation as a witch, aren't you?'

'I've heard the rumours, indeed,' Isaac replied, his voice softening. 'But I've always found it hard to believe. To me, she appeared more as a lonely soul in need of compassion than a wicked enchantress. And doesn't our faith teach us to extend kindness to those less fortunate?'

Sister Agnes's eyes widened, trembling with fear. 'I've heard she was the devil incarnate. During her time within our walls, strange occurrences plagued this place.'

'Like what?' Isaac inquired, trying to suppress a chuckle.

Sister Agnes leaned in closer, her voice barely above a whisper. 'Phantom pregnancies, women giving birth well before their due dates, and unexplained deaths,' she confided, glancing around to ensure no one could overhear. 'And sometimes, Meg would be nowhere to be found. But whenever her bed was empty, a big brown rat would scurry through the rooms, making the poor women shriek. And whenever she returned to her bed, the rat was gone.'

Isaac tried to hide the scepticism in his voice. 'So you can confirm that Meg was indeed here and had given birth?'

'Oh yes, I can confirm that for certain,' Sister Agnes replied, her tone low and secretive. 'Did you know she was a prostitute?' She nodded towards an imaginary presence beside her. 'She used to walk the country lanes waiting for the pubs to close, preying on drunken men for a fumble in exchange for a couple of shillings. Ghastly woman.'

'Let's remember our dear own Mary Magdalene had a past too before we judge too harshly,' Isaac said sternly. 'And Jesus loved her as if she was his own sister.'

'Well, one of these poor fellows was taken in by her. A constable at the time apparently. Wife at home waiting for him. His reputation would be shattered if anyone knew. He'd be long gone now of course. Well, Meg got pregnant and confronted him. He of course wanted nothing to do with her and insisted she gets rid of the baby. And apparently she even tried to end her pregnancy herself but to no avail. So she came to us. And we looked after her for a few months, helped her give birth and then a few days after the little boy was born, she left and he was adopted by a local family.'

'Did she see the child at all while he was within your care?' Isaac asked.

'No. We try to avoid that. It's not fair on the mother or the baby to start building a bond. But in her particular case, we made sure she couldn't see him. We didn't want her placing a hex on the poor child.'

'And who adopted him?'

'It was a local family. The Ashtons. The lad will have grown up and will probably have a family of his own by now of course.'

'And what did they name him, do you know?' Isaac felt a bead of sweat pour down his forehead.

'Oh yes, I'll never forget that particular child. Given it was Meg Shelton's child. They called him Francis.'

Isaac's eyes widened, horrified by the admission.

'Why are you telling me this?' Isaac asked. 'I thought you had a vow of silence when it came to those who required your support?'

Sister Agnes laughed. 'Yes, in most cases. But if you were the son of a witch, wouldn't you want to know? If he's in danger, the least we can do is help him. And I'm sure God will forgive me for that.'

Isaac thanked Sister Agnes and left the convent. As he walked home, he considered everything he'd learned. He passed what was left of the Cavendish farm towards the small cottage in the distance where his dear young friend, James, was tending to his vegetables. Little did he know that his departed best friend, Meg Shelton, was in fact his long-lost grandmother.

Chapter 20

6 months earlier

In the dimly lit ambiance of their quaint kitchen, Sarah Ashton gently guided her son to the bench. James, sensing the weight of anticipation, lowered himself with hesitant grace. His mother, a picture of poised determination, stood before him, her husband's reassuring grip intertwined with hers. Their smiles, bright as the moon in a cloudless night, brought an air of expectancy upon the household.

'We come bearing news,' Sarah whispered, her voice carrying the weight of hidden worlds. James, suspended in a moment of taut hope, held his breath, his heart aflutter with a mixture of excitement and apprehension.

'We're expecting a baby,' Francis declared, his voice a symphony of jubilation. Beside him, Sarah beamed with radiant eagerness, her eyes alight with the promise of new beginnings. They turned to James, their gazes full of hope and expectation, yearning for him to embrace the burgeoning joy that swelled within their hearts.

'Oh, I see,' James murmured, his tone a sombre melody in the midst of their jubilation. With a heavy heart, he lowered his gaze. His response cast an air of silence over his once exuberant parents, their buoyant spirits deflating like a punctured balloon.

'Are you not pleased for us?' Sarah inquired, her words tinged with a hint of confusion as her eyes darted between her son and her husband. 'You're going to be a big brother.'

'I just can't help but wonder where the baby will fit. I'm already sharing with Grandma,' James said softly, his words laden with the weight of an overcrowded home.

His grandmother's recent arrival, a necessity born of her frailty in advancing years and the void left by her husband's death, had already stretched their living space thin. With only two bedrooms to accommodate them all, James found himself sharing cramped quarters with his grandmother, a situation that often ignited the fiery frustration of adolescent solitude denied.

'Lower your voice, please. We can't risk unsettling my mother,' Francis urged in a hushed tone. 'She raised me, and now it's my turn to care for her.' His smile, a beacon of familial duty, softened the tension in the room, though Sarah's expression failed to conceal her inner reservations as she pondered how long they would have to put up with her mother-in-law, especially with a baby on the way.

Sitting beside her son, Sarah embraced him, her touch a soothing balm to his troubled thoughts. 'Remember, Grandma won't be with us forever,' she murmured softly, her words carrying the weight of reassurance. 'And the baby will be by our side in our room for quite some time. By the time they need their own space, you'll have completed school, embarked on a journey towards independence, and perhaps even begun to contemplate a place of your own.'

'So you can't wait for me to move out?' James grumbled.

Sarah sighed softly, her gaze tender yet tinged with sadness at her son's interpretation. 'It's not about getting you out of our home, James,' she replied, her voice gentle yet firm. 'It's about acknowledging that life moves forward and circumstances change. We're navigating these transitions together, as a family, each step of the way.'

'Listen, son,' Francis said, his voice a gentle reassurance amidst the whirlwind of emotions. He settled beside James, his touch a grounding force upon his knee. 'Your mother deserves this happiness. She's endured more than her fair share of heartache.'

His words carried the weight of their shared history, a past marred by the devastating loss of four children, leaving James as the sole survivor of what could have been a larger family. Sarah and her husband, in their unwavering determination, saw in this impending arrival a beacon of hope, a chance to mend the wounds of the past. James, grappling with his own conflicting emotions, understood the depth of his mother's longing for this final opportunity to nurture another life. Yet, amidst his sympathy, a selfish twinge of apprehension stirred within him, prompting him to ponder the extent to which his own life would inevitably be altered by this new addition.

'Congratulations, Mother,' James murmured, his embrace tinged with a hint of formality, a barrier he struggled to breach amidst the complexities of their shared emotions. 'May I go out and spend some time with my friends?'

'Of course,' Sarah replied. 'Just keep away from that Meg Shelton!'

As James sprinted down the familiar lane, a rush of conflicting feelings churned within him, propelling him further away from the jubilation that circled his home. To his parents, this impending addition was joyous news, a light amidst the shadows of past sorrow. But for James, it represented an intrusion, a disruption to the delicate equilibrium of his existence as an only child.

His parents' insistence on dictating on who he could spend time with only fuelled his sense of rebellion, especially when it came to Meg Shelton, a beacon of solace in a sea of uncertainty. In her embrace, James found the warmth and affection he craved. His parents' preoccupation with the impending arrival left him feeling adrift, yearning for the maternal love and care that Meg effortlessly bestowed upon him.

Ignoring his mother's warnings, James veered towards the outskirts of town, his steps guided by a rebellious determination. As he reached the borders, he found himself standing before the weather-beaten façade of the decaying cottage nestled in the shadow of Lord Cottam's opulent manor. The stark contrast between the two structures was a visual reminder of the gaping divide that separated their worlds.

With a firm knock on the cottage door, James braced himself for the familiar creak of hinges and the warmth of Meg Shelton's welcoming embrace. Here, amidst the crumbling walls, he found solace, a refuge from the expectations within his own home. And as the door swung open revealing the dimly lit interior, James stepped across the threshold, ready to immerse himself in the comforting familiarity of Meg's presence.

Meg's heart ached at the sight of James's tears, a stark contrast to the vibrant energy he usually exuded when he visited. With a gentle touch she guided him inside, offering a comforting seat and a steaming cup of tea.

As James poured out his heart, the weight of his parents' revelations hung heavy in the air, mingling with the bitter taste of his own resentment. Meg listened attentively, her understanding gaze a silent reassurance in a world fraught with uncertainty.

Meg's voice, soft and reassuring, broke through the haze of James's turmoil. 'Oh, my dear,' she murmured, her words carrying the weight of a lifetime's worth of understanding. 'It may not seem easy now, but trust me, a new life is a blessing beyond measure. Your mother's joy, though it may be hard to see amidst your own worries, is a testament to the beauty of new beginnings.'

'Did you ever have children?' James asked, sniffling and wiping the moisture from his cheeks.

'I did, yes,' Meg said solemnly. 'But I wasn't cut out to be a mother. Thankfully other families are desperate to be parents. And so I don't need to worry about my own.'

As James bowed his head in silent reverence, he felt a profound sense of empathy wash over him, an acute awareness of the pain and anguish that Meg had endured in her journey through life. In that moment, he realised the depth of her unspoken sorrow for the offspring she'd left behind.

A sombre realisation settled over him, casting a new light on his own circumstances. He couldn't help but feel a surge of gratitude for the blessings that his parents enjoyed, for the precious gift of a family that they had been granted.

'Is your grandmother still living with you?'

'Yes, she is,' James confirmed with a sigh, grateful for the change in conversation. He recounted the challenges of sharing his space with his grandmother, describing the ups and downs of navigating his new normal. Meg listened attentively, her expression a mask of understanding, though she couldn't help but feel a twinge of sadness at James's apparent frustration.

'Your grandmother is probably the same age as me,' Meg chuckled. 'And yet here you are with no complaints spending time with me.'

'It's just different. And *we* don't share a room! I've had my own room my entire life. And now I have to share with my grandmother. It's just not fair.'

Meg approached the window. Her fingers delicately traced the outline of a potted plant, its golden petals unfurling like rays of sunshine captured in bloom. She lifted the radiant creation and presented it to her young companion with a quiet solemnity.

'Here, take this,' she whispered.

James accepted the offering with a furrowed brow, his gaze flickering with uncertainty. 'What's this?' he asked.

'It's a plant.'

'I can see that. I mean what's it for?'

'Take it with you,' Meg insisted, her voice a gentle command wrapped in the warmth of her conviction. 'Give it to your mother. Let this flower be a harbinger of happiness and tranquillity within your home.'

James grumbled in response. 'My mother said not to see you again,' he muttered, his words heavy with the weight of their strained relationship.

'But is she going to turn away such a beautiful flower?' Meg countered, her tone laced with gentle persuasion.

'I suppose not,' James conceded with a shrug, the tension in his shoulders easing slightly.

'Now go, and reunite with your mother and grandmother,' Meg urged, her voice soft with hope. 'May this pot plant bring health and happiness to all who breathe in its scent.'

With a heartfelt embrace, James bade farewell to Meg and set off homeward bound, the pot plant cradled close to his chest.

As he approached his doorstep, exhaustion mingled with anticipation, his heart fluttered with uncertainty. But as his mother's eyes lit up at the sight of the flower, a spark of hope ignited within him.

'Oh, James, is this for me?' his mother exclaimed, her joy palpable as she accepted the gift from his outstretched hands. 'It's beautiful. Thank you,' she whispered, pressing a kiss to his cheek before calling for her husband to share in the moment.

Francis nodded appreciatively, his smile reflecting the warmth of his wife's delight. But as James revealed the true origin of the present, a shadow fell over their happiness, his mother's reaction veering unexpectedly into anger and suspicion. 'It's from Meg. It's for you.'

'I don't want it!' she exclaimed, her voice trembling with emotion as she moved to discard the plant. 'I won't accept a flower from a witch!'

Francis intervened. 'My love, this is a gift. It brings us no harm,' he reasoned, his words a gentle plea for understanding.

Reluctantly, Sarah conceded, placing the pot by the window with a heavy sigh. Though she harboured doubts and suspicions, she knew that her assumptions would make her look ungrateful and well... a little mad.

As the evening sun dipped below the horizon, casting a warm glow over the Ashton household, Sarah served a hearty dinner, and the family gathered around the table to celebrate the news of the upcoming arrival. Laughter and joy filled the air as they shared stories and dreams for the future.

Afterwards, as the dishes were cleared away and the candles flickered low, James bade his family goodnight and made his way to bed. In the quiet of his room, he approached his grandmother's bedside, her frail form a stark reminder of her numbered days.

With a tender kiss upon her cheek, James whispered a soft goodnight, his hand encased in hers. Despite the weariness that etched lines upon her face, her eyes sparkled with love and affection as she wished him sweet dreams.

As dawn broke, painting the room in soft hues of morning light, James awoke to a profound stillness that hung heavy in the air. The familiar rhythm of his grandmother's breath, a comforting lullaby that had echoed through the night, was conspicuously absent. With a sense of urgency, James hurried to her bedside, his heart pounding with a mixture of fear and disbelief.

As he reached out to touch her, the truth washed over him like a cold wave crashing against the shore. His grandmother lay still, her chest unmoving and her hand cold to the touch. A sense of overwhelming loss threatened to engulf him as he realised that she had slipped away in the silence of the night.

In a frenzy of panic and despair, James called out for his parents, his voice cracking with emotion. They rushed to his side, their faces etched with a mixture of shock and grief as they beheld the scene before them. In that instant, without a word spoken, they knew that their beloved matriarch had departed this world, leaving behind a void that could never be filled. Together, they gathered around her bedside, their tears mingling with the soft light of dawn as they mourned the loss of her cherished soul.

Two days later, beneath the sombre gaze of St. Anne's Church, the Ashton family gathered to bid farewell to their beloved grandmother. Reverend Isaac, his voice a solemn melody in the stillness of the sanctuary, led the congregation in a heartfelt tribute to the departed.

Though she had not been a member of the congregation of St. Anne's, the grandmother had found solace and shelter within the homes of two of Reverend Isaac's parishioners in her final days. In a gesture of compassion and grace, Reverend Isaac granted them the blessing of laying her to rest within reach of their residence.

As the mourners gathered around the graveside, the air heavy with grief and remembrance, Reverend Isaac's words honoured the life and legacy of the departed grandmother. And as they lowered her into the earth, beneath the watchful eyes of the heavens above, Sarah's hand instinctively fluttered to her tummy, a sudden twinge of discomfort rippling through her like a bolt of lightning. The mourners, their grief momentarily eclipsed by concern, gasped in alarm as they witnessed the expectant mother's distress.

Francis, his heart lurching with fear, reached out to steady his wife as she doubled over, her face contorted in pain. With a low moan escaping her lips, Sarah clutched at her abdomen, her breath coming in ragged gasps as she struggled against the wave of agony crashing over her.

With hurried steps, they ushered Sarah back to the familiarity of her home. As James tenderly helped his mother out of her black coat, his heart skipped a beat at the sight of crimson droplets staining her leg.

'Oh, Mother,' he breathed, his voice thick with concern as he pointed towards the troubling sight. 'Have you injured yourself?'

Sarah's face paled at the sight, her hand instinctively reaching down to touch the source of the bleeding. A wave of dizziness washed over her as she struggled to comprehend the sudden onset of pain and discomfort.

In that moment, as the gravity of the situation settled over them like a heavy shroud, James and his father exchanged worried glances, their hearts heavy with fear for Sarah's well-being. As Sarah crumpled onto the bed, her sobs echoing through the room, the weight of her grief bore down upon her like a crushing weight. With each breath, she felt the pain of loss reverberating through her very being.

Beside her, James and his father stood silently, their hearts heavy with sorrow as they bore witness to Sarah's raw agony. In the face of such profound loss, there were no words that could offer solace, no gestures that could ease the pain of a mother's broken heart.

As Francis retreated to the kitchen in search of solace, his heart heavy with the burden of his wife's anguish, James followed in his wake, a silent shadow trailing in his father's footsteps. As they stood together in the quiet of the kitchen, the weight of their shared sorrow hung heavy in the air.

'Is Mother going to be alright?' James asked.

With a heavy sigh, Francis turned to his son, his voice tinged with a sorrowful resignation. 'I don't know, son. But there will be no brother or sister for you anymore,' he murmured, his words a painful acknowledgment of the shattered dreams that now lay in ruins. 'Your mother is going to be sad for a long time.'

As James absorbed his father's words, a sense of helplessness washed over him, his heart heavy with the weight of his mother's grief.

But as Francis's gaze fell upon the potted plant given to them by Meg Shelton, a sudden fury seized him, his grief giving way to irrational anger. With a primal roar, he lunged towards the plant, ripping it from its soil with a violence that shocked his son to the core.

'This!' he bellowed, his voice trembling with rage. 'This house was full of happiness until you brought this hex into our home! Your witchy friend cursed it!'

James recoiled in shock, his eyes wide with disbelief as his father's accusations rang out in the stifling air of the kitchen. 'Father, don't be ridiculous,' he protested weakly, his voice barely above a whisper.

But Francis would not be swayed, his mind consumed by the irrational fear and grief that threatened to consume him. He thrust the torn stem into his son's trembling hand, his words a bitter condemnation of the innocence that had unwittingly brought about their downfall.

'I bet you wanted all this to happen,' he spat, his voice dripping with venom. 'You wanted your room back to yourself. Well, I hope you're happy. Your grandmother is dead and so is your sibling.'

Before James could respond, his father's hand closed around his collar, wrenching him towards the door with a violent force. In a blur of motion, he found himself cast out into the cold embrace of the night, the weight of his father's accusations ringing in his ears like a damning echo of his own guilt.

As he stood alone on the doorstep, the shattered remnants of the potted plant clutched tightly in his hand, James felt the sting of betrayal burn hot in his chest. And as he watched the door slam shut behind him, cutting him off from the only home he had ever known, he knew that the darkness that now surrounded him was not merely a reflection of the night, but an omen of the storm that raged within his own fractured soul.

Chapter 21

Isaac inhaled deeply as he made his way towards the illustrious Cavendish farm. Along the path, he passed the opulent abode of John, the prestigious owner of the estate, and ventured towards the modest cottage nestled at the rear – a sanctuary for the Ashtons. The weight of his investigation bore down on him, a burden of weariness creeping into his bones. How many souls must he cast suspicion upon before vindication blessed his efforts? And in this labyrinth of deceit, how would he unravel the enigma of the true culprit? Could he coax the confession from their lips, admitting complicity in the tragic demise of Margery Hilton?

Isaac rapped on the weathered door, anticipation mingling with apprehension as it swung open to reveal Francis, unexpected yet familiar. His initial assumption shattered like glass against the reality of Francis's presence during the day – a poignant reminder of the farm's recent misfortune, its once-thriving fields now reduced to ash by the merciless blaze that consumed John's crops. Isaac's thoughts drifted to the Ashtons' struggle, grappling with the harsh reality of diminished income.

'Hello, Vicar,' Francis greeted, his voice a mixture of politeness and curiosity. 'If you're in search of James, I regret to inform you he's at school.'

Isaac paused, recalibrating his intentions. 'Actually, it's you I've come to see,' he confessed, watching as surprise etched itself across Francis's features. Though a familiar face at St. Anne's, Francis's involvement in parish affairs remained minimal – a stark contrast to Sarah's diligent contributions, her steadfast devotion to the church evident in her unwavering commitment to its every need.

'Perhaps you better come in,' Francis offered, gesturing his guest to step over the threshold. 'Tea?'

Isaac nodded, gratitude evident in his eyes as Francis set about preparing the comforting brew. 'This is rather unexpected,' he remarked, his tone a blend of hospitality and curiosity. 'How can I assist you?'

'It's a delicate matter, Francis,' Isaac began cautiously.

'Is it my son? Is he in trouble?' Francis's concern flickered across his face.

'No, not at all,' Isaac reassured him. 'But something has come to light, and I wanted to inquire about your family, particularly your parents.'

'How intriguing.' Francis handed Isaac his tea before settling into his own seat at the table. 'They've both died now. You'll recall my mother's funeral at your chapel earlier in the year.'

'I remember,' Isaac replied solemnly, his thoughts briefly returning to the sorrowful time, intertwined with the memory of Sarah's loss of her baby, as well as her mother-in-law. 'It was a trying period for you both.'

'Indeed, the worst few days of my life,' Francis confessed. 'But what exactly do you wish to know about my parents?'

'Were you close to them?' Isaac broached the subject delicately.

'Of course,' Francis responded with a hint of confusion. 'As you're aware, my mother spent her final days with us. Why do you ask?'

'Did they ever discuss your birth with you?' Isaac pressed, his voice measured.

'Yes, it was quite the tale,' Francis chuckled. 'Mother was in church when her waters broke – it was quite the scene apparently.'

'I see,' Isaac acknowledged, swallowing past the lump in his throat. 'So she never hinted that perhaps you might be...'

'Might be?' Francis echoed, brows furrowing in bewilderment.

'...adopted?' Isaac finished, the word hanging heavily between them, pregnant with implication.

Francis's eyes widened, a flicker of disbelief crossing his features. Isaac allowed the silence to stretch, watching for any reaction from his host.

'I beg your pardon?' Francis's voice held a tremor of disbelief.

'Did your parents ever give you any indication that you might be adopted?' Isaac repeated, his gaze steady.

'No, of course not!' Francis exclaimed, his chair scraping back as he recoiled in disbelief at the vicar's audacious accusations. 'I was their flesh and blood. How could you even suggest such a thing?'

Isaac held his ground, his expression grave. 'Recent developments have shed light on the sudden demise of Margery Hilton. In my pursuit of truth, my investigation led me to St. Paul's Convent. Are you familiar with it?'

'Of course, my parents were devout Catholics,' Francis replied with a trace of irritation. 'We visited the church next door many times in my youth.'

'After speaking with the nuns, I learned that Margery once sought refuge there in her youth. As you may know, the convent aids young unmarried mothers who are unable to care for their children, often arranging adoptions.'

'And what does this have to do with me?' Francis demanded, his patience wearing thin.

'Margery gave birth to a son, and according to the nuns, that child was adopted by the Ashton family, whom they named Francis,' Isaac revealed, his words heavy with implication. 'I believe that child could be you.'

Francis scoffed, his disbelief palpable. 'Don't be absurd! How dare you come into my home and hurl such accusations? There must be countless Ashtons in the vicinity. It's hardly a unique name!'

'True,' Isaac conceded, 'But the parallels in this case are too striking to ignore, Francis. And if Margery was aware of the connection, it would explain her interest in your son. He would be her grandson by blood.'

'She was a batty old woman. Her interest in my son was unusual. But everyone in the town found her crazy.'

'But you can't deny James and Margery were remarkably close. I wondered if their relationship was due to a natural bond which only a grandmother and grandson could develop. Even if neither were aware of it.'

'James was drawn to her because she offered him things for his garden. He's a misunderstood child, a bit of a loner,' Francis said, his tone defensive. 'And she showed him attention. Any attention in this town would have caught his interest. It just happened to be that eccentric old woman.'

'Since this revelation came to light, I can't help but notice the familiar eyes of Miss Hilton in both James and yourself,' Isaac remarked thoughtfully. 'There are mannerisms I see in all three of you. And when I reflect on your dear mother before her passing, I recall practically no family resemblance between you. Are you certain there's never been a hint of doubt over the years?'

Francis pondered the question, memories flooding back from his childhood. 'There was something,' he admitted with a lump in his throat. 'There was always something slightly off. My parents showered me with love, but I never quite felt as if I belonged. Like there was a difference between me and the rest of my family. They told me I took after my maternal grandparents, who died before I was born. I never questioned it after that.'

'Perhaps this could explain it,' Isaac suggested gently.

'But if it's true, how could my mother keep it from me?' Francis's voice trembled with emotion. 'I spent so much time with her in her final days. Why wouldn't she tell me about my true heritage?'

'Maybe she wanted to protect you,' Isaac offered.

'And you believe that woman could be my mother? I find it hard to believe,' Francis protested.

'The timelines align, I'm afraid,' Isaac confirmed.

'But I treated her so terribly... I...' Francis trailed off, guilt weighing heavily on his conscience.

'You...?' Isaac prompted, leaning forward in anticipation.

'Well, Sarah and I, we banned her from seeing James. We banned her from our home,' Francis confessed.

'But you didn't...' Isaac's voice trailed off.

'Didn't what?' Francis asked, confusion knitting his brow.

'...hurt her,' Isaac finished.

'God no, why would I do that?' Francis shook his head vehemently.

'Your son mentioned that she was murdered by a relative. I'm just eliminating potential relatives,' Isaac explained.

'But I didn't even know she was a relative. So why would James?' Francis shrugged.

'A valid point,' Isaac conceded.

'Wait, why does James know that Meg was murdered? And by a relative?' Francis's eyes widened in realisation.

'He was supposedly there. But whatever he saw, he's refusing to tell anyone. I thought he might be protecting someone. I thought he might be protecting you for a moment,' Isaac admitted.

'Or he's scared of someone...' Francis suggested.

'I feared that too.

Chapter 22

3 months earlier

'Come on, James,' Meg called, her voice a siren's song luring him into mischief. Another day, another farm. This time, it was the Darwen dairy farm, nestled amidst rolling fields dotted with black and white cows. In the fading light of dusk, the pastoral scene took on a tranquil aura. The day's labour had ended, and the milkmaids had retired from their duties, leaving behind the serene ambiance of the countryside.

Meg seized the boy's hand and hurried him through the field, their footsteps a rushed rhythm against the soft earth. In her arms she cradled a clay jug, a prized possession from her humble cottage. James trailed behind her reluctantly, a sense of apprehension knotting in his stomach. He feared the consequences of their escapade – reprimands from his parents or additional chores doled out by a stern farmer played on his mind. If he thought cleaning the chicken coop was arduous, the prospect of dealing with cow manure was an entirely different challenge altogether.

'What are we doing here?' James groaned, his reluctance evident in his voice.

'We need milk, of course! What did you think we were coming for? Prime steak? A leather jacket?' Meg chuckled, brandishing the jug before him like a trophy.

'If you wanted milk, I could have brought some from home. We have plenty,' James protested.

'I'm self-sufficient,' Meg declared with a mischievous glint in her eye, a statement that elicited a wry smile from James, considering their current endeavour hardly fitted the definition of self-sufficiency. 'Besides, this is far more fun. And it's a victimless crime. I'm only taking what I need, James. And these farms earn a pretty penny from all this cattle. What do I have? Nothing!'

She approached one of the cows, her movements fluid as she knelt down, using her staff for support. With practised ease, she began to tug on the udders, eliciting a steady stream of milk into her jug. A smile of awe and gratitude touched her lips as she marvelled at the abundance of Earth's natural resources.

'Come on, James!' she called out, her voice carrying across the field. 'There's plenty of cows. Two hands make light work and all that...'

James hesitated, casting a wary glance at the towering figures of the cows surrounding him. Slowly, he approached one, but it regarded him with suspicion and ambled away.

'You need to walk over with confidence, James!' Meg encouraged, her voice buoyant with determination. Yet, despite his efforts, James's attempts proved futile.

'Never mind,' Meg declared, her jug now nearly full. 'I've got what I need.'

Turning around, James caught sight of Meg sucking the last remaining drops directly from the udder. He couldn't help but gag at the sight, wondering about the hygiene of such an act.

'Waste not, want not,' Meg quipped with a grin, as if sensing his discomfort.

Confident they had gathered enough, they began to make their way across the field towards the road. Suddenly, a voice pierced the air from behind them.

'Oi!' they heard, causing them to freeze in their tracks. Farmer Darwen was charging towards them, his shotgun gripped tightly in his hand. 'Bring that back, you thief!' he bellowed, his voice filled with fury.

'Come on, let's get out of here!' they whispered urgently to each other as they scurried away from the farm. Once they were out of sight, they slowed down and strolled leisurely towards Meg's cottage. Inside, she served them both some haggis with vegetables, and they dined together in the cosy warmth of her home.

A knock on the door interrupted their meal, and they exchanged puzzled glances before Meg went to answer it. Standing there was Lord Cottam, holding a bunch of tomato plants, soil dropping from the roots.

'What do you think you're doing?' he demanded, his voice stern. 'What did I tell you about growing things on my land?'

'I have nowhere else to put them,' Meg pleaded. 'Please, I'll starve if I can't find a way to grow my own food.'

'From what I hear, you steal from our neighbours,' Lord Cottam accused.

'I wouldn't need to if I was given space to grow my own,' Meg grumbled.

Lord Cottam thrust the plant into her hand and brushed the soil off his fine suit. 'Then move somewhere where you can grow your own, in that case,' he snapped before storming off.

Meg slammed the door shut in frustration, and James couldn't help but feel sympathy for her.

'I can't believe he treats you like that,' James said, shaking his head in disbelief.

'Oh, I'm used to it,' she shrugged. 'His mother was far worse.'

'Why? I thought his parents liked you,' James said, recalling their previous discussion about Meg's relationship with the late Lord Cottam.

'His father did, but his mother couldn't stand the sight of me,' Meg explained. 'She would tell me to stand down whenever I was on duty to serve her. And she'd hit me if her husband wasn't around.'

'Why did you put up with it?' James asked, appalled.

'She was a troubled woman, and she was jealous of me,' Meg replied simply.

'Why was she jealous of you?' James furrowed his brow.

'Hey, I might not be the prettiest, but there's plenty of things I have that she didn't,' Meg said defiantly.

'Like what?' James inquired.

'Lots of things. The will to run away from a wedding I didn't want to attend, for one,' Meg quipped.

'Do you ever think about what life could have been like if you had gone ahead with the marriage to Lord Alnwick?' James asked, curious.

Meg pondered his question for a moment, gazing out the window towards the mansion. 'I'm sure I would've been treated better, and I wouldn't have worried where my next meal was coming from. But no, it's far greater to be free than rich,' she concluded.

'Do you ever think about the family you could have had?' James asked softly.

'I had an opportunity to have a family. But they were both taken away from me shortly after I gave birth to them,' Meg explained.

'Both of them?' James gasped.

'Yes, two. Both boys. I was a single woman with no money. They're much better off without me,' Meg said sadly.

'Do you ever wonder what happened to them?' James asked, his curiosity piqued.

'Oh, I know exactly what happened to one of them,' Meg replied, her eyes lingering on James before turning back to the window. 'The other, I have no idea. He'll be grown up by now, with a family of his own, no doubt. I hope he's happy wherever he is.'

'The one you know about, have you ever told him?' James asked.

'No, I'd never want him to know. He's happy and has no idea his mother was not his blood relative. I'm not going to take that away from him. And I'm hardly the most popular person in town. Who would want to find out that this supposed hag was their mother?' Meg explained.

'I'd love it if you were mine!' James assured her with a smile.

'I'd be old enough to be your grandmother,' Meg laughed.

'Even better!' James exclaimed. 'So who is he? This illegitimate son of yours?'

Meg looked at him with caution, unsure of how he would react to the truth. But seeing his kind and gentle demeanour, she felt a glimmer of trust.

'All right, I'll tell you. But you must promise me you'll never tell a soul,' she said, her tone serious.

'I won't, I promise!' James assured her eagerly.

Meg smiled and gestured towards the dirty dishes and pots. 'Do me a favour, wash up those for me, and I'll tell you.'

Chapter 23

Isaac waited outside the school gates, waiting for the children to disperse from a day of learning. A bell rang and dozens of boys flooded out of the doors, kicking balls and playing chase across the yard.

'James!' Isaac called when he spotted his young friend. He looked up and smiled when he saw the friendly vicar.

'Reverend! What a surprise! What are you doing here?'

The other children looked on, confused as to why James was being summoned by the local vicar. They knew him well. He'd attended many assemblies to teach them about the Christian religion and they had a weekly sermon in his church on a Wednesday morning where they sang hymns and read prayers together.

'I wanted to talk to you,' Isaac explained and nodded towards the church across the road. 'Fancy joining me in the vestry for a chat?'

'Sure.' James shrugged. He waved at Henry and William, who were too busy playing kickball to care that their pal was leaving. They walked towards the church. It was a crisp sunny day. There was a chill in the air which suggested winter was close. Before long they would be singing Christmas carols again. The years seemed to go by faster and faster as Isaac grew older. He wondered how much longer he'd be serving the Lord from Earth before he'd hopefully sit beside Him in Heaven.

In the vestry, Isaac made some tea and sat at the table beside James, who was looking a little daunted by the vicar's invitation. He wondered if he was in trouble.

'Now, James, I want to ask you some delicate questions,' Isaac said calmly, shuddering as he heard his voice repeating the same line he'd spread around town over the previous days. He shook his head, ridding himself of the embarrassment.

'Of course,' James said, his hands beginning to shake as he picked up his tea.

'Margery Hilton… your friend Meg,' Isaac began. James nodded curiously. 'Did you know that she had children?'

James nodded. Isaac's eyes widened.

'How did you know?'

'She told me.' James shrugged, perplexed by the vicar's insight into Meg's private life.

'What did she say?' he asked, stroking his beard and staring at the young boy, wondering what secrets he harboured.

'She had two boys. Both now raised by other parents.'

'Did she tell you who those boys were?'

'She knew one of them. The other she couldn't tell me.'

'And why was that?' Isaac leaned in.

'Well she didn't know who he was. Just that he'd been brought up by another family.'

'But you know the name of the other boy?' Isaac asked, his heart racing.

'Yes.' James avoided the eye of the vicar.

'And who was that, James?'

'I can't say.' James shook his head.

'Why not?'

'Meg promised me not to tell a soul.'

'But Meg's gone now, you can surely share now? It won't harm her to tell me.'

'No but it wasn't just about her. It was about her son too. She didn't want him to know. But regardless, I promised a friend and I'm telling you, I won't break that promise.'

Isaac nodded his head, admiring the young boy's commitment to Miss Hilton. He scratched his head, wondering how he could get the boy to expose the name.

'What if I told you I knew the boy's name who Meg gave birth to?' Isaac said.

'I'd ask how you came to know about it.'

'I found out from the nunnery where Meg was staying.'

James's eyes widened, aware that the vicar was probably telling the truth and not just trying to catch him out.

'So now you know. And you'll know how important it is that he never finds out.'

'But he does know, James,' Isaac explained.

'Pardon?' James gasped. 'How?'

'I went to see him today. I told him what I'd discovered.' Isaac watched as James fidgeted in his chair and his face reddening.

'You shouldn't have done that, Isaac,' James shouted. Isaac knew he was angry. James never called him by his real name, but always with a respectful Reverend, despite the friendship they'd developed.

'I'm sorry but I had to know more and I felt he was owed an explanation. We all deserve to know where we came from. The truth is important, James.'

'How did he take it?'

'Well he was surprised. He didn't believe me at first but he soon came around. How did you feel when you found out?'

'Equally surprised. It's quite the scandal, that's for sure. It could upset a lot of people if people found out. But I guess now he knows.'

'James...' Isaac said quietly. 'I have to ask you something. And I want you to be honest. Did you kill Meg?'

He gasped. 'What?

In the dimly lit room, tension hung heavy, thick as fog rolling in from a distant shore. Isaac's voice cut through the silence like a knife, each word deliberate, laden with an unspoken weight. 'It might have been an accident. I won't judge you. I just need to know,' he reiterated, his gaze steady on James.

James, his features twisted with disbelief, shot back, his voice trembling with emotion, 'Why on earth would I kill my friend? My only friend really at the time!'

Isaac's mind raced, piecing together fragments of a puzzle shrouded in darkness. 'You might have been furious to discover who she really was. Who her long-lost son was,' he reasoned, his words hanging heavy in the air.

'Why would I care who her son was?' James countered, his voice edged with confusion.

Isaac pressed on, unravelling the tangled threads of a hidden truth. 'Well, because it made her your grandmother. I would understand if it came as a shock and you reacted impulsively. It would alter your entire history,' he explained, his voice softening with sympathy.

As realisation dawned, a heavy silence settled over them, suffocating in its intensity. James, his voice barely a whisper, confessed, 'What the hell do you mean? What do you mean, she was my grandmother?'

Isaac's heart sank as he realised the depth of his revelation. 'We have reason to believe that your father was Meg's long-lost son. I'm sorry you found out this way, this was not my intention,' he admitted, his voice laced with regret.

In the aftermath of truth laid bare, James grappled with the weight of a newfound identity. 'She had two sons,' he revealed, his voice hollow with grief. 'She knew where one of them was. But had no idea what happened to the other.'

Silence stretched between them, a chasm of unspoken words and lost opportunities. 'I'm in shock. She was my friend. And now she's my... grandmother,' James murmured, his voice thick with emotion.

'It seems so,' Isaac agreed, his own voice heavy with sorrow.

As James wrestled with the implications of his newfound lineage, Isaac recounted the journey of discovery that led them to this moment, his words a sombre melody in the dimly lit room.

In the quiet aftermath, James stood at the window, his gaze fixed on the tombs that held the secrets of his past. 'I'm glad I got to know her,' he confessed.

'She thought the world of you, regardless of whether she knew about your connection or not. That's a wonderful thing to hold on to,' Isaac offered, his words a beacon of solace in the darkness.

Yet, as the shadows lengthened and the truth loomed large, Isaac couldn't shake the gnawing question that lingered in the depths of his mind. 'I know you've been very guarded about the identity of Meg's other son,' he ventured, his voice tentative. 'But I wondered if you'd be happy to share this information with me. It could be important.'

James hesitated, his resolve wavering. 'I promised Meg that I would never tell,' he confessed, his voice heavy with guilt.

Isaac's heart sank, the weight of uncertainty pressing down upon him like a stone. 'Still, don't you think he has a right to know? Now you're in his shoes, do you not feel he should know, knowing what you do now about your connection to Meg?' he pressed, his voice tinged with urgency.

'I suppose.' As James turned to leave, his words hung in the air like a whispered prayer. 'It's Lord Cottam,' he revealed and closed the door behind him.

Chapter 24

34 years earlier

'My courses came again,' Lady Cottam whispered, her voice choked with tears, the weight of unfulfilled dreams heavy upon her. 'I am once again without child.'

'I'm sorry, my love,' Lord Cottam murmured, his fingers gently tracing lines through her hair. 'We can always try again.'

Tears glistened in Lady Cottam's eyes as she spoke of years of fruitless attempts. 'We've been trying for years to no avail. And soon my age will prevent me from bearing any child. I will never be able to give you an heir.'

With a tender embrace, Lord Cottam drew her close, their hearts heavy with the ache of longing unmet. Together, they sat in silent contemplation, their minds drifting to the future they had envisioned but had never come to pass.

'It seems there is potentially another way,' Lord Cottam ventured, his voice tinged with hesitant hope. 'We could consider adoption.'

'Adoption?' Lady Cottam's breath caught in her throat, disbelief mingling with a flicker of possibility. 'But no, it would never be ours.'

Lord Cottam's eyes sparkled with determination as he outlined a plan born of desperation and love. 'Nobody else would know. We could keep you in hiding for a few months. Everyone would believe that the child was ours. And we could ensure it was a boy too.'

'But it's not just about others,' Lady Cottam protested, her voice wavering with uncertainty. 'How would I ever love a child who I hadn't carried?'

'You would find a way,' Lord Cottam replied, his voice soft but resolute, a promise woven through the words like a thread of hope.

The Cottams' bedroom exuded an air of timeless elegance, a sanctuary of comfort nestled within the grandeur of their estate. At the heart of the chamber stood a magnificent four-poster bed, its carved mahogany frame adorned with intricate scrollwork and draped in sumptuous fabrics of deep burgundy and gold. A pair of plush armchairs nestled near the fireplace, and above the mantel a portrait of the Cottams in happier times gazed down upon the room, their smiles frozen in a timeless embrace.

'Where would we find such a child?' Lady Cottam's voice trembled with uncertainty, her heart heavy.

Lord Cottam's gaze softened as he sought to reassure her. 'There are plenty of convents in the region. They take in all sorts of people. Single mothers who are unable to care for their child.'

A flicker of dismay crossed Lady Cottam's features as she recoiled from the suggestion. 'I don't want my child to be the fruit of some common prostitute,' she declared, her voice tinged with indignation.

'Of course we don't,' Lord Cottam hastened to assure her, his tone soothing. 'We can inquire about their backgrounds. We can ensure the child comes from a respectable lineage.'

'But what if he doesn't look like us?' Lady Cottam's fear rang clear in her voice, her worry etched in the furrow of her brow. 'I want him to look like us. Otherwise, people will suspect.'

With a gentle touch, Lord Cottam took her hand, his eyes filled with understanding. 'Let's go and explore the convents, see what's available. There's no pressure to commit. We can ensure that the child we choose fits our criteria.'

Lady Cottam's shoulders sagged with exhaustion. 'I'm afraid I'm too tired and fragile to consider this now, Edward.' she admitted. 'You go and look without me.'

Edward left the comfort of his home and mounted his horse, setting off towards St. Paul's Convent. As he approached the imposing structure, memories of his school days flooded back, a mix of nostalgia and trepidation swirling within him. Recollections of stern-faced nuns and the sting of rulers on his disobedient wrists danced at the edges of his consciousness, but as he neared St. Paul's, a sense of calm washed over him, soothing the lingering echoes of his past.

Upon arrival, Edward was warmly welcomed by Sister Mary, who graciously led him on a tour of the immaculate facilities. His eyes took in the pristine surroundings, noting with admiration the careful separation between the new-borns and their prospective parents. The distant cries of infants filled the air.

'Do any of them take your fancy?' Sister Mary inquired, her gaze gentle as it swept over the rows of tiny faces nestled in Moses baskets. Edward found himself lost in contemplation, pondering the futures of these innocent souls and the weight of the decisions being made on their behalf.

'Do you have any boys?' he ventured, his heart yearning for an heir to carry on his legacy.

'Just one today,' Sister Mary replied, leading him to a crib where a cherubic boy with bright blue eyes awaited. As the child was placed in his arms, Edward felt a pang of uncertainty gnawing at his heart. Despite his best efforts, he couldn't shake the nagging feeling that this child wasn't meant to be his son.

'I'm sorry,' he murmured, his voice tinged with regret. 'He just doesn't feel like mine.'

Sister Mary offered words of reassurance. 'It can take time to form that connection,' she explained gently. 'Even we grow to love them, even when the bond isn't immediate. It breaks our hearts when they leave, but we know they're going to better homes where they will be adored. That is God's will.'

Mindful of his wife's desire to be involved in the decision, Edward hesitated, contemplating their next steps. 'My wife would want to meet the child too,' he admitted.

Sister Mary nodded understandingly, her expression sympathetic. 'Does it need to be a boy?' she inquired, her gaze flickering towards the other cribs, to the children she struggled to find homes for. 'We have some lovely little girls as well.'

Edward hesitated, his thoughts consumed by the weight of familial expectations. 'I'm afraid it does,' he confessed. 'I need an heir to my estate.'

Acknowledging his concerns, Sister Mary offered a compassionate suggestion. 'Why don't you return with your wife? You can see the children together and make a decision as a family. There may be more boys by then. New-borns arrive frequently.'

'Thank you for your time, Sister Mary. I assume I can rely on your discretion?' Lord Cottam asked, fearful of the rumours which would swirl through the neighbourhood if anyone discovered his fragile wife could not conceive.

'Of course, Lord Cottam. Nobody will ever know that you have visited.'

With gratitude in his heart, he bade farewell to the convent, and passed the Ashton family, who were making their own parenthood journey. They glanced at each other familiarly and nodded respectfully but refrained from speaking. They had a shared understanding that this was a private voyage they were all embarking on.

He climbed onto his horse and urged it forward, setting off down the private road that wound its way out of the estate. Approaching the steel gates of the convent, he caught sight of a solitary figure emerging from its confines. Dressed in a sombre black cloak, her wild brown hair framing a face marked by sorrow, she stood alone, bearing the weight of her pain like a heavy cloak.

'Hello!' he called out, his voice cutting through the stillness of the air. The woman glanced up, her eyes reflecting a profound sadness that tugged at his heartstrings. Her features, though striking, were marred by a prominent nose.

'Hello,' she replied softly. Edward dismounted his horse and approached her, his heart heavy with empathy.

'I've just visited the convent. May I assume you've just made a delivery?' he inquired gently, speaking in riddles to protect her reasons for leaving the sacred place. His eyes searched hers for confirmation.

'I have,' she murmured, her head bowed in silent grief and shame. Tears streamed down her cheeks.

'How did you end up here?' Lord Cottam pressed, his voice tinged with compassion.

'I became pregnant, and I'm not married. I have nothing to offer a child,' she confessed.

'Do you have family who can offer you support during these dark times?' he inquired.

'None who will acknowledge me. I was once part of the Hilton family, but they have disowned me.'

Edward was astonished. The Hiltons were a prominent family, their name synonymous with wealth and status. To encounter one of their own cast aside and forgotten stirred a mix of emotions within him.

He had dined with the Hiltons countless times, mingling in their world of opulence and privilege. The revelation that this woman, standing before him in her moment of vulnerability, was once a part of his world left him reeling. Here was a woman, stripped of her status and cast aside by those who should have embraced her. In her, he saw not just a fallen noble, but a fellow human being in need of solace and support.

'You must be Margery then?' Edward inclined his head respectfully, recalling the tale of her departure ahead of her wedding to Lord Alnwick. He too had been on the cusp of journeying to Northumbria as a guest of honour at the time. The message from the family that the wedding had been called off came just in time.

'The very same, although most people call me Meg,' she replied.

'It's a pleasure to meet you, Meg.' Edward extended his hand, which she accepted with a gentle shake. As they exchanged pleasantries, the gears in his mind began to turn. He realised he was in the presence of a woman of noble birth, descended from an esteemed lineage.

'Did you have a little boy?' he inquired, his thoughts drifting to the child he had held moments earlier.

'I did,' she confirmed, a tear escaping her eye as she spoke. 'If you are looking to adopt, I'd be honoured if you took him home. I know he would be well looked after in your family's care, Lord Cottam.'

He winced inwardly, realising he hadn't introduced himself formally, though he was accustomed to being recognised as a nobleman amongst the villagers. With a reassuring smile, he replied, 'Please, call me Edward. I assure you, any child of yours would be well looked after in my home.'

As he glanced back at the convent considering whether he should rescue the little boy, a nagging feeling gnawed at him. Despite the allure of adopting a child with such esteemed lineage as Meg's, he couldn't shake the doubt that lingered within him. When he picked up the baby boy inside the convent, he just didn't feel the love and joy which a parent should feel when handed their child for the first time.

'Actually, Meg, I have a proposal...' he began, his mind racing with a new idea.

He arranged for Meg to ride back to the estate. Upon their arrival, her eyes widened in awe at the sight of the grand sandstone building that stood before them, flanked by a quaint white cottage nestled within the grounds.

Lord Cottam assisted Meg as she dismounted the horse, leading her into the cosy confines of the cottage. With its simple furnishings and warm ambiance, it offered a humble yet comfortable sanctuary.

'Some of our staff have used this in the past. It isn't much, but it's something,' Edward explained, gesturing towards the interior.

'I'd be honoured to live in such a lovely cottage,' Meg replied gratefully, her eyes filled with a quiet appreciation for the generosity extended to her.

'Make yourself comfortable. I need to see my wife,' Edward informed her before departing to seek out Lady Cottam, leaving Meg to acclimate to her new surroundings.

Edward ascended the grand staircase of his ancestral mansion, the weight of his newfound proposal heavy on his mind. Entering the bedroom, he found his wife still nestled in bed, tears staining her cheeks as exhaustion etched lines of weariness on her face. Her hopeful gaze met his as he approached, a silent question lingering in the air.

'I have an idea, Nell,' he began, leaning in to kiss her sweat-dampened forehead.

'What is it?' she inquired, her voice tinged with a mixture of curiosity and apprehension.

Edward proceeded to recount his visit to the convent, detailing the encounter with the young woman and the child she had left behind. Nell listened intently, her expression shifting from anticipation to incredulity as she processed his words.

'You can't be serious?' she gasped.

'I am very serious,' Edward affirmed, his conviction unwavering. 'It would be perfect, don't you think? Meg is one of our kind.'

'Not anymore!' Nell protested vigorously, her objections ringing loud in the room.

'But she was born into our world,' Edward countered, his voice calm yet resolute. 'She may have lost her way, but she still carries the history of the Hilton family. Surely, if we turn away commoners from marrying into our families because they can never truly be one of us, then the same must apply in reverse.'

'Why can't we just adopt her little boy?' Nell queried.

'Because he doesn't look like either of us,' Edward explained patiently. 'And it just didn't feel right. But we could have one of our own. Our flesh and blood.'

'*Your* flesh and blood,' Nell retorted bitterly. 'It wouldn't be anything to do with me.'

'You will love him as your own,' Edward reassured, his tone gentle yet firm. 'And at least he will look like me. Nobody will question his lineage.'

'I'd have to think about it,' Nell grumbled, her reluctance evident. 'Where is she now?' she inquired, her curiosity piqued.

'In the cottage,' Edward replied, gesturing towards the house nestled within the grounds.

'You gave her our cottage?' Nell gasped, her anger flashing in her eyes.

'We can't let her carry our baby while living on the streets,' Edward reasoned. 'We could take care of her, make sure she's well-fed and warm. We can ensure our baby is healthy.'

'I want to meet her,' Nell declared.

Together, hand in hand, they descended the stairs and made their way to the cottage, where Meg awaited, a potential stream for their hopes and dreams of parenthood.

'My God, she's ugly,' Nell remarked, her words cutting through the air like a sharp blade. She wrinkled her nose in distaste, as if the sight of Meg was repulsive to her senses. Meg lowered her head, the sting of the insult familiar to her from a lifetime of harsh judgments.

Edward winced, feeling a flush of embarrassment at his wife's callousness. 'This is a great opportunity for us, Nell,' he interjected, attempting to quell the tension with a soothing touch to her back. 'Meg will be giving us the gift of life. The best gift anyone could give us.'

Nell's gaze turned towards the mansion they had just departed, her expression hardened. 'Your father gave us this house,' she retorted, her tone tinged with bitterness.

'But it's all material things,' Edward countered gently, his voice filled with earnest conviction. 'Nobody can give us a child. It's a wonderful offering. Nothing could ever come close.'

'How do we know she's up to the job?' Nell continued, her scepticism palpable as she scrutinised Meg as if she were an object on display.

'She's just had a baby. We know she's capable,' Edward replied, seeking to reassure his wife despite her dismissive demeanour.

Nell subjected Meg to another once-over, her scrutiny bordering on dehumanising. 'Very well then. If this is what you want,' she accepted with a sharp glare at her husband, 'I don't want anything to do with it until the baby is born. Do I make myself clear? And I don't want to know how the baby is conceived. And the second the baby is born, she must be gone.'

With that, Nell stormed off, leaving Meg and Edward alone in the wake of her abrupt departure. 'I'm sorry about that,' Edward said. 'She's rather upset at the moment as she can't have a baby herself, but I know as soon as she meets the child she'll be full of joy and love. The Nell I know and love will be back.'

'I understand,' Meg replied quietly.

'Are you not going to find this too hard? You've just had to say goodbye to one baby and now you're going to hand over another,' Edward queried, concern evident in his tone.

'It'll be incredibly hard, but I have little choice,' Meg admitted, her voice tinged with sorrow. 'I have nowhere to live, and you've already said you'll compensate me well.'

'Don't mention compensation to my wife,' Edward cautioned, his voice low and urgent. 'She will go mad if she finds out you're getting paid as well as having a place to live.'

'Mum's the word,' Meg agreed with a wry smile. 'Quite literally in this case.'

Over the ensuing months, Edward observed Meg's transformation from a frail, delicate girl to a radiant mother-to-be. He made daily visits, bearing gifts of fresh fruits, vegetables, and the choicest game meat from his hunts. Both Meg and Nell remained secluded in their chambers, with servants prohibited from entering either room.

'Lady Cottam is with child, but her pregnancy has taken its toll, leaving her quite unwell. Therefore, she will not be receiving visitors for the time being. Only I will attend to her. Do you understand?' Edward declared to their staff and any guests to the estate. When Nell sought respite outdoors, she strolled the grounds with a cushion tucked beneath her dress, a precaution in case she was spotted.

'I'm renovating the cottage,' Edward informed the housekeepers, deflecting inquiries about its use. The windows were obscured with old newspapers to deter prying eyes, and he occasionally accompanied Meg on long walks, both concealed beneath voluminous cloaks to hide her blooming bump.

During their excursions, Edward grew to appreciate Meg's wit and charm. She regaled him with tales of her misadventures in town, and they exchanged gossip about mutual acquaintances from her time at the Hilton estate. Edward developed a platonic fondness for his newfound friend, a sentiment that contrasted sharply with his strained relationship with his wife, who had grown increasingly bitter. He clung to the hope that the arrival of their child would mend their fractured bond.

In the dead of night, a frantic knocking roused Edward from his slumber. With the staff gone and his wife asleep, he hurried downstairs to find Meg trembling in the rain.

'My waters have broken,' she announced breathlessly. 'The baby is coming.'

Bringing her inside, Edward wrapped her in a towel before summoning Nell. 'Come downstairs!' he called out.

Together, the three of them laboured to ensure a safe delivery. When the new-born's cries echoed through the house, Nell swiftly claimed the child, pressing him to her chest with a tender kiss. As Meg watched, exhausted and drained, her heart ached at the sight of yet another infant torn from her arms mere moments after entering the world.

'She can leave now! Her task is done,' Nell commanded, her voice sharp and authoritative. Edward hesitated, torn between his duty to his wife and his compassion for Meg.

'But, Nell,' he protested, 'she needs time to recover, and the baby will need her milk. Surely she can stay in the cottage for a while longer.'

Relenting at the sight of her wailing child, Nell grudgingly agreed. 'Fine, but only temporarily. I don't want her getting attached.'

The next morning, Edward visited Meg bearing gifts of flowers and food. She lay in bed, her expression sombre as she mourned the loss of her son, now residing next door.

'What did she name him?' she inquired wearily.

'Bartholomew. After the Apostle,' Edward replied.

'A strong name for a strong boy,' Meg remarked with a bittersweet smile. 'I'll be out of your hair as soon as he's strong enough to no longer need me.'

'Meg, you've given me the greatest gift,' Edward insisted earnestly. 'I can never thank you enough, and I won't allow you to return to the streets.'

'I'll manage,' Meg assured him, though her eyes betrayed a deep well of sadness.

'No, I won't have it. What kind of man would I be if I were to allow that to happen? In exchange for your kindness to my family and for giving me my son, I want you to have this cottage. For as long as I live, and beyond, I want you to have a home,' Edward insisted, his voice firm and resolute.

'What about your wife?' Meg asked, her expression tinged with scepticism.

'Leave her to me. We will appreciate having you around. You can help us out on the estate, and we'll need someone to help care for Bartholomew. And you'd be able to see him grow,' Edward explained, his tone reassuring.

'That would be painful, but at the same time, I think I'd like that. To keep an eye on him, even if he's not mine anymore,' Meg admitted, her voice filled with mixed emotions.

'You can be his guardian angel,' Edward said tenderly, reaching out to rub her arm. He placed a gentle kiss on her cheek, expressing his gratitude once more before returning to his home, where he embarked on his new journey of fatherhood.

Chapter 25

As dusk descended upon the Lancashire countryside, casting long shadows over the rolling hills and verdant valleys, Pendle Hill loomed in the distance like a silent sentinel guarding ancient secrets. In the small village nestled at the foot of Pendle Hill, whispers of the past echoed through the cobblestone streets.

Quaint cottages with thatched roofs and whitewashed walls lined the streets. Windows glowed warmly against the gathering darkness, and smoke spiralled from chimneys.

As Isaac approached the village inn, he couldn't help but notice the wary glances of the locals, who regarded him with a mixture of curiosity and suspicion. It was clear that outsiders were not always welcome in this close-knit community, especially those who seemed too eager to uncover the secrets of Pendle Hill, which the neighbourhood seemed keen to forget.

In The White Bear, a 17th-century pub nestled in the village of Nelson, Isaac found himself face to face with the Bishop of Lancaster. The venerable stone structure, erected in 1607, bore witness to generations of whispered tales and local gossip, particularly those tinged with the spectre of witchcraft that had once haunted the nearby villagers.

The Bishop of Lancaster cut a striking figure in his white choir dress, complete with puffy sleeves and a black rochet draping elegantly over the top. Atop his head perched a white curly wig. As he sat, sipping on a tankard of ale graciously provided by Isaac, the atmosphere in The White Bear seemed to hold its breath, curious to hear the conversation taking place in the corner by the two religious men.

'Thanks for meeting me, George,' Isaac said, his tone respectful yet comfortable. Despite the bishop's authoritative status, which far surpassed that of a mere vicar, their relationship transcended formalities, allowing them to converse on a first-name basis.

'Of course, Isaac,' George replied, his interest piqued at the mention of discussing witches. A few heads turned, overhearing their whispered conversation. Despite the witch trials being consigned to history, the mere mention of their presence still struck a chord of unease among the locals, a reminder of darker times lingering in the collective memory.

'In my village, there lived a woman known as Margery Hilton, or as some called her, Meg Shelton. She was a beggar, often resorting to pilfering food from local farmers just to survive. Some say that she had cast curses upon our village, but in truth, she seemed like any other ordinary woman,' Isaac recounted.

'You speak of her in the past tense. Has she left the village?' George inquired.

'In a manner of speaking. She died recently,' Isaac replied.

'So, what's the problem?' George shrugged.

'Since her burial, her body has mysteriously reappeared several times. While I suspect it's the work of a troublemaker from our midst, my parishioners are convinced it's something supernatural,' Isaac explained.

George's eyes widened, captivated by the unsettling details of Isaac's story. 'And do you believe there's any truth to it?'

'What do you think, George?' Isaac countered.

'I'd say it's rather sacrilegious to entertain the notion of anything otherworldly occurring,' George replied.

'And I concur,' Isaac nodded.

'But your parishioners aren't budging?' George raised an eyebrow.

'No, they strongly oppose her burial in the church grounds, fearing she's still cursing the town from beyond the grave. I'm at a loss on how to handle it. So, I've come seeking knowledge on the background of this fear, hoping to reason with them or debunk their irrational beliefs,' Isaac admitted.

'It's a wise decision, and you've come to the right place,' George reassured, glancing out the window towards Pendle Hill, a site steeped in Lancashire's witchcraft history. 'But why approach me?'

'Your role gives you oversight of the Lancashire parishes and you are based in Lancaster, where I know the trials took place.'

'Indeed they did, at the castle.'

Isaac remembered visiting Lancaster for the first time. The imposing silhouette of Lancaster Castle stood sentinel atop its rocky perch. From the cobbled streets below, the castle loomed like a silent guardian, its centuries-old stones bearing witness to a lifetime of history. Within the castle's walls, there was a maze of chambers and corridors. The Great Hall had a majestic timber roof and intricate carvings, while the dungeons below told tales of darker days of penance and torture.

Lancaster Castle stood as both a court of law and a fortress of punishment, its formidable presence a stark reminder of the consequences for those who dared to disobey the country's strict laws. Beyond its formidable walls, the gallows stood as a chilling reminder of the ultimate fate awaiting those deemed guilty by the law. Isaac couldn't help but shudder as he envisioned the morbid spectacle that had unfolded countless times before – a gathering of spectators, their gloomy curiosity piqued as they watched condemned souls meet their end on the hangman's noose.

'So, what can you tell me about this dark period of history?' Isaac inquired, his voice tinged with curiosity.

'From my understanding, people have always harboured a fear of evil forces beyond our mere mortal endeavours. However, King James I's ascension to the throne seemed to intensify those fears,' George began, shaking his head in disbelief. 'Upon his coronation, Catholicism was outlawed, and adherents faced severe punishment, sometimes even death. And then, with Guy Fawkes's attempt on his life, King James's resolve to root out dissenters and punish those who did not adhere to the Protestant religion only grew stronger. Catholics were demonised, and witchcraft often became a scapegoat for those who simply wished to practise their faith in their own way.'

'I feared religion might have played a part in it. It's so sad, especially as we read from the same Bible and pray to the same God,' Isaac lamented.

'Indeed it is,' George agreed solemnly, bowing his head. 'The Witchcraft Act was enacted in 1604, making sorcery illegal and punishable by death.'

'But how did they prove someone was a witch?' Isaac pressed.

'That's the perplexing thing about it. Hearsay was accepted as evidence, so anyone could accuse anyone else. There didn't need to be any tangible evidence. There were even

243

instances of rebellious children returning home late, covered in dirt, and concocting stories of witches kidnapping them as excuses for why they weren't home in time for dinner,' George explained.

'They took the testimony of children?' Isaac gasped in disbelief.

'Many times. It's astounding. What were we thinking? Moreover, there were cases of warring families fabricating tales of witchcraft to eliminate their rivals. Here in the Pendle area, for instance, the Chattoxes and Demdikes were prominent families in the town. Both grandmothers were referred to as cunning women, undertaking ambiguous roles such as brewing healing potions or claiming to find lost items for a fee; of course the cunning women would steal them knowingly and then approach the bereft families claiming they'd discovered their lost possessions.'

'And these two rival families would accuse each other of witchcraft?' Isaac surmised.

'Exactly that. They engaged in a fierce competition, with accusations flying back and forth. The court proceedings were farcical as well. Defendants were denied legal representation, were uninformed of the charges until appearing in court, and were coerced into guilty pleas, which were then used against them,' George elaborated.

'Did they resort to torture?' Isaac asked, his expression filled with horror.

'No, it was technically illegal to use torture for confessions, though it may have occurred nonetheless. Instead, plea bargains were employed. Defendants would receive lighter sentences if they pleaded guilty,' George clarified.

'So when did this finally cease?' Isaac inquired with curiosity.

'While the Witchcraft Act remains in law today, it's rarely invoked nowadays. After King James's death, the enthusiasm surrounding catching Catholics and witches subsided. The monarchy was no longer actively hunting down those who deviated from the Protestant norm they had imposed on the country. Fortunately, by the century's end most people had moved on, though pockets of fear still linger in society,' George explained.

'It's still prevalent in Woodplumpton,' Isaac remarked.

'Indeed, it seems so. I hope the law will be completely abolished soon. It's a nonsensical law that has led to the execution of countless innocent individuals due to baseless rumours,' George concluded with a note of solemnity.

'And were these punishments confined to Lancashire?' Isaac asked.

'No, it happened everywhere, but Lancashire seems to have carried a particular burden of witchcraft. The capital believed Lancastrians were a rebellious bunch. And I suppose in some ways we are,' he chuckled. 'However it goes beyond England itself. There is hearsay that the same is occurring across the pond in America. There have been witch trials in Salem, near Boston. So it seems it's a global issue.'

'What would you advise I do, George? The villagers seem adamant.' Isaac voiced his concern, seeking guidance from his superior.

'I think, in this case, you should appease them. If this poor girl is causing such grief for those she tormented when she was alive, perhaps taking the appropriate steps to relocate her remains outside the church grounds would be wise. Part of being a vicar is to listen without judgment. If moving her outside the church boundaries helps ease tensions, then I'd encourage it. After all, she's not aware. I assume she has no family to protest the move?' George suggested.

'The family she does have are part of the crowd who want her erased from the town's history,' Isaac replied solemnly.

'Then there's nothing to worry about. Although I imagine moving her won't be a pleasant task,' George remarked sympathetically.

'Don't worry. I've had to put her back in the ground a couple of times already,' Isaac confessed, his stomach turning at the memory of shifting the decaying corpse. But then he changed the conversation to another pressing matter. 'I have reason to believe she was murdered, but I'm struggling to uncover the truth of who did it.'

'Maybe that's best left to God to deal with when they die,' George suggested gently.

'You're saying I should leave this alone?' Isaac asked, surprised by his boss's advice.

'You're a vicar, Isaac, not a law enforcer. Let the appropriate authorities handle that,' George reminded him.

'They don't seem interested. She was found crushed beneath an oak barrel in her home. Nobody suspects anything more sinister,' Isaac explained.

'So maybe that's what happened,' George suggested, his tone sombre.

'No, there's a boy who says he was there, but he seems too frightened to say anything about it,' Isaac countered.

'Then that's for his conscience to deal with, not yours,' George concluded.

'Thank you, George. I appreciate your time tonight,' Isaac expressed his gratitude, shaking the bishop's hand before finishing his ale and leaving the pub.

It was the dark wee hours of the morning when Isaac returned to Woodplumpton. Exhausted but knowing he needed to pray before sleep, he detoured to St. Anne's. However, as he walked through the gates, he sensed something was amiss. Rushing to Margery Hilton's grave, he found the tombstone overturned and smashed on the ground. A hole gaped where her coffin had been interred.

Margery's body was gone.

Chapter 26

1 month earlier

A buzz of excitement filled The Wheatsheaf as a large crowd gathered, reminiscent of the bustling atmosphere during their New Year's Eve celebrations the previous December. The owners, Agnes and David Robinson, exchanged a knowing glance, realising they hadn't seen such a turnout in months. With more patrons than chairs, many stood around, engaging in lively debates about the latest controversies gripping the village.

Agnes swiftly locked the doors, ensuring no eavesdroppers could disrupt the animated discussions within the pub. Meanwhile David rubbed his hands together eagerly, contemplating the anticipated takings from the sales of ale. Despite the barrels running dry, he took comfort in the ample supply of spirits he had on hand to keep the festivities going if needed.

All the men from the village had gathered, responding to the summons of a select committee of women led by Sarah Ashton, Joan Clitheroe, and Mrs Norris. Over the past few days, these women had diligently circulated handwritten notes throughout the borough, urging locals to come together and discuss what to do about the local nuisance, Meg Shelton.

Two notable absences were observed. The first was Constable Kirkham, deliberately excluded from the meeting to ensure open discussion without the influence of law enforcement. As they convened, Constable Kirkham was patrolling the streets of Preston, a detail they had carefully noted from his rota.

The other absentee was Reverend Isaac, purposely omitted due to his perceived sympathy towards Meg. The women knew Isaac had a soft spot for the troubled woman and didn't want his religious ethics to sway their decisions. Knowing it was Sunday evening and Isaac would be occupied preaching to a smaller congregation at St. Anne's, they strategically scheduled the meeting to coincide with his service.

'I've had enough,' Sarah began, her voice trembling with anger and frustration. 'She's caused too much pain during this time. She's cursed my baby and my mother-in-law.'

'She killed my wife!' John Cavendish roared, slamming his tankard onto the table with a resounding thud. 'And continues to steal from my land.'

'My milk's gone sour,' Farmer Darwen grumbled, his brow furrowed in irritation. 'I caught her stealing it, and ever since, what I have left over has never been the same. It's disgusting. Even the freshest of my produce has come out with a vinegary taste.'

'It really has,' Mrs Norris chimed in, her face scrunching up in distaste as she recalled her morning cereal.

'And I can't even breed new cows as they've suddenly become barren!' Farmer Darwen continued, frustration evident in his voice.

'I haven't seen an egg being laid for weeks,' John added, his tone heavy with concern.

'Are we going to let this evil witch ruin our lives? Are we going to continue to let her kill our loved ones and curse our livelihoods? We'll starve to death at this rate,' Sarah declared passionately, banging her knuckles on the table for emphasis. Rising to her feet, she fixed the men with a determined gaze. 'What are we going to do about her?'

'I say we kill the witch!' Joan Clitheroe declared boldly, and her words met with a resounding cheer from the gathered crowd. 'Don't just stand there! Let's get her!'

The mob cleared out of the pub, their fervour palpable as they left David and Agnes to tidy up the abandoned tankards. John, Francis, and the other farmers armed themselves with pitchforks. Meanwhile, the women took charge, igniting beacons of fire to light their way.

With a sense of purpose driving them forward, the group marched down the lane with determined strides, their collective determination echoing through the night air. Each step brought them closer to their target, fuelled by a potent mix of anger, fear, and the desperate need for justice. As they advanced, the flickering flames cast eerie shadows upon their faces, transforming them into avengers in the unfolding drama of the night.

Sarah assumed the lead position, her fiery torch held aloft as a beacon for the resolute vigilantes. Seeking to stir the zeal within the angry mob, she initiated a chant, and swiftly the assembled throng echoed her words in unison. Their unified voices reverberated through the darkness.

'Beneath the moon's watchful eye, we rise,

With hearts ablaze and vengeance in our eyes.

Pitchforks raised, our spirits high,

As flames dance bright against the night sky.

For too long, we've borne the pain,

Of curses cast and lives in vain.

Now we march with purpose clear,

To cast out evil, banish fear.

With each step, our voices ring,

A chant of justice, let it sing:

By fire's light, and pitchfork's might,

We'll rid our land of darkest blight.

No more shall Meg's shadow fall,

No more shall she haunt our hall.

With courage bold and hearts aglow,

We'll cleanse our village, make it so.

So onward, onward, brave and strong,

We march together, right the wrong.

With fire and fury, we shall be free,

From the grasp of witchery, we'll break free!'

It took nearly an hour for the mob to reach Meg Shelton's cottage, their chant dwindling to a simple yet chilling mantra: *'Kill the witch!'* As they neared the Cottam estate, the sight of candlelight in the stone mansion gave pause. A silhouette of Lady Cottam flitting about the house reminded them of the human lives that must not be disrupted in their quest for vengeance. Sensing the need for caution, Sarah hushed the crowd.

Turning their attention to the small white cottage within the estate grounds, where Meg Shelton resided, Sarah led the mob with quiet determination. Approaching the cottage with stealth, she peered through the window but found no sign of its occupant. With a silent nod, she conveyed her plan to the eager crowd.

Gathering wildflowers from Lord Cottam's garden, Sarah approached the cottage door with feigned innocence, a guise of peace masking the violence brewing within. Knocking softly, she prepared to deceive Meg Shelton with a false gesture of goodwill.

The mob's anticipation reached a fever pitch. Each member licked their lips in anticipation of the torment they would inflict upon the old woman. Some fantasised about pulling at her hair, while others envisioned tearing her limbs apart. Those armed with pitchforks eagerly anticipated spearing them into the witch's frail body.

But Sarah harboured a different desire. She longed to witness the witch's pleading eyes, to see her grasp at her empty womb, a painful reminder of the life she had taken from a mother-to-be. As she banged on the door, Sarah stood poised, ready to bear witness to the culmination of their collective fury. But there was no answer.

Sarah knocked a little louder, her heart pounding with uncertainty as Meg Shelton's continued silence left her perplexed. Glancing around at the others who had gathered behind her, she shrugged her shoulders in confusion.

'Maybe she went out?' she whispered, her voice barely audible over the rustling of leaves in the night breeze.

'Go in!' John urged, his tone edged with impatience.

'I'm not going in alone!' Sarah replied, her voice tinged with fear. 'Who knows what she could do to me in there. For all we know, she's anticipated our arrival and summoned a spell!'

'I'll come with you,' offered John, his grip tight on his pitchfork. Together, they cautiously turned the knob on the rickety door and slowly pushed it open, wincing at the loud creak it emitted. Peering into the dimly lit room, they searched for any sign of the old woman.

'Meg?' Sarah called out, her voice echoing into the empty space.

'Look!' John whispered, pointing towards a large oak barrel overturned on the floor, a pair of feet visible from underneath. The sight made Sarah's blood run cold.

They crept closer, John handing Sarah his pitchfork before rolling the barrel aside. Beneath it lay Meg Shelton, her face distorted and lifeless. Meg's cold, lifeless eyes gazed distantly into the unknown, reflecting neither the light nor the shadows of the room.

'She's dead,' John declared, and Sarah gasped in horror. 'She's been crushed.'

'What should we do?' Sarah whispered, her voice barely above a whisper.

'I'll place the barrel back over her, and we'll leave. We'll pretend we were never here,' John decided, his tone sombre.

Sarah nodded, her mind reeling with shock as John carefully replaced the barrel over Meg's body. With a heavy heart, they quietly exited the cottage, closing the door behind them.

As the bewildered crowd emerged from their hiding spot, Sarah shrugged, her voice hollow as she delivered the news. 'She's not in.'

Disheartened, the defeated mob began the sombre journey back to Woodplumpton in silence, their enthusiasm replaced with a heavy sense of remorse. Walking alongside John, Sarah felt his arm wrap around her in a gesture of comfort.

'Are you all right?' John asked softly, concern evident in his voice.

'I'm fine,' Sarah replied, though her paleness and trembling betrayed her true feelings. 'Seeing her like that... I realised I couldn't have been a part of it. Her murder.'

'I felt the same. It's a harsh dose of reality,' John admitted.

'What got into us?' Sarah pondered aloud, her guilt weighing heavily on her conscience.

'We were angry. Mob mentality. She's caused nothing but trouble for this village for decades,' John reasoned. 'But now she's no longer our concern.'

'We went to kill her,' Sarah reiterated, her voice filled with disbelief. 'But someone beat us to it. The question is... who?'

Chapter 27

Isaac found little respite in sleep, the evening's tumultuous events swirling relentlessly in his mind. The inexplicable disappearance of Meg's body weighed heavily on him, a perplexing mystery with no easy solution. He couldn't shake the disbelief that such a desecration could occur, especially within the sacred confines of his church.

As he tossed and turned, Isaac contemplated the bishop's advice to let go of the matter, to relinquish control and allow events to unfold as they may. Yet, a sense of responsibility gnawed at him. This was his business now, a stain upon God's holy ground that demanded his intervention.

The thought of other graves being disturbed, of unsavoury souls being unearthed, filled him with dread. Would this sacrilege continue unchecked, threatening the sanctity of all those laid to rest? He couldn't stand idly by and watch as the peace of the deceased was violated.

With a heavy heart, Isaac sought solace before the altar, his prayers a plea for divine guidance in the face of uncertainty. In the quiet sanctuary of the church, he sought strength to confront the challenges ahead and protect the sanctity of those who rested in eternal slumber.

What confounded Isaac most was the sheer cruelty of it all. Meg had long departed this world, and while some whispered of her posthumous presence lingering among the town's inhabitants, there was no evidence to support the notion that she was responsible for the myriad curses attributed to her.

John Cavendish's devastating loss, such as the fire that ravaged his fields, could be attributed to numerous factors.

Forest fires were not uncommon in the area, sparked by the sun's relentless heat or careless campfires set by reckless youths. Moreover, in a farming community where competition was fierce, John had no shortage of rivals vying for dominance in the market. Who's to say one of them didn't sabotage his crops to gain an advantage?

The soured milk and barren hens he could not fathom. However concerning Sarah's losses; her mother-in-law was elderly and ill, and no doubt the stress of caring for the elderly woman, mixed with the common occurrence of miscarriages upon young women was the answer to why she lost her child. Surely they couldn't blame Meg Shelton for two seemingly innocent deaths?

As Isaac pondered the complexities of the situation, he couldn't help but question the validity of the accusations levelled against Meg. Were they merely scapegoating her for misfortunes beyond her control, perpetuating a cycle of fear and superstition? Or was she exactly what they said she was? A common witch. The truth remained elusive, buried beneath layers of suspicion and uncertainty.

Evidence seemed to hold little sway in the face of rampant superstition and hearsay, a reality that echoed the dark days of the Pendle Witch Trials a century prior. In those harrowing times, innocent women were condemned based on little more than rumours and accusations, their fates sealed by the pervasive fear of witchcraft.

Margery Hilton, flawed though she might have been, did not deserve to be branded as an evil witch. Isaac couldn't help but reflect on the injustice of it all, the arbitrary nature of judgment that condemned so many to their untimely demise.

Recalling his conversation with George the previous evening, Isaac felt a profound sense of gratitude that Margery had not lived in an era plagued by such hysteria a century before. If she had, there was little doubt that she, like countless others, would have faced trial and execution under the oppressive grip of the Witchcraft Act.

As he mulled over the implications of history's dark chapters, Isaac couldn't shake the sobering realisation that progress was not inevitable, and that the spirit of ignorance and fear still loomed large in the hearts of the men and women in the village. It was a sobering reminder of the fragility of justice and the enduring need for vigilance against the forces of prejudice and intolerance.

A solemn knock disrupted Isaac's silent communion with the divine. With reverence, he rose from his knees, bowing his head before the crucifix, and made his way to the door. Outside, the rain poured relentlessly, casting a veil of darkness upon the world, while a shadowy figure stood drenched within its embrace.

'Lord Cottam,' Isaac greeted his guest warmly, though concern flickered in his eyes. 'Do come in. This is a surprise.'

He nodded in acknowledgment, his demeanour fraught with unease as he stepped inside, shedding his drenched hat and shaking off the rain. His appearance was dishevelled, as if he had encountered something unsettling. The sight before Isaac was an unusual departure from the norm. Bartholomew Cottam, a man known for his unwavering professionalism and impeccable grandeur, stood before him in disarray. Rarely did a hair stray from its perfect place, and his garments were always of the finest quality. Yet now, he appeared dishevelled and shaken, a stark contrast to his usual composed demeanour.

'What can I do for you, Bartholomew? You don't look well,' Isaac inquired, using his guest's first name in acknowledgment of the informal atmosphere. While he preferred more formal titles during official duties, it seemed appropriate given the circumstances.

'I need to confess,' Bartholomew declared, his voice heavy with urgency.

'I'm afraid I'm not Catholic, Bartholomew,' Isaac replied gently, his concern evident. 'You'd need to seek guidance from a priest if you're looking for a formal confession.'

'It can't be anyone else, it has to be you,' Bartholomew insisted, his eyes pleading. 'You'd be the only one who would understand. And it would only feel right that I would confess it to you.'

Isaac's heart went out to his troubled guest. 'My goodness, Bartholomew, this must be weighing heavily on you. You can confide in me, but please understand that I can't offer you absolution in the same manner as a Catholic priest. I can't prescribe a few Hail Marys and send you on your way. Do you understand?'

'What can you do for me then?' Bartholomew's voice trembled with desperation.

'Well, I might be able to offer you some solace,' Isaac reasoned gently. 'A problem shared is a problem halved, as they say.'

'Nothing could make this better, Isaac. I've done some horrendous things,' Bartholomew confessed, his anguish palpable.

'I can pray for you,' Isaac offered, his tone compassionate. 'And help you seek forgiveness from God. Only He can grant you salvation, my friend.'

'That may have to do. I can't live with this secret anymore,' Bartholomew admitted, his voice breaking with raw emotion. Isaac watched in astonishment as tears flowed freely from the typically composed Lord Cottam, a rare display of vulnerability that spoke volumes as to the weight he carried on his shoulders.

'Please, have a seat.' Isaac guided Bartholomew to a pew, positioning himself beside him with a comforting hand placed gently on his arm. 'What is weighing so heavily on your heart?'

'You won't divulge this to anyone, will you?' Bartholomew pleaded, his voice tinged with desperation.

'Your secret is safe with me,' Isaac assured him, gesturing with a symbolic zip of his lips.

'It's about Meg Shelton,' Bartholomew confessed, drawing a deep breath before continuing.

'Ah, Meg Shelton,' Isaac acknowledged, sensing the gravity of the forthcoming revelation.

'It turns out... she was my mother,' Bartholomew divulged, his voice thick with emotion.

Isaac's demeanour softened, a blend of astonishment and sympathy reflecting in his expression. 'I had an inkling. I learned of it recently, from someone she confided in.'

'And who might that be?' Bartholomew inquired, his voice wrought with apprehension.

'I'm bound by confidentiality, as I am with you,' Isaac responded solemnly.

'But they might suspect...' Bartholomew trailed off, his nerves palpable.

'Suspect what?' Isaac probed, his brow furrowing in concern.

'It was me,' Bartholomew confessed, his voice barely a whisper.

'What do you mean?' Isaac pressed, though he already had a hunch.

'I...' He cleared his throat and turned away. 'I killed Meg Shelton.'

Chapter 28

1 month earlier

The grandeur of Lord Cottam's manor stretched out before him, a majestic testament to centuries of wealth and privilege. Nestled amidst the rolling hills of the countryside, the manor stood as a beacon of aristocratic elegance, its towering spires and ivy-covered walls casting a shadow over the lush landscape below.

As Lord Cottam approached the imposing gates, wrought-iron tendrils curling upwards towards the heavens, he felt a swell of pride rise within him. This was more than just a home; it was a symbol of his family's legacy, a bastion of tradition and prestige that had endured through the ages.

The gravel crunching beneath his feet echoed in the stillness of the afternoon. To his left, manicured gardens stretched out in a riot of colours, a tapestry of blooms that danced in the gentle breeze. To his right, dense forests whispered secrets of ages past.

As Lord Cottam ascended the steps to the grand entrance, flanked by weathered stone statues of long-forgotten ancestors, his gaze fell upon the unsightly cottage that marred the otherwise pristine landscape. The cottage, a testament to his father's misplaced generosity towards Meg Shelton, stood in stark contrast to the elegance of the manor. Its thatched roof sagged with neglect, the once-white stone now obscured by a thick blanket of moss.

With a grunt of frustration, Lord Cottam cursed his father's foolishness for including such absurd terms in his will. The sight of the dilapidated cottage served as a constant reminder of his father's misguided generosity, a burden that he now bore unwillingly.

In his father's final days, anticipation brewed within Lord Cottam as he looked forward to the impending eviction of the old hag from his estate. His mother's tales painted Meg Shelton as a persistent nuisance, a thorn in their side who had caused years of frustration until her dying day. Meg's presence had not only sparked fear within the town but had also invaded their very home, casting a shadow over their once-peaceful abode.

As Lord Cottam recalled his mother's eagerness to rid their estate of Meg's troublesome presence, a sense of righteous indignation fuelled his resolve. With each passing day, he licked his lips in anticipation, relishing the thought of breaking the news to her and marching her off his property, reclaiming what was rightfully his.

But then, like an unwelcome ghost, the family lawyer stepped in and shattered Lord Cottam's hopes with the terms of inheriting the Cottam estate. Meg Shelton, it seemed, would have a home for life, courtesy of his father's inexplicable soft spot for the old witch. Try as he might, Lord Cottam couldn't fathom why his father had harboured such sentiment for a woman who, according to his mother, was nothing short of a nuisance.

According to his mother's accounts, Meg had been stealing from the property, meddling in everyone's affairs, and criticising Lady Cottam's attempt at bringing up Bartholomew himself. At times, he even entertained the notion that his father might have had a secret affair with Meg, but upon glimpsing at her ghastly attire, prominent nose, and warty complexion, such a possibility seemed ludicrous. After all, how could his father have found this woman attractive when his own wife, Nell Cottam, exuded beauty and grace?

Nell's soft complexion, cascading blonde locks, and slender figure made her the epitome of desirability, which even her own son could admire. And as he pondered the stark contrast between his mother's elegance and Meg's grotesque appearance, he couldn't help but feel a surge of resentment towards the woman who had been granted a lifetime of shelter on his family's estate.

After poring over the terms of his inheritance and consulting with his lawyer, Lord Cottam realised that while he was indeed obliged to provide Meg Shelton with a home, there was no stipulation dictating that it had to be comfortable. His father's oversight in this matter struck Lord Cottam as nothing short of foolish.

With a sense of grim determination, Lord Cottam resolved to exploit this loophole to his advantage. While he couldn't outright evict Meg from the estate, he could certainly make her existence as unpleasant as possible within the confines of the agreement. After all, his father's sentimentality had no place in the ruthless world of estate management.

With cold fortitude, Lord Cottam refused to allocate resources to maintain the upkeep of Meg Shelton's abode, allowing mould and damp to seep insidiously into the walls while water trickled relentlessly through the leaky roof. To some, it might have seemed as though he was cutting off his nose to spite his face as the cottage marred his land, but in Lord Cottam's mind, it was a calculated move designed to hasten Meg's departure from the estate.

As the decaying cottage deteriorated further under his neglectful gaze, Lord Cottam harboured plans to demolish the building as soon as Meg vacated its decaying confines – or, failing that, upon her eventual demise.

Whichever came first.

In addition to his neglect of the property, Lord Cottam imposed further restrictions upon Meg's autonomy. He barred her from planting vegetables on the estate grounds, asserting his ownership over every inch of land and denying her any claim to its bounty. Though he knew she would struggle to feed herself without the vegetable patch she had tended for so long, he remained unmoved, convinced that she could always relocate if she found his rules too burdensome.

Furthermore, Lord Cottam erected barriers to Meg's entrance to the property, forcing her to navigate an additional half-mile to reach a side entrance instead of using the main gates. It was a deliberate act of inconvenience, a means of wearing down the old hag's resolve and ensuring that every step she took served as a reminder of her unwelcome status on his estate. At the very least, if it didn't entice her to move, it might tire her out and make her death arrive much sooner.

Just the day prior, Lord Cottam implemented yet another decree, spurred by the sight of an unexpected visitor entering Meg Shelton's domain. The boy, bearing gifts of fresh vegetables and offering assistance around the home, struck Lord Cottam as a peculiar child indeed. What business did this stranger have with Meg, and why would she befriend someone so much younger than herself? Such questions only added to the enigma that was Meg Shelton, a woman already steeped in mystery and eccentricity.

Determined to maintain his iron grip on the estate's affairs, Lord Cottam intervened, delivering the news to Meg that she was henceforth forbidden from entertaining visitors on the premises. He cited security concerns as justification for this new rule, though in truth, his motives were driven more by a desire to exert control over her increasingly isolated existence.

As Lord Cottam's gaze swept over the eyesore that was Meg Shelton's hovel, his attention was drawn to an irregularity – a small patch of earth where she had once again begun to grow her own vegetables. With clenched fists and a face contorted with rage, he felt a surge of fury wash over him.

Without hesitation, Lord Cottam stormed towards the cottage, his footsteps echoing like thunder on the path. His anger boiled beneath the surface, ready to erupt like a volcano of wrath upon his unruly tenant.

Banging furiously on the door, he awaited her response with mounting impatience. When Meg finally appeared, her sheepish demeanour did little to quell his rage. She stood behind the door, peeking out cautiously as if anticipating the storm that was about to descend upon her. But despite her attempts to shield herself from his wrath, Lord Cottam was prepared to unleash hell upon his defiant tenant.

'What the hell are those vegetables doing there? What have I told you about growing anything on my land? Now tear them up before I do,' Lord Cottam bellowed, a fleck of saliva shooting out and landing on Meg's prominent nose.

'I'm sorry, Lord Cottam, but I'm becoming older and less and less agile by the day. I had a friend who brought me food but you've banned all my visitors. If I don't grow something soon, I'm afraid I'll starve to death.'

'Then why don't you just go ahead and move somewhere else then?'

'But I have nowhere else to go,' Meg whimpered, revealing a rare glimpse of vulnerability.

'As if I care what happens to you,' Lord Cottam shrugged indifferently.

'Why don't you come in? I'm sure we can come to some sort of compromise which would suit us both?'

Though he was hesitant to enter the old woman's home, Lord Cottam nodded, intrigued to see what other rules she might have broken. Had she snuck in that boy? Or that girlfriend she used to harbour? Removing his hat and placing it on the table, he glanced around, gagging at the musty stench that permeated the air.

'You've not been looking after this place, Meg,' he remarked with disdain. 'If you can't maintain the property, you'll have to find somewhere else to live.'

'I've tried my best,' Meg assured him. 'But unfortunately, some of the issues are the building itself. It needs work. Please, I've not asked for much from you. I'm so grateful I can stay here. Your father was ever so kind to me.'

'I don't know why. My mother was right, you are a nuisance,' Lord Cottam retorted sharply.

'It breaks my heart that your mother despised me like she did. I did everything I could for her. I gave her everything I had.'

'What possibly could you offer her? You have nothing!'

'That's quite right. Now I have nothing. But once I had the only thing she didn't have.'

'And what was that?' Lord Cottam inquired, heckling a lone laugh.

'The ability to conceive,' Meg explained calmly.

'What the hell are you talking about, woman? My mother gave birth to me. While you...' He trailed off, his gaze sweeping over Meg's haggard appearance.

'Bartholomew,' Meg began, using his given name.

'It's Lord Cottam to you. How dare you use my Christian name. We're not friends. We're barely even acquaintances. I am your landlord and you will have respect for me.'

'We're closer than you could possibly ever imagine, sir.'

'I don't understand. Spit it out, woman. Stop talking in riddles.'

'Your parents struggled for years to have a baby. And when I met your father, he asked me if I would perhaps have his child and give the baby to your mother.'

'Don't be absurd!' Lord Cottam banged his fist heavily on the table, rattling its contents.

'I'm afraid it's true. I am your mother,' she explained calmly.

'You're lying!'

'I promise you, I am not.'

Staring into Meg's eyes, Lord Cottam felt a surge of disbelief and confusion. Despite her claims, he couldn't shake the feeling of scepticism. How could this old woman possibly be his mother?

'You ghastly woman. How dare you say these things!' he exclaimed, his emotions roiling within him.

'I promise you it's true. Nell was desperate.'

'Take my mother's name out of your filthy mouth!'

In a rush of fury, Lord Cottam pushed Meg backward, causing her to fall and strike her head on an old wooden barrel before collapsing to the floor. Reality crashed down upon him as he realised the gravity of his actions. Rushing to her side, he felt for her pulse, only to find that there was none. Meg lay still, her chest unmoving.

He had just pushed over an old lady; regardless of her faults she was still a fragile human being, and now she lay before him, lifeless and silent.

'Oh my God,' he whispered, his voice barely audible above the pounding of his heart. 'I've killed her.'

Frantically, he scanned the room for a means to conceal his heinous deed, his eyes darting from one corner to another in search of an escape from his predicament. And then, like a beacon of salvation amidst the chaos, he spotted the heavy wooden barrel. With trembling hands, he lifted it and closed his eyes, steeling himself for the dreadful task ahead. With a sickening thud, he dropped the barrel over her lifeless body, the weight of his actions settling heavily upon his soul.

Grabbing his hat in haste, he cast one final glance around the room, ensuring that no trace of his presence remained. Satisfied that he had covered his tracks, he fled the scene, his steps quickening as he made his way back to the safety of the manor.

As he returned to the opulent halls of his family home, the sounds of laughter and play echoed around him, a stark contrast to the turmoil raging within his own mind. His children ran past him, their joyful voices a painful reminder of the innocence he had shattered with his actions.

Lady Cottam approached him, her eyes alight with warmth and affection as she pressed a tender kiss to his cheek.

In that moment, he felt a surge of guilt and shame wash over him, knowing that behind his loving gaze lay a truth he could never confess.

She exuded an air of refined elegance that seemed to radiate from her very being. With porcelain skin as smooth as silk and delicate features that spoke of aristocratic lineage, she had a beauty that captivated all who beheld her. Her eyes, a mesmerising shade of sapphire blue, held a depth of wisdom and grace, framed by thick lashes that fluttered with every graceful movement. Her hair, a cascade of golden locks that shimmered in the light, fell in loose waves around her shoulders, adding to her angelic aura.

'You're all sweaty,' she remarked, her hand cool against his feverish forehead.

'I've just had a long walk,' he replied smoothly, masking the turmoil within him with practised ease. 'I've been hunting, and it was quite a trial today.'

'Without your gun?' Her gaze lingered on his empty hands, a silent question hanging in the air.

'No wonder I didn't kill anything,' he chuckled, forcing nonchalance into his tone. She raised an eyebrow, a flicker of suspicion dancing in her eyes, but she chose to let the matter slide.

Later that evening, as his wife immersed herself in the activities of the drawing room and the laughter of their children filled the air, he found himself drawn to the window of his bedroom, his gaze fixed on the cottage below. In the cloak of darkness, he pondered the fate of the woman lying within its walls, a shroud of guilt enveloping him like a suffocating fog.

The distant sound of chanting pierced the night, sending a shiver down his spine. Peering out into the darkness, he beheld the ominous sight of the townsfolk of Woodplumpton, their torches casting flickering shadows across the land as they advanced towards his estate. Fear gripped him tightly as he watched their approach, his heart pounding with dread.

With bated breath, he observed as the mob descended upon Meg Shelton's humble abode, their fervent whispers blending with the night air. Time seemed to stand still as he awaited their discovery, his pulse quickening with each passing moment. Then, as swiftly as they had arrived, they departed, leaving behind an eerie silence that echoed in the depths of his soul.

Days stretched into endless nights as he wrestled with the weight of his deception, the ghost of Meg Shelton haunting his every waking moment. Unable to bear the gnawing uncertainty any longer, he dispatched one of his loyal servants to investigate the cottage, feigning concern for the elderly woman's well-being.

The shrill cry that pierced the air spoke volumes, confirming his worst fears. Meg had been found, her lifeless form a silent testament to his darkest secret.

'She's been crushed to death by an oak barrel.' confirmed the servant.

Even as Lord Cottam grappled with the guilt that threatened to consume him, a perverse sense of relief washed over him. His plan had succeeded and his secret remained buried beneath layers of deceit.

But deep down, he knew that the truth would always linger, a shadowy spirit haunting the corridors of his conscience, waiting to be unearthed from the depths of his darkest secrets.

Chapter 29

Within the confines of St. Anne's Church, a hushed reverence enveloped the space, like a sacred veil draped over its inhabitants. The air was heavy with the scent of aged wood and burning candles, mingling with the faint aroma of incense that lingered from the morning service.

The pews themselves bore the marks of centuries of worship, their polished surfaces worn smooth by the countless faithful who had knelt in solemn contemplation. Isaac sat on a pew, absorbing Lord Cottam's story. After all his searching, he had finally found her killer. And he lived no further than a few feet away from where she was found. How foolish, he thought, that he hadn't considered him as his first suspect. But Lord Cottam was so graceful, well rounded and put together. He was a noble man and a stickler for the law. Now he sat before him confessing his sins, that he had broken the sixth commandment.

Isaac thoughts swirled like a tempestuous sea. Lord Cottam's confession hung heavy in the air, a damning revelation that shattered the illusion of nobility and grace that had once cloaked the man in an aura of respectability. The man seemed the epitome of virtue, his demeanour polished and refined, his adherence to the law unwavering. Yet beneath the veneer of gentility lurked a dark and sinister truth, a truth that now lay bare before him.

As the weight of Lord Cottam's words settled upon him, Isaac couldn't help but feel a sense of profound disappointment. Here was a man who had broken one of the most sacred of commandments, a man who had taken a life in cold blood, all while masquerading as a pillar of society.

But even as Isaac grappled with the enormity of Lord Cottam's confession, a steely resolution ignited within him. No matter how well-crafted the façade, no matter how carefully concealed the truth, justice would always prevail.

'I killed my own mother,' Lord Cottam sobbed, his voice heavy with remorse.

'Bartholomew...' Isaac placed a comforting hand on his visitor's arm. 'It was an accident. The only crime you've really committed is trying to cover it up. I'm sure you didn't mean to kill her.'

'I can't say for certain, Vicar. I was so angry, Isaac.' Bartholomew wiped a tear from his eye. 'There have been so many times that I wanted that old woman dead. And I had a burst of rage, and now she's gone. I have her blood on my hands.'

'You're a decent man, Bartholomew. I just can't see it in you that you have the ability to kill another human. Not on purpose anyway.'

'And yet I have.'

'You pushed her, yes. But you'd just discovered the most shocking secret, which completely altered life as you knew it. Your mother was not whom you thought she was.'

'Can you ever forgive me, Reverend?' Bartholomew pleaded.

'It's not for me to forgive,' Isaac explained. 'You have to ask for forgiveness from God. And you also have to seek forgiveness in yourself.'

'I think the latter will be quite difficult. I've not slept since. I keep waiting for someone to find out. And I heard you were asking questions. I felt you getting closer and closer.'

'I was far off the mark,' Isaac confirmed.

'You won't tell anyone, will you?'

'I won't, no. You've told me as your vicar. I'll take this to the grave with me. However, I do feel you should own up to your involvement. If only to unleash the burden of the weight which is bearing down on you.'

'Thank you, Vicar.'

'There is something you should know though,' Isaac said. 'There is someone who knows it was you. You weren't alone in the cottage that day.'

'That's impossible.' Bartholomew shook his head.

'I'm afraid not. They may have been hiding, given you had banned visitors from the residence.'

'Who is it?' he barked, before his eyes widened with acknowledgement. 'The boy? James?' Lord Cottam gasped.

'I'm not at liberty to say.'

'Do you think they will tell anyone?' His eyes widened with the stark realisation of the potential consequences looming ahead – a hanging at Lancaster Castle.

'I doubt it. The person hasn't even told me who was responsible for Meg's death. I think they are scared. And now I know it's you I can understand why.'

'Whatever do you mean?' Lord Cottam gasped.

'You are of the aristocracy, sir. A nobleman. Who would believe a mere pauper? It is a huge accusation, and few would take it seriously. If you were like the rest of us, perhaps it would be believed. It wasn't long ago that people believed a lot stranger accusations. But no, I think your secret is safe, for now anyway.'

'I see.' Lord Cottam lowered his head in solemn acknowledgment of the weight of his actions.

'Why don't we pray?'

They knelt side by side before the altar, their gazes fixed upon the crucifix suspended above. Lord Cottam closed his eyes in quiet reflection as Isaac offered prayers for his soul.

'O merciful Father, who art in heaven, we gather before thee in humility and contrition. We beseech Thee to grant Thy grace and forgiveness to Lord Bartholomew Cottam, who stands before Thee burdened with the weight of his transgressions. Guide him in the path of righteousness, that he may find solace in Thy mercy and redemption in Thy boundless love. Grant him strength to face the consequences of his actions with courage and humility.

'May he find peace in the knowledge of Thy forgiveness...,' Isaac continued. '...and may Thy divine light illuminate his path as he seeks to atone for his sins. Bless him with Thy divine guidance and protection, that he may walk in Thy ways and be restored to the fullness of Thy grace. We also lift up to Thee our dear sister Meg Shelton, whose life was taken prematurely. May she find eternal rest in Thy heavenly embrace, and may her soul be granted peace and tranquillity in Thy presence. We offer this prayer with hearts open to Thy mercy and compassion, trusting in Thy infinite wisdom and love. Amen.'

'Amen,' Lord Cottam murmured, crossing his head, chest, and shoulders.

As they stood and embraced, Isaac gently urged, 'You should return home to your family, Bartholomew. And please, find it in your heart to forgive yourself. This was a tragic accident. I can't help but think Meg held a deep love for you. Why else would she have remained at the estate to witness your life unfold? She would want you to release yourself from this burden of guilt.'

'Thank you, Vicar,' Lord Cottam responded, moving toward the doors.

Isaac's curiosity got the better of him. 'By the way,' he called after Lord Cottam, who paused and turned back. 'What prompted you to confess now?'

Lord Cottam drew a deep breath before answering, 'Well... I fear my birth mother may not be as forgiving of my role in her passing. It's as if she's haunting me.'

'Haunting you?' Isaac's eyes widened in astonishment. 'What do you mean?'

'I believe the locals may be justified in their fears,' Lord Cottam replied gravely. 'For when I departed my home this morning, her body lay upon the grass outside the manor, as if she had risen from her grave.'

Chapter 30

As the sun ascended above the horizon, its gentle rays cast a warm glow over the tranquil landscape of Woodplumpton. In the heart of the village, nestled amidst quaint cottages and verdant meadows, lay James's vegetable patch.

Rows of vibrant greenery stretched out, each plant standing tall and proud, reaching for the heavens. Lush tomato vines sprawled across the earth, their crimson fruits peeking out from beneath verdant leaves. Alongside them, sturdy stalks of corn swayed gently in the breeze, their golden ears promising a bountiful harvest.

Intermingled with the familiar crops were lesser-known treasures: slender green beans dangling from delicate tendrils, vibrant carrots bursting forth from the soil with earthy vitality, and plump courgettes nestled among broad, glossy leaves.

As James bent down to pull up the last of the day's rewards, a shadow cast over him.

'Hello, James,' came a voice from behind. 'I think you and I need a little chat.'

He turned around to see that a tall figure stood above him, glaring down with suspicious eyes.

'Vicar,' James said, staring up at Isaac.

The pair walked over to the church and took a seat on a bench across from the empty tomb of Meg Shelton. As dusk descended upon Woodplumpton, casting long shadows over the sleepy village, the graveyard lay silent and still beneath the fading light. Nestled within the embrace of ancient oak trees, the burial ground exuded an air of solemn tranquillity.

At the heart of the cemetery stood the empty tomb. Surrounding it, rows of graves stretched out into the distance with flowers resting at their feet.

'I know who killed Margery Hilton,' Isaac said. James glanced at up at him, surprised by his revelations.

'How?' James gasped.

'He told me himself,' Isaac confirmed. 'He came to see me. He couldn't hold on to the guilt anymore.'

'So now you know the truth. Lord Cottam murdered his own mother.'

Isaac felt relieved they had the same person in mind. He didn't want to betray Bartholomew's trust and had held back his name until James revealed it himself. If only he had manipulated James into believing the killer had confessed earlier, he wouldn't have needed to go on a wild goose chase. But his faith prevented him from taking advantage of the boy.

'Murder is a strong word, James.' Isaac gave the boy a reproachful glance. 'He pushed her in rage. Her death was an accident. He was devastated that he had killed her.'

'Then why did he continue to want her removed from the graveyard? It hardly showed remorse for what he did.'

'He hated coming past here and being reminded of what he had done to her,' Isaac said. 'I imagine most people would feel the same. He is deeply saddened for what he did. He wishes he could take it all back.'

'Well, he could have let her rest in peace,' James grumbled.

'As could have you,' Isaac replied.

'What do you mean?' James asked, shocked by the vicar's accusations.

'I know it was you who unearthed Meg's body.'

Silence hovered over them as James took in Isaac's revelation. He bowed his head.

'How did you find out?'

'Only you knew who killed Meg Shelton. And somehow her body ended up on Lord Cottam's estate. And I don't believe she crawled there herself. It didn't take much time to put two and two together. Why did you do it, James?' Isaac inquired, his voice laced with concern.

'I wanted him to feel remorse for what he did,' James explained. 'He wouldn't admit it himself, and no one would ever believe me. But I thought if I could frighten him enough, he might confess. The first few attempts didn't work, so I had no choice but to make a statement by placing her on his own land. I knew he'd be alarmed once he saw her near his home.'

'And what about the other townsfolk? You've terrified the entire neighbourhood,' Isaac pointed out.

'They deserved to be scared,' James retorted, his voice rising. 'They treated her terribly her whole life. I wanted them all to feel afraid, even though Meg was gone.'

'But digging up her body? Didn't you realise that it would only reinforce the belief that Meg was a witch? How could you do this to your friend?' Isaac pressed, his brow furrowed with concern.

'Meg once told me that if people believed she was a witch, she was content to let them hold on to those prejudices,'

James replied. 'She hoped it would instil fear in them and perhaps only then they'd leave her alone.'

'But they haven't left her alone, have they? The town wants her body removed from here,' Isaac pointed out.

'They wanted that long before I started digging her up,' James countered.

'How did you know Lord Cottam killed his mother?' Isaac asked. 'He's sure that the house was empty.'

'I was hidden. He banned me from visiting her at the cottage. So when he knocked, I crawled under the bed and heard everything. I was too scared to come out after that. Or to say anything. Nobody would believe me if I did.'

'I see...' Isaac nodded. 'I have another question. The fire at the Cavendish farm...'

'That was me,' James admitted, his voice heavy with remorse. 'I was furious with John. He wouldn't stop calling Meg a witch, despite her being dead for weeks. I wanted to get back at him.'

'But it cost him his livelihood. And it's cost your own family too. Your poor father can barely make ends meet now. You've hurt your own family as a consequence. I'm sure Meg wouldn't want that for the man who we now know is her son,' Isaac remarked, his tone tinged with sadness.

'I didn't know that at the time. But honestly, it was partially an accident. I just wanted to burn a few of his crops. But the fire got out of hand, and before I knew it, his entire field was in flames. I ran away because I was so scared of what might happen,' James confessed.

'And so you let your dear friend take the blame. Oh, James, what has happened to you?' Isaac asked, his voice filled with sorrow.

'I don't know,' James admitted, bowing his head. 'I'm so angry, Reverend. They hurt her so much, and I wanted to hurt them back. Meg isn't here to stand up for herself, but I am.'

'Well, it needs to stop. Now,' Isaac declared firmly.

James nodded in agreement. 'It will, I promise.'

'It explains why you always had mud on your trousers. I always thought it was from your vegetable patch,' Isaac remarked.

'My mother thought the same,' James confessed.

Isaac's mind turned to the logistics of the exhumations, which had previously made him overlook this boy's part in the theatrics of Meg's reappearance.

'How on earth did you manage to dig her up and carry her to Lord Cottam's estate?' Isaac inquired.

'I had help,' James replied sheepishly.

'Who?' Isaac pressed.

'William and Henry,' James admitted, swallowing the lump in his throat. 'It's one reason I'm back in the fold. They were making fun of my friendship with Meg. So I told them I didn't care for her anymore and asked if they'd like to help me pull a prank on the town. They were in. And William's family has a horse and carriage, which he took after they went to bed. It was relatively easy to organise once we had that.'

'And you smashed up her gravestone? Why?' Isaac asked, looking at the broken stones beside the empty tomb with sadness.

'That was William. He brought a sledgehammer as well as a spade and went too far. I felt awful watching him, but I couldn't speak up, otherwise they'd know how I really felt,' James explained, swallowing the lump in his throat.

'It's rather cowardly, James. If Meg were here, I wouldn't be surprised if she was disappointed in you too,' Isaac remarked.

'I know, I'm sorry,' James replied, his voice filled with regret.

'And you'll need to ask for God's forgiveness too. But I can help you with that,' Isaac offered.

'Thank you. Will you tell anyone?' James inquired.

'That depends...' Isaac said mysteriously.

'On what?' James pressed.

'Whether you do what I say,' Isaac replied.

'I'll do whatever you ask me,' James agreed.

'All right, I have a plan. But I'm going to need your help,' Isaac revealed.

'Anything,' James nodded enthusiastically.

'First things first, I'll need you to allow me to tell Lord Cottam that you knew about his part in her death and your role in moving her body...'

James swallowed the lump in his throat, wondering what plans Isaac had up his sleeve.

The Wheatsheaf pub exuded a cosy warmth as soon as one stepped inside, offering respite from the chill of the autumn evening. The low hum of chatter and laughter filled the air, blending with the low hum of a folk musician in the corner.

The walls, adorned with framed paintings of local patrons, bore witness to decades of camaraderie and conviviality. A row of polished wooden tables, illuminated by the soft glow of candlelight, invited patrons to gather around and share stories over tankards of ale.

Behind the well-worn bar, decorated with brass railings and rows of gleaming glasses, stood the genial figure of the owner, David, deftly pouring drinks and engaging in friendly banter with the regulars.

In the corner, a crackling fire cast a warm, flickering light across the room, inviting weary travellers to settle into their stools and unwind with a drink in hand. The occasional burst of laughter or clink of glasses added to the convivial atmosphere, creating a sense of camaraderie that was as comforting as it was familiar.

Isaac stepped into the dimly lit interior of The Wheatsheaf pub, finding the townsfolk gathered around the bar, exactly as he had anticipated. They had insisted on his presence, initially proposing the church as the meeting place, but Isaac suggested the local public house for a more relaxed atmosphere. Plus, he admitted to himself, he could use a whisky or two to steady his nerves.

As he scanned the room, he noted the familiar faces of the regular patrons. Mrs Norris sat with Juno nestled on her lap, while Margaret Parr and Joan Clitheroe engaged in lively conversation with the rest of the townsfolk. However, two notable absences stood out – Sarah Ashton and her husband, who had distanced themselves since the revelation of Francis's maternal heritage.

'Vicar!' John Cavendish called out, spotting Isaac's arrival. 'Thank you for joining us. We have urgent matters to discuss regarding Meg Shelton.'

'What can I do for you?' Isaac took a seat. David swiftly brought him a glass of whisky, which Isaac eagerly gulped down while his neighbours filled him in on the latest developments.

'As you know...' Joan Clitheroe began, her voice tinged with apprehension, '... Meg Shelton has once again risen from her grave. She's now ventured beyond the confines of the graveyard and made her way to the Clifton estate! What horrors will she bring upon us next?'

'It's true. We can't continue like this,' John nodded in agreement. 'We need to deal with that witch once and for all.'

Isaac turned to his housekeeper who was tenderly stroking her dog. 'What do you think, Mrs Norris?'

'I agree,' she replied, her tone respectful in Isaac's presence. 'We can't allow her to keep resurfacing. And it's not fair on you, Vicar, to keep having to rebury her. I can't help but wonder what this is doing to your back.'

'How diplomatic of you,' Isaac said with a smile, acknowledging her tact.

'Come on, Vicar. We need your help here. This needs to end. Once and for all,' Joan urged, echoing the sentiments of the group.

Isaac took another sip of his whisky, savouring the rich flavour. 'Well, as it happens, I've resolved the matter.'

'You haven't just reburied her again, have you?' John interjected sceptically.

'No, not at all,' Isaac reassured them. 'Last night, under the cover of darkness, Lord Cottam respectfully brought Meg Shelton's body back to Woodplumpton on his horse and carriage. And we found a plot for her.'

The crowd murmured in suspicion, but Isaac pressed on. 'To prevent her from rising again, we buried her upside down. So if she does decide to crawl in the night again, she'll only be going further and further down.'

'Straight to hell, I hope!' Joan cheered, her voice filled with a mix of fear and defiance.

'And just in case she manages to turn around, we've placed a large boulder on top of her grave. It took three of us to put it there, so I doubt a feeble woman like Meg Shelton could move it.'

The sceptics in the group still seemed unsure, but Isaac remained steadfast. 'Go and see for yourselves if you don't believe me.'

'We shall!' The townsfolk rose from their seats and made their way to the churchyard, anticipation evident in their determined strides.

As they approached Meg's grave, they were met with the sight of the large boulder, a symbol of their collective effort to put an end to the terror. Isaac observed the relief and gratitude on their faces.

'And Lord Cottam's priest from the chapel on his estate personally came over to bless the ground, freeing it of any spirits,' Isaac added, providing the final reassurance.

'Thank you, Vicar,' John said, patting Isaac on the back. 'We appreciate you addressing our concerns and taking action.'

Across the road, James observed as the crowd dispersed from the graveyard, and Isaac winked at him, a silent acknowledgment of their shared understanding. As Isaac returned to the church to offer his prayers, he reflected on the wisdom of the Bishop of Lancaster, who had advised him that sometimes appeasing the concerns of his parishioners was more pragmatic than challenging their deeply held beliefs. Lighting a candle for Margery Hilton, he offered a silent prayer for her peace.

Exiting the church, Isaac cast one last glance at Meg's grave. 'Oh, Margery,' he chuckled softly. 'You're still stirring up trouble from beyond the grave. What a character you were, and still are.'

With his coat pulled tightly against the evening chill, Isaac made his way back home, reassured that Margery Hilton, also known as Meg Shelton, was finally at rest.

Chapter 31

Present day

Speeding down the M6, Mason gripped the back seat of Marvin's brother's car, his knuckles turning white with tension. Callum, at the wheel, kept his eyes fixed on the road ahead, his grip firm on the steering wheel. Beside him, his younger brother leaned forward, hands pressed against the glove box. Sensing Mason's anxiety, Kyle, seated beside him, shot a nervous glance in his direction.

'The grave...' Mason's voice quivered '...it was empty.'

Kyle's nod mirrored the unease that swept through them. The image of the vacant tomb lingered in their minds, unsettling in its implications. What was even more chilling was the tunnel, an unexpected passage leading deeper into the earth than the standard six-foot depth, before curving eastward out of sight.

'You don't think...' Kyle's voice trailed off, a shiver running down his spine. '...that she might have crawled her way out?'

'I don't know about that...' Marvin's face drained of colour, his words heavy with dread. '...but certainly deeper into the ground. God knows where she is.'

'So, the stories Reverend Thomas told were true. She really was a witch.' Mason's voice trembled as he contemplated the terrifying possibility.

'We have to tell someone!' Kyle's voice cracked with urgency.

'Don't be an idiot!' Callum snapped, his hand darting back to deliver a sharp punch to Kyle's leg from the driver's seat, eliciting a screech. 'We shouldn't have been there tonight. It was illegal what we did. We can't tell anyone.'

'I wish we weren't there,' Mason admitted, his throat tight with fear.

'Just forget you've seen anything,' Callum commanded, his gaze piercing through the rear-view mirror to meet Mason's eyes. 'Put it out of your mind. We must never speak of this again, do you understand?'

Mason nodded silently, his gaze drifting out the window to the distant silhouette of Pendle Hill, steeped in the history of seventeenth-century witch trials. Behind it, the full moon cast its ethereal glow upon the countryside, shrouding it in mystery. Above, the stars twinkled, whispered reminders of departed souls. As they left the borough behind, Mason couldn't help but wonder if there was more to the world than met the eye, a realm of secrets and shadows lurking just beyond reach.

The events of the evening had left an indelible mark on him, a reminder of the thin veil that separated the familiar from the unknown. Glancing back once more at the moonlit landscape, he questioned what other secrets lay hidden beneath the surface of their seemingly ordinary world. With a heavy sigh, he turned his gaze forward, steeling himself for the uncertainties that awaited them all.

Epilogue

Isaac and James stood side by side in the eerie stillness of the graveyard, enveloped by the darkness of the night. The distant sound of a horse-drawn carriage echoed through the silence, drawing closer with each passing moment. As the moon cast its ethereal glow upon the scene, the carriage emerged from the shadows, its presence growing more pronounced with every creak of its wheels.

'Lord Cottam,' Isaac murmured softly as the carriage came to a halt, his voice barely above a whisper in the night air.

Bartholomew acknowledged him with a solemn nod, his gaze shifting nervously between Isaac and James. 'Isaac,' he replied in a hushed tone, his apprehension palpable. Turning to James, he offered a nod of recognition. 'James.'

'Hello, sir,' James responded respectfully, his own unease mirrored in his demeanour. Despite the newfound revelations that had brought them together, a lingering tension hung between them, their shared secrets looming large in the silence. They stood at a crossroads, bound by the weight of their concealed truths, each acutely aware of the delicate balance that held their fates in the balance.

'Well, let's get the old dear back in her rightful place, shall we?' Lord Cottam smiled, finally offering her a more respectful name than he had in recent years. He walked to the back of his carriage and removed a blanket. Beneath, a wooden casket lay. Together, with the aid of Lord Cottam's groundsman, Oscar, they carefully carried the coffin into the graveyard towards an empty tomb.

They lowered the casket into the ground. Lord Cottam grabbed some wildflowers and scattered them on top of the coffin, took off his hat, and bowed his head. Together they stood around the grave and said their silent prayers.

'Will someone not want this plot one day?' asked Bartholomew, glancing around the small area of land with limited space for the increasingly older parishioners who would be seeking out their own place of rest in due time.

'This plot is already assigned,' Isaac smiled.

'To whom?' James asked curiously.

'Me,' Isaac chuckled. 'Perks of the job. When I go, I get a free plot in the grounds. This is my spot.'

'That's very clever of you, Vicar,' Lord Cottam sniggered. 'However, when you do go, won't they find the space is already taken?'

'Very well observed, Bartholomew. I hope that time won't be anytime soon. But if it is, she's eight feet down while the standard is six. Plus I have these, if you wouldn't mind giving me a hand?'

Isaac walked over to the side of the church, and the other gentlemen followed, finding slabs of rock resting against the church wall. With solemn determination, they carefully lifted the heavy stones and rolled them into the grave. They winced as they heard the crack of the wood beneath the weight, but they all knew it was necessary for Meg's eternal peace.

'If they dig down, they'll feel the rock against their spade and assume they'd hit the bottom and won't go any further,' Isaac winked.

'Your cunning astounds me, Vicar. Maybe we could offer a final prayer for her?' Bartholomew suggested.

'Good idea,' James agreed.

As Isaac stood at Meg's graveside, surrounded by the silent shadows of the night, he bowed his head in reverence, his heart heavy with the weight of their shared secrets and the mysteries that had unfolded. With a gentle sigh, he began to speak, his words a whispered invocation to the heavens above.

'Dear Heavenly Father, we gather here tonight, beneath the watchful gaze of the moon and stars, to offer our prayers for the soul of Margery Hilton, known to us as Meg Shelton. Though her earthly journey may have been fraught with hardship and sorrow, let her spirit find solace in Your eternal embrace. Grant her peace, dear Lord, and release her from the burdens of this world. May she find rest in the eternal light of Your love, where pain and suffering hold no sway. Let her soul soar free, unfettered by the chains of mortal existence, and find sanctuary in the arms of Your mercy.

'As we stand here...' Isaac continued '...surrounded by the quiet embrace of the night, we ask for Your guidance and wisdom. Help us to seek forgiveness for our transgressions and to find redemption in Your boundless grace. May we learn from Meg's trials and tribulations, and strive to live our lives with compassion, kindness, and understanding. In Your infinite wisdom, O Lord, You know the secrets of our hearts and the depths of our souls. Hear our prayers, we beseech You, and grant us the strength to face the challenges that lie ahead. And may Meg's memory live on in our hearts, a beacon of hope and a reminder of the power of forgiveness and redemption. Amen.'

They filled the grave and carefully replaced the patches of grass to conceal their handiwork. The site remained unmarked except for a solitary flower, a tribute from James to the woman whose final resting place they had just prepared. But their task was not yet complete.

Moving to where Meg had once lain, they continued to dig, creating the illusion that she might have somehow found her way deeper into the earth. 'Just in case any nosy neighbours come snooping,' Isaac remarked with a chuckle. The men rolled a sizable boulder, transported on Lord Cottam's carriage, and positioned it over the tomb. Stepping back, they wiped sweat from their brows, feeling a sense of accomplishment tinged with fatigue.

'How are you going to tell the townsfolk?'

'In the pub, I think. That way I won't need to lie in God's own house. I'll pray for forgiveness after. Now only we know the true location of Meg's burial. So if she reappears, I'll know who to blame.' Isaac remarked, his gaze firm as he looked at James. The young man nodded, his head bowed in remorse for his past actions.

'Well done, boys,' Lord Cottam commended. 'A splendid team effort. I believe we have honoured her memory well.'

With handshakes exchanged, they parted ways, each returning to their respective homes. Isaac made his way back to the vicarage, casting a glance at the night sky. In a moment of whimsy, he winked at a particularly bright star, feeling a sense of connection with Meg's mischievous spirit. He believed she would approve of their unconventional burial, once again defeating the townsfolk from beyond the grave.

As Isaac made his way back to the warmth of the vicarage, he couldn't shake the feeling of overwhelming peace that finally settled over him. The events of recent days had been turbulent, revealing layers of secrets and darkness hidden within their small community. But now, as he looked up at the stars twinkling in the night sky, he felt a sense of closure.

Meg Shelton, once feared and misunderstood, now rested in eternal slumber, her spirit finally at peace. And as the night embraced Woodplumpton with its gentle embrace, Isaac couldn't help but feel a glimmer of hope for the future, knowing that even in the darkest of times, there was always a path to redemption, forgiveness and, as he'd learned from Meg... always room for a little bit of mischief.

Note from the Author

I never expected to write a historical novel set so far in the past. While I had covered the Second World War in *Camp* and the era of Abraham Lincoln's life in *The Exhumation*, none of my novels had ventured so far back in time. I initially doubted my ability to infuse enough insight and relatable references into the novel, especially given that every part of normal life in the 1600s and 1700s differs so vastly from my own today. However, I'm grateful for the wealth of online resources which have proved invaluable in aiding my research.

Meg Shelton, or Margery Hilton as she is known in the records, was a real parishioner of St. Anne's Church and was believed to be a witch within the town. While little is known about her true identity, rumours have been passed down in folklore for centuries, some of which I'll cover at the end of this book.

Given how limited the information there was about her, I've used what I could find and combined it with a little creative embellishment. I've written for you my interpretation of her life and who Margery Hilton truly was. In my opinion, she was merely a poor elderly woman, resorting to stealing food for survival, which led to the local farmers accusing her of witchcraft, a common occurrence during the seventeenth and eighteenth centuries. Thankfully, the days of arresting and executing witches had long passed when the accusations against Meg arose. Every other character in the novel is completely fictional.

I first learned of Meg's story when I was a child, when my parents took me to see her grave. I visited again when I was eighteen, and my friend Matthew Rossall, who had a keen interest in her story, took me there en route to a local pub. In the graveyard is the large boulder covering her grave for all to see, with a small plaque beside it referencing who is buried beneath it. Across the road, in The Wheatsheaf pub which still stands today, there is a tribute to her story with some information regarding the rumours which surrounded her. And more recently I ventured to the church as part of a circular walk around rural Lancashire.

When I shared my visit to Woodplumpton with my friend Gemma, she suggested it would make an interesting plotline for my next book. I didn't think anything of it at first. After all, how could I write about a group of people with whom I had literally nothing in common, when it came to their everyday living? But as I read over Meg's biography and the rumours which swirled around her, a story began to form in my mind. So thank you, Gemma!

What startled me the most was, despite the gaps in time and the way we live our lives, just how much these characters resonated with me today. The fear around people who are different from us continues. The lies spread around different religions, races, genders, and those fleeing war continue to be the subject of fear-mongering within tabloid newspapers and from our political parties today. And the ableism of Meg's appearance and her disability is still a source of comedy and fear within television and modern tales today. The Pendle Witch Trials may be over, but the fear of the unknown, speculation, and casting out people in society remains. You can even look to the current thirst of 'cancel culture' to see that witch hunting remains prevalent.

I do hope you enjoyed the book. While local historians might argue that I've taken some creative liberties, my goal was to create an engaging story with compelling characters, and I hope I've delivered that. Thank you sincerely for taking the time to read it!

David Hatton

What we know about Meg Shelton...

Meg Shelton died in 1705. She is buried at St. Anne's Church in Woodplumpton, Lancashire on the outskirts of Preston. She's apparently buried beneath a large boulder in the church grounds, where a nearby plaque reveals that she was known as the Fylde Hag. Little is known about her life, but she is rumoured to have had the ability to shapeshift into different animals.

There are tales of her turning into a duck when she was caught stealing milk from a local farmer. And during a bet with her landlord whom she had asked to build her a new cottage, she apparently transformed herself into a hare, but he released his hounds and chased Meg, biting her in the chase. According to legend, she transformed back into a human upon being bitten and supposedly she walked with a limp. It is said that she had a wart on her face and a large protruding nose, with locals comparing her appearance to that of a witch.

Farmers have claimed that she placed curses on their crops and turned milk sour. When she died, she was buried in St. Anne's Church, however her body kept rising from the ground overnight, which led the locals to believe she had crawled out of her grave. Eager to solve the problem, it is said that the townsmen decided to bury her upside down, so that if she did continue to crawl in her grave, she would dig deeper into the depths of hell, rather than disturbing the local villagers. A large boulder was placed on top of her tomb to prevent her rising again.

She died in her home where she was found crushed beneath a large oak barrel. Some believe it was God's way of punishing her. Others believe she was murdered by an aggrieved farmer. Whilst there are some who simply believe it was a tragic accident.

There are numerous reasons why Meg Shelton might have had a different name. She could have fled a family who wanted nothing to do with her. Or her name might have been changed under the whispers of folklore as Shelton isn't too dissimilar to Hilton. It is equally possible that her name in the records could have been incorrect.

There are also many reasons why she could have been dubbed a witch. The first is that she was a poor, peculiar looking beggar, quite eccentric with a notable limp. Women who didn't fit the norm in the 1600s and 1700s were often branded witches. Local farmers might have accused her of being a witch as she was stealing from their farms. At the time, the Witchcraft Act continued to be law until 1745 when it was repealed, however it was rarely enforced during Meg's lifetime, though the fear of witches and the accusations continued. She could have also been a midwife or been simply intelligent, or disobedient, as men used the retribution of witchcraft to keep women in their place during the seventeenth century.

There is also another possibility. There are some rumours that she had in fact birthed a child of a local aristocratic gentleman who was unable to conceive with his wife. Supposedly she gave the child over to the married couple who raised the son as if he were their own. It is possible that jealousy on his wife's behalf had led her to spread rumours that Meg was a witch.

We will never know the true story of Meg Shelton. And we don't know if she continues to be under the boulder at St. Anne's Church today. But her story continues to excite people up and down Lancashire, and beyond. In research for this novel,

I found websites and podcasts from people in America who were equally enticed by Meg's story.

Pendle Witch Trials

The Pendle Witch Trials in Lancashire are among the most infamous trials in history, dating back to 1612. Twelve individuals were accused of witchcraft in the vicinity of Pendle Hill, charged with the alleged murder of ten people through black magic. All but one of the accused were tried at Lancaster Castle, where ten of them were found guilty and subsequently hanged.

The Witchcraft Act of 1542 established severe penalties, including execution, for those found guilty of sorcery. Legal proceedings of the time admitted hearsay as evidence and often relied on the statements of children. Accused individuals were frequently uninformed of the charges against them prior to trial, and confessions, often obtained under duress, were used against them.

The climate of fear surrounding witches can be traced back to the reign of James I, who enforced Protestantism in England, leading to the execution of many Catholics. Following an assassination attempt by Guy Fawkes, the government intensified its crackdown, often using accusations of witchcraft as a means to target the Catholic community. Although the Witchcraft Act remained in force after James's death, prosecutions for witchcraft dwindled, and by the end of the seventeenth century, the act was largely abandoned, though rumours persisted.

Lancashire was particularly prone to witchcraft rumours, with the county often associated with rebellious behaviour. The Witchcraft Act was frequently utilised to maintain social order and punish those who deviated from accepted norms. The act was eventually repealed in 1736.

Most of the accused individuals in Lancashire were women from two prominent families in the Pendle Hill area: the Demdikes and the Chattoxes, known for their manipulation of local villagers. Competition between these families often led to accusations against each other, although it was not uncommon for individuals, including children, to accuse and testify against their own family members.

Salem Witch Trials

Across the pond, in Massachusetts, USA, a series of trials occurred in the town of Salem between 1692 and 1693, during which over two hundred individuals were accused of witchcraft. Thirty people were convicted, with nineteen of them ultimately executed by hanging. Remarkably, these American trials unfolded at a time when the United Kingdom and Europe were moving away from such prosecutions.

Accusations primarily targeted young teenage girls, with the youngest alleged witch being just four years old. The fear of witchcraft stemmed largely from religious discord, as many individuals had fled to America seeking refuge from religious persecution amidst the ongoing conflicts between Catholics and Protestants. However, despite the promise of religious freedom in their new land, similar anxieties regarding witchcraft began to emerge.

Salem became a focal point for witchcraft accusations, driven in part by the contentious relationships within the population. Disputes between neighbours often led to false accusations against perceived enemies, mirroring patterns seen in England. Like their counterparts across the pond, the Salem trials relied heavily on hearsay and rumours as evidence against the accused.

With thanks

- To Gemma Coll, who gave me the idea to write this book. I hope it is a good option for your book club!

- To my parents and to my friend, Matthew Rossall, who took me to see Meg Shelton's grave when I was younger. Little did I know that it would inspire a book!

- My partner, David, who accompanied me on a trip back to Meg's grave and who continues to be supportive despite often being ignored when I'm in 'writing mode'.

- To everyone who has bought my books, told their friends and written reviews!

DID YOU ENJOY THIS BOOK?

Please leave a review on Amazon or Goodreads! It really helps out authors. And please tell your friends and share the links on Social Media with your followers!

About the Author

David Hatton was born in Preston, Lancashire. Over the years, he has called various places home, including Manchester, Leeds, Chicago, and Horwich, until finally returning to his Lancashire roots in 2022. Currently, he resides in Buckshaw Village. An established writer with seven novels to his name, David contributes regularly to the Lancashire & North-West Magazine, where he also mentors young aspiring writers and has been on a panel of judges for their school competition for young creatives. His voice has reached audiences through BBC Radio Lancashire, Manchester Talk TV, and Radio Leyland. David has also shared his insights at literary festivals, notably the Stonyhurst Literature Festival. Beyond the world of writing, he enjoys country walks, finishing with a well-deserved pint in a pub. In his personal life, David lives with his partner, who is also called David, and his two adopted cats, Buck and Eddie.

Website: www.david-hatton.uk

Insta: @davidhattonbooks

Facebook: dhattonbooks

Also by David Hatton

The Return

Beverly Hahn has the shock of her life when her husband knocks on her door, ten years after he was declared dead in the September 11th terrorist attacks. How will she tell her children? And how will she face those who supported her through the grief she had no entitlement to feel?

*****

"An intriguing and moving story about love, loyalties, betrayal, deceit and forgiveness."

*****

"Enjoyed the book from start to finish."

*****

"Enthralling novel"

*****

"A fantastic debut"

Available on Amazon

The Medium

When Michael Walker is approached by a psychic medium claiming to know the whereabouts of his missing wife, he has to choose between his beliefs in science and the desire to find the love of his life. But is the medium everything she claims?

*****

"Kept me guessing right to the end."

*****

"The characterisation is rich, layered, and trickled through to the reader just enough to keep you guessing."

*****

"A real page turner!"

*****

"Every chapter was gripping!"

*****

"I couldn't put it down!"

Available on Amazon

The Catfish

Rachel McCann has left the corporate world of law to open her own independent practice. Her first client is a mother whose son has been catfished online by a vigilante group: The Predator Hunters. In a world where a criminal trial is outweighed by the wrath of social media, how far can Rachel go for her client who will stop at nothing to protect her son's honour?

*****

"A great choice for a book club!"

*****

"A timely story."

*****

"A fast read with a great plot and great characters."

*****

"The premise is strong and it's well worth the trip."

*****

"Started off with a bang and didn't stop!"

Available on Amazon

The Exhumation

In 1876 the body of Abraham Lincoln was taken from his tomb in Springfield, Illinois. 130 years later grave robbers have ransacked the tomb again. Detective Darnell Jackson is on the case to find the former president's body. As Jackson becomes more emotionally involved in the case, he discovers the secrets that America has hidden away for far too long. Should Detective Jackson reveal the darkest secrets of their former leader and risk destroying his legacy forever?

*****

"The Exhumation is both gripping and sensitively handled."

*****

"The story is fast and easy to read."

*****

"It is really enjoyable and the characters are strong"

*****

"David Hatton masterfully blends history with detective crime fiction in The Exhumation"

Available on Amazon

Camp

1925 - a curious George Taylor has left Britain behind to explore the gay capital of Europe: Berlin. But just as he's starting to settle into his new home, an upcoming election threatens the liberated lifestyle for which he'd moved to Germany for.

The Nazi Party are gaining popularity across the country and their ruthless leader, Adolf Hitler, is determined to punish homosexuals across the nation and beyond. Is George's life coming to an end just as it's only truly begun? Nobody can imagine the horrors that await him and his friends.

*****

"A page turning addictive read that takes you on a huge emotional journey."

*****

"A really beautiful story and one that made me cry."

*****

"A compelling and emotional story detailing the plight of those in the death camps who wore the pink triangle whose history and suffering has been rarely told."

*****

"Outstanding read!"

Available on Amazon

It's the End of the World as We Know It

Six friends decide to come together to witness the end of the world.

But as their lives intertwine, circumstances threaten to destroy the bonds which they once believed were unbreakable.

If they don't want to die alone, they need to work together to mend their ties of friendship.

Perhaps it's their last good deed in this world...

*****

"Terrifying and thought-provoking!"

*****

"

"Another brilliant book by David Hatton."

*****

"If you like pre-apocalypse and friendship that puts them in situations to test their loyalty, then you give this book a chance to read."

Available on Amazon

Printed in Great Britain
by Amazon